Absolute Cornelia

Lucretia Bingham

ABSOLUTE CORNELIA

Lucretia Bingham

Rand-Smith Publishing
ASHLAND

Absolute Cornelia

Print ISBN: 978-1-950544-04-2

Digital ISBN: 978-1-950544-05-9

Registered with the Library of Congress

Rand-Smith Publishing
www.Rand-Smith.com

Ashland, VA

Printed in the USA

Contents

Part I

ABSOLUTE HONESTY

Chapter 1

By age seven, Cornelia had seen many fish die, gasping for air, quivering as their brilliant colors faded to flat. She had seen chicken bodies running around spurting blood from their neck after her stepfather swiftly chopped off their head with a whack. She had even seen mother rabbits devour their screaming young. Her own mother, Nevin, thought it part of her children's education to witness birth and death. Both were bloody and hard to forget.

After her divorce, Nevin and her new husband Ray took Cornelia and her brother Nathan to live what was promised to be a wonderful life on an isolated island in the Bahamas. They learned to milk goats, chop brush with machetes, weed acres of land, and cook meals for themselves when their mother got the blues. After their chores, they often raced down to the back harbor where they chased elusive stingrays and rainbows across low-tide flats.

No matter how idyllic their new life seemed, the children missed their father, Cornelius Woodstock (C.W.), who they hadn't seen since the messy divorce. Maybe "missed" is the wrong word since they didn't know him well enough to miss him, but they were curious about their real father. Their stepfather Ray had plans of teaching them how to work but no desire to play the traditional fatherly role in their lives. He quipped he had already raised four children of his own so why would he want to do it again?

When Nevin and Ray finally ran out of money to sustain their new wonderful self-sufficient life, C.W. demanded a visit from the children in return for larger monthly checks. Nevin broke the news to the children, "You are going to spend some time with your father."

Then she added, "I've told you before, your father is rich but cheap. Very cheap." The children looked at each other with expressionless stares. They knew not to question anything their mother said. It only made her go into hysterics.

Even though they hadn't seen him in three years, C.W. greeted them at the Detroit airport, not with hugs, but with little black leather books in which he immediately instructed them to write down their "guidance" from God. Cornelia was initially excited to undertake the task since at seven years old, she was still mastering her writing skills. They all then quickly boarded an overnight train heading north and then rode a ferry to the island where C.W.'s group "The Moral Absolutes" had their summer headquarters.

At the ferry dock, they were greeted with great fanfare. A chorus of women and men wearing costumes that represented cultures from all around the world sang about a wind of love and unselfishness that was sweeping the world. A carriage pulled by bell-festooned horses carried them up the hill to the large conference center where four towers snapped with pennants that each proclaimed one of the four Moral Absolute standards by which, their father instructed, they now must live: Absolute Honesty, Absolute Unselfishness, Absolute Purity and Absolute Love.

Cornelia and Nathan were shell-shocked from the extensive travel, not to mention being overwhelmed by the presence of their father. Several times, Cornelia found herself just staring at him as they traveled, studying his features, wondering what it would be like to spend time with her real father. Both children were unsure what to make of this new experience, but at first glance, Dad's "group" seemed on the right track. Honesty, unselfishness, purity, and love didn't sound threatening or scary at all.

At the entrance, without any warning, the children were separated from each other and their father, and all were whisked off to separate quarters. When Cornelia met her 19-year-old roommate, who wore a stern expression and a lumpy nose, homesickness churned her stomach and heart. Initially when her father had told them they were coming to an island, she had been excited, but this island seemed much different from the one she'd just left. Where the Bahamas was warm, relaxed, and intoxicating, this island was chilly, tense, and foreboding.

After their grand arrival, the children expected there would be many new friends to play with. Instead, they were mostly ignored. The children thought that maybe it was because the annual Moral Absolute conference was underway. In attendance, there were 2,322 adults, and only three children, including the Woodstocks. The other child was a bossy, pudgy little girl who mostly clung to her chaperones who cooed over her while her mother saved souls in Africa.

They quickly learned it was their father who was of interest to the group not them. They knew from what their mother had told them that C.W. came from fourth-generation wealth. His great-grandfather had built railroads and steel mills; his grandfather had built factories all over the world. His own father had collected valuable art and managed the family fortune, but C.W., it seemed, had very little fire in his belly to do any of that. One thing he did inherit from his father was an affinity for art. In fact, truth be told he preferred his oil paints to people. Yet, in his forties, awkward and alone, a hunger for spiritual meaning had emerged. The Moral Absolutes gave him a sense of purpose, filling his life with meaning and direction. Now he would see to it that his children were exposed to the Moral Absolute standards as well.

Once on the island, Horace Baker, the leader and founder of the Moral Absolutes, sat him next to world leaders in his special VIP dining room. He flattered him and cajoled him. He told him he was "meant" to give large donations to the cause.

The children were left pretty much alone, but they were expected to work. In the bowels of the conference center, Nathan unloaded boxes off trucks, then sent them trundling up conveyor belts to the kitchen. He soon learned to hide in the walk-in freezers whenever an older man arrived to discuss his "guidance" and possible impure thoughts.

Cornelia worked a housekeeping shift where she yanked sheets into tight corners and replaced the toilet paper after every guest left, even if only a few squares had been used. According to the head housekeeper, Mrs. Rogers, that attention to detail was a form of Absolute Love.

With no playmates and no books to read but the bible and Moral Absolute literature, there was little to entertain Cornelia after her housekeeping shift was done. She took to wandering the halls of what had once been a grand hotel. Rows of a seemingly endless number of rooms lined the hallways lavishly decorated with carpet and wallpaper prints that had once been on trend but now were faded and peeling at the corners.

As she encountered more of the group members, most were ready to greet her with a smile. But her odd responses unsettled them. First of all, she never smiled back. Just fixed them with an uncompromising gaze from out-sized almond shaped eyes with irises as dark as her pupils. Adults tended to fidget under this intense scrutiny. But some just tried harder.

"Aren't you pretty," said one woman.

Cornelia snorted, then one side of her tight-lipped mouth turned down, highlighting a sharp bony slant to her cheekbones. "I don't really think so."

"Well, of course you are," said the woman, already wishing she hadn't engaged. Cornelia thought the woman cooed like the doves outside her window in the islands. The sound made her mournful, an annoying reminder that this island was nothing like home.

"Actually, if you really want to know," Cornelia said, "I'm the opposite of pretty. My mother is pretty. She has curly hair. Mine is lank. She has pink cheeks. Mine are sallow. Her profile is perfect. Everyone says so. I recently learned that I have my dad's flat nose and cheekbones, we might even have Native American ancestors."

"Oh," said the woman and gasped like a fish back home.

"My mother says I'll never be the belle of the ball. So I had better develop character. Do you think I have character?"

"I should say you do," said the woman before fleeing down the hall.

Others whispered she was difficult. The postman said she had thrown a tantrum when he told her, for the third time that day, that there were *still* no letters from her mother. Mrs. Rogers sniffed that the child was self-will run riot. Cornelia had screeched when told that her housekeeping schedule couldn't be changed so she could have every meal with her brother. And then she had stamped her foot and run out the door, leaving without sharing her "guidance."

After hearing music and voices from one of the rooms, Cornelia started attending the general meetings held in the great hall. It was the one grand new addition to the old hotel. Modeled after a giant teepee, its yard-thick rafters smelled freshly of pine and vaulted many stories high. Cornelia liked the way the light beamed down from a row of tiny windows at its very pinnacle. She sat in the shadowy back of the giant room and listened to every word. She heard confessions of adultery. Of drunkenness that made men throw up on the streets. And of jealousy that made sisters tear each other's hair out.

As she listened, her look was solemn. She was a tensile child, some might call her frail, but there was a surprising strength in her limbs. She held herself alert at all times, never leaning back against the chair. She often rocked up onto her tiptoes as if she might take flight at any moment.

"I see you're here again," said a woman who sat down next to her.

"My mother would say I have a morbid fascination with these meetings," said Cornelia.

"Well, I don't know about morbid," the woman laughed, "I'm sure you're learning *lots* of interesting things."

Cornelia's eyebrows rose as she darted her an assessing glance. "Well, my mother says my father didn't teach us how to ride bikes or to tie our shoelaces or to throw a ball or comb our hair. But just recently," she said this last word carefully as if she had just added it to her vocabulary, "I guess he is trying to teach us how to listen to God."

"That's *wonderful*," said the woman, "and what do you think of our fearless leaders?" She nodded her head toward the dais where Horace Baker was flanked by two men, Hall Hamden and Hadji Nehru.

She looked toward the dais and considered her answer. Horace seemed child-like, she thought. It was said he had a divine connection to God like no other. Sometimes, as if he had been given cookies for a snack, he beamed when someone spoke. Then, with his bald head and large ears, he looked like an elf. But when he thundered and disapproved and spoke of sin, she thought, his beady eyes and weak chin made him look more like a ferret. "Horace looks kind of weaselly."

"Oh my," said the woman and leaned away from her.

"And Hall Hamden's head is too big for his body. But my roommate thinks he's awfully good-looking. I don't know about that. I think he smiles too much. I call it the Absolute smile. The truth is I don't know if he's smiling or snarling."

"That's enough now," said the woman, squirming and looking around.

"I'm only trying to be absolutely honest, you know." And Cornelia fixed her with a stern look, "Don't you want to know what I think of Hadji?"

"I guess I do." She tittered.

"I like him. His hair is shiny. And his skin is golden. He's East Indian, you know. His grandfather was a famous guru. And he's not a kid like me. But he's not a grown-up like everyone else." She sighed, "He's a teenager. And I like the way he flicks his hair back off his forehead. Like this." She raked her lank bangs back up off her face, exposing a wide domed forehead. But she did not smile. "But most of all I like what he says."

The woman pushed at the arms of her seat to stand. "Well, I have to go now. Lovely chatting with you." Cornelia dipped her chin and the glare that shone out from beneath the protuberant brows and perfectly arched eyebrows reminded the woman of a diving hawk. The woman sank back down in her seat. "Tell me then. What do you like best about what Hadji says?"

"I liked best what he said about the four Absolute Morals. Absolute Love means you forgive your neighbor for being different. Absolute Purity means you have a fire in your gut to cure the hurt in the world. Not like Mrs. Rogers who says, when she talks about purity, that all women are the same under the sheets whether you look like Snow White or the wicked witch, like she does."

The woman gasped but Cornelia prattled on. "Hadji says Absolute Unselfishness means that you put others' needs first. And share your bread with them. I guess that being absolutely unselfish means I have to accept that Daddy probably loves Horace more than he does us."

"Certainly not," whispered the woman, "I'm sure your father loves you very much."

"Well, I'm just being absolutely honest you know. And by the way, Hadji says Absolute Honesty means being willing to admit that people and countries have made mistakes and that by making amends, and by loving them and saying you're sorry first, you can make a difference in each of us, and then our families, and then our countries and finally the whole world." She waved her hands to include the whole meeting hall. "So, I have to love you all. Even if I don't." Her head sank. She inhaled deeply, shook herself, rocked up onto her toes and turned abruptly toward the woman, "Namaste," she said, putting her hands in the prayer pose. She bowed slightly in the woman's direction "May the divine in me recognize the divine in you. Namaste. That's what Hadji says."

"Oh," said the woman and fled.

That night, for the first time in weeks, Cornelia and Nathan had dinner with their father in the general dining room. Cornelia looked around at the hundreds of tables covered with starched tablecloths, surrounded by thousands of people eating. She picked up her stainless-steel fork. "How come," she asked C.W., "you get to eat in Horace's dining room? My roommate Gertrude says they have fine bone china and sterling silver in Horace's dining room. How come you always get to eat there and we don't? Mummy wouldn't like if she knew you weren't spending time with us."

Nathan kicked her under the table. "He *is* spending time with us."

"I mean like every day," said Cornelia.

C.W. didn't answer. He cut his grey meat up into tiny pieces, which he then chewed and chewed, too much, thought Cornelia. "All is well," he intoned.

Cornelia noticed that he had a very large head, and his shoulders were too broad for his skinny body. And he twitched before he spoke. "Things are going right along," he said. His shoulders hitched as if someone had admonished him.

"Things are *not* going right along," said Cornelia, "I want to go home. I miss Mummy. And the dogs. And books that I can read. I hate it here. Everyone's always talking about *lusting* after their neighbors, whatever that means. And how they *need* to take a walk because the demon of wanting a drink is chasing them. Are there really demons like that here? If so, then I *really* want to go home. Like, right now." Despite her best efforts, Cornelia's chin wobbled. She blinked furiously to fight back tears.

Nathan looked at her in astonishment. He was always amazed, he often told her, by how she couldn't just let things be.

"Demons chase all of us." C.W. set down his fork and splayed his long fingers out over the pristine tablecloth. But he couldn't look at his children. He never even touched them, Cornelia thought, he never tucked them into bed, he only taught them how to say their prayers and to write down their guidance in little black books.

"Well, if those demons chased me, I'd never let them catch me. I'd just run faster." Nathan laughed and managed to get a smile from Cornelia.

When she smiled, though she didn't know it, her pinched face let loose and lit up like a paper unfurling in a warm flame. But then Cornelia looked back at C.W. and the frown returned. "But why, Daddy? Why do demons chase everyone? Are they fire-breathing devils like Horace says?"

"Well, no but...."

"Then what do you mean?" Her black eyes drilled into him.

"God has a plan for all of us. We just have to ask."

"What's his plan for us? What's his plan for Mummy? Why does she have no money when you have so much?"

"God disposes as he sees fit," said C.W., poking tiny wipes of his napkin at the corners of his mouth, his eyes darting around to all the other tables.

"Mrs. Rogers asked me today why my Mummy had sent me in a dress that was two sizes too small. She said it wasn't decent for my knees and thighs to be showing all the time. I told her it was because my mummy had no money for new clothes. Then she just shook her head like I was making up a story. I wasn't. It's true." Cornelia's tone got shrill.

Nathan jammed a whole bunch of food in his mouth until his cheeks bulged like a chipmunk's. He scraped his chair back, "May I be excused?"

"No, you may not." C.W.'s tone was stern. His face folded into disappointed lines. "God disposes where he sees fit. My guidance tells me it would not be wise for me to send more money to her at this time. Particularly when you're here learning about the right way to live."

"What does that mean? That she lives the wrong way? And if she doesn't live the way you want she gets no money? That what she says."

"Cornelia," Nathan rolled his eyes at her, "She asked us not to talk about that. May I *please* be excused?"

"No, you may *not*!" shouted C.W., bringing censuring looks from nearby tables.

Knowing that it wasn't wise, but unable to stop now that she had started, Cornelia hammered away. "And I think it's weird that I have to stay with such an old roommate. Why can't I stay with Nathan? We're used to sleeping in the same room."

"It's not proper. It can open you up to thoughts of impurity."

"What?" said Nathan, "That's disgusting. She's my sister. And we're just little kids."

C.W. chose not to answer that. Instead he said, "Besides your roommate isn't old. She's a very nice young farm girl from Idaho."

"She's 19 and I'm 7. And her voice is all flat."

"You need to learn to curb your tongue. It's not loving to comment critically on your roommate's accent."

"I thought we were supposed to be absolutely honest."

"Well we are but..."

"Besides, she's always mooning after Hall Hamden."

"What?" C.W. shot her a quizzical look and she knew she had finally hit a sore point.

"She says he's righteously good-looking, that his face must be blessed in the Lord's eyes and that he's always hanging around the kitchen, making her nervous so she can't stop breaking the yolks of eggs when they're supposed to stay together to be fried. She says he makes her go all hot and bothered and then she gets all flushed and goes and undresses in the closet so that I can't see that she has big boobies."

"She does?" Nathan's jaw dropped open.

"Yeah, just like Mummy."

"That's enough," C.W. slammed the palms of his hands down on the table and stood up, almost knocking over his chair. "You," he pointed a finger at Nathan, "can be excused."

Nathan shoved back his chair and bolted from the room.

"And you," C.W. pointed his finger at Cornelia, "Will come with me to have guidance."

He grabbed her by her bony wrist and yanked her out of the room, then down the hall to a private sitting room overlooking the lake. He jammed her black book at her. "Sit down. Pray for forgiveness and guidance. The business of other men and women is *no* business of yours."

She sat. Her throat swelled as if a bloated toad was jammed at the apex of her lung. It hurt when she breathed. He sat down across from her. His face was stern and frozen. He snapped open his black book.

She looked out the window at the lake where the moon studded spangles onto black waters. Somewhere maybe her mummy was looking at the same moon. She knew that her grandfather had called C.W. a living statue. Her mummy had told her that. She felt the first twinge of shame. Why was she so hateful? Why did she say things that upset people? What about her words had transgressed the four Absolute Moral standards? She hadn't been dishonest. She hadn't been impure. She didn't think she had been selfish. Well, maybe a little bit when she wished she could eat in Horace's dining room with C.W. and Nathan. But she had to admit she didn't absolutely love her roommate Gertrude. She tossed and turned too much at night. She got all sweaty along her upper lip when she talked about Hall Hamden. So, after five long minutes of silence, when C.W. asked her to share, she did her best.

"I'm sorry I was selfish about wanting to eat in Horace's dining room."

"Apology accepted. Anything more?"

She squirmed, "I guess I was unloving toward Gertrude. I guess I owe her an apology."

C.W. nodded his head in approval. "Maybe a living amends?"

"What's that?"

"That's when you do something nice for the person. Or do something they ask you to do whether you want to or not."

"Like she's been asking me to go riding with her? Even though Mummy says I shouldn't go riding with anyone else, I should go?"

"That would be good. And my guidance is, as always, that all is well," he intoned, "All will go along."

But her father was wrong, Cornelia thought a few days later. All was not well, all was not just going along.

Chapter 2

It had all started out so wonderfully. They had left the lodge at an early hour. As soon as they were outside, Gertrude's stern demeanor changed. She became all giggly and over-enthusiastic, a little bit, thought Cornelia, like her own mother Nevin when she was in one of her giddy, "let's have a wonderful adventure" moods.

"Will I be back in time for housekeeping duty?" she asked Gertrude.

"Oh, never mind that," Gertrude waved her hand, "Who cares about that old biddy Mrs. Rogers?" Out of her prim shirt dress and stuffed into tight jeans, Gertrude looked almost pretty. Though her nose still looked as lumpy as a potato, the brisk lake air brought out roses in her cheeks.

"I like you in jeans," Cornelia said.

Gertrude blushed, "First time I've been in jeans in weeks. I used to live in blue jeans. Come on, let's run."

They ran wildly down the hill to where the stables were next to the lake. It was a big lofty building with soft wooden floors and piles of fragrant hay, and Cornelia could have stayed there for hours just listening to the horses chomping on their oats and stomping their feet and inhaling the yeasty smell of their sweat tempered by the fresh air blowing in off the lake.

The man in charge of the stable chose an old gelding for Cornelia. Gertrude chose a black glossy mare for herself, one who pawed at the sawdust and tossed her head when the bit went in.

"Make sure to keep the child on the lead," said the stableman.

Gertrude tossed her head. "We'll be fine."

At first it had all been magical. Following dutifully along on his lead, Cornelia's horse clopped along down a soft dirt trail that meandered next to the sparkling waters of the lake. She was thrilled to be riding. She quickly adapted to the horse's rhythm, rocking back and forth, lulled by the slow and steady gait. But then they turned inland and steeply uphill and suddenly the saddle seemed slippery and the earth a very long way below. It was at that moment that she firmly grasped the saddle horn.

Gertrude curled around and called back over her shoulder, "Isn't this the best? Don't you just love it? Wait until you see the view from the top!"

As promised, the view was certainly magnificent. Down below, the Lodge's four Absolute Moral pennants snapped in the breeze, and the sapphire lake stretched until the horizon absorbed the sky and it was all a huge silvery bowl of light.

But then they turned into a thick pine forest and Gertrude picked up the pace. Dark and gloomy woods stretched out on either side of the path. The air was brisk and sharp with pine resin, swooshing past Cornelia's ears, burning her cheeks, and roaring up into her nose in an almost painful rush. Beneath her, the big gelding slammed into a trot, banging her up and down in a most uncomfortable manner. She clung harder to the saddle horn. How had the peaceful gait turned so rough? And why? The only time she had ridden before was at a carnival. This new experience was alien. Once more she was reminded of her mother and of how her promised "wonderful adventures" often turned scary.

Ahead of her on the bridle path, Gertrude seemed to be one with her horse. No air appeared between her rump and the horse's back. She turned and trotted back toward Cornelia and with a wild toss of her head, said "I'm going to unlatch you now. I want to go a little faster. But you hold him back and you'll be fine." And before Cornelia could protest, Gertrude leaned down and unclipped the lead. Then she turned and kicked her horse into a gallop, fast disappearing around a curve in the trail.

Cornelia's horse stood quietly for a moment, staring at the fast disappearing duo, then everything went silent for a split second before he lurched back into a banging trot. The air rushed past; the wind burned her cheeks; the pine trees swept by in a green blur; and every bone in her body was rattled. Just when she thought her jaw was going to break, her horse's trot smoothed out into a wonderfully rocking canter.

She grinned. She was flying! Exhilaration bubbled through Cornelia. Then, with no warning, once again everything changed.

The horse staggered, then stumbled. Cornelia was pitched forward and over head. And then she was truly flying. For one long soaring moment, she paralleled the ground. Time stretched out like taffy, endlessly unfurling, until the ground flew up at her, and she slammed into an embankment.

Stunned, she lay there without moving, looking back at her horse. Some fifteen feet away on a patch of bright green grass. She felt a thudding of hooves, that came to a halt with a squeak of leather as Gertrude jumped off her horse and ran to her side.

"What happened?" She cried out, "How did this happen? Everything was going so well." Gertrude yowled and broke out into a storm of weeping. Her tiny potato nose turned white at the tip and dark red splotched her face. "Are you okay?"

Cornelia was too stunned to answer. She was keeping very still. Every part of her hurt. She was afraid that, like Humpty Dumpty, she had cracked and would never come together again.

"Are you hurt? You can't be hurt. They'll blame me." And again, she howled. But she did lean down and examine Cornelia. When she came to her wrist, Cornelia squealed. Gertrude made her wiggle her fingers.

"Never mind. I know it hurts, but I'm sure it'll be fine. As long as you can wiggle your fingers." Suddenly all business, Gertrude wiped her nose with her shirt, whipped off the red kerchief from around her neck, then carefully folded it into a triangle, turning it into a primitive sling.

"I am so sorry," she said, "This is all my fault. I don't know what got into me. I just wanted to go fast. I should never have...." Her words trailed off.

Cornelia blinked and tightened her lips, determined not to cry.

"I promise you," Gertrude held up her pinky toward Cornelia's good hand, "I promise you we'll walk the whole way back."

And they did. And except for the searing pain shooting up and down Cornelia's arm, everything went well. The stableman wasn't there when they got back. Gertrude quickly unsaddled the horses and put them in their stalls, while Cornelia sat on a corner bench, gritting her teeth to keep them from chattering. Then they started the long walk back uphill toward the lodge, which towered over them. The sun had already slipped behind the steep hillside, and there was a sudden dark chill in the air.

When they finally got to the main entrance, Gertrude looked down at her watch and gasped, "I was due in Horace's dining room twenty minutes ago. I've got to run." She looked down at Cornelia, "You'll be fine, you've got to be fine. I just know it. Look, ask the lady right over there," she nodded at the lady behind the reception desk. "She'll help you find your Daddy and he'll take you to a doctor." She led her over to the reception desk. But the lady was on the phone with someone and waved at them to wait.

Again, Gertrude looked at her watch.

"I'll be fine," said Cornelia, "Just go."

Cornelia sat down on a bench and waited for the woman to get off the phone. But when the woman finally did, she seemed to have forgotten all about Cornelia because she too looked down at her wristwatch, gulped, then dashed off down the hall as if tied to a string that was pulling her away.

Cornelia sat quietly for five minutes more until a man ambled down the hallway and took his place behind the desk. After he finished shuffling some papers he looked up and saw her watching him. "Can I help you?" he asked, but without waiting for her answer, brightly continued, "Where are you supposed to be right now? Why are you just sitting there?"

She said nothing, hoping he would note the sling on her arm. She was afraid if she spoke she would start bawling.

"Don't you have a schedule?" He persisted. "We all have schedules."

Cornelia nodded.

"Well, what is it?"

And now she could tell he was getting annoyed, as grown-ups will with children who don't talk. Just as annoyed, she thought, as when she talked too much. And so she whispered, "Housekeeping?"

"Well, go along then." He waved his fingers at her, and then turned to look out the door as a carriage drew up and spilled out a bunch of newcomers.

She thought about trying to find her father, but she had no idea where he was actually staying in the giant building. She didn't have the energy to climb the seven flights to her room, so she wandered down the hallway and found the housekeeping room, which was empty, and sat down in one of the chairs and stared out the window at the lake which looked steely grey now and as wrinkled as damp clothes left overnight in a basket. She wondered who was hanging out the clothes to dry at home now that she was no longer there to do her chores. Cornelia fell into a dazed slumber until she heard the twist of a door knob. She awoke with a start and gasped in pain as she pushed with her hurt arm away from where she had been slumped.

"Where have you been?" Mrs. Roger said, "You missed the housekeeping meeting. Rudy here had to cover for you." She motioned to the pudgy young girl behind her, flanked by two young women.

Cornelia held up her sling. "Gertrude took me riding. And I got hurt."

"That sling doesn't look very professional. What did the doctor say?"

She shook her head. "I didn't go to the doctor."

"Why didn't Gertrude take you to the clinic?"

"She said I was okay. That I could wiggle my fingers."

"Okay then, I guess it can't be so bad then, can it now? *Do you think* you need to go to the doctor?" Mrs. Roger's chin lowered, and her eyebrows rose.

Tears stung the corners of Cornelia's eyes, but she gritted her teeth and blinked them back. She shook her head.

"So." Mrs. Rogers glared at her. "No doctor, no malingering. Horace says when we don't honor our duties we're not being absolutely loving. As I said, we already covered for you. But one room still remains to be done and I expect you can manage that, even if your arm does hurt just a teeny bit." She cackled and shared knowing glances with the other women.

The pudgy girl simpered and cut her eyes toward Cornelia who grimaced back.

"And after you're done," said Mrs. Rogers, "I would like you to have Quiet Time for exaggerating to get out of working. Funny thing how everyone gets 'cramps.'" She frowned at the young women cowering next to her. "And headaches and imaginary hurts just when there's work to be done. So go along now, room 2211, up on the second floor."

Cornelia trailed along the second floor until she found room 2211 way down at the end. Then she located the housekeeping closet, took out a fresh batch of sheets, a cleaning caddy and plodded back to the room, being careful to do everything with her right hand. It was a tiny room along the backside of the giant structure, with no view of the lake. She guessed it was fated to be the room of someone not very important, someone who would not be dining in Horace's special dining room. She cleaned the toilet with one hand, changed the roll of toilet paper, rinsed out the sink and cleaned the mirror, but when it came time to make the bed she realized there was no way she could do it with only one hand. When she tried, her wrist throbbed with pain. In frustration, she flung out her good hand and, to her dismay, clipped the china lamp sitting on the bedside table.

It teetered for one long second, then tumbled over and crashed down onto the floor. As her heart hammered, she stayed silent and listened, but no one came running. She kicked the broken pieces under the bed, sure that at any moment, Mrs. Rogers would be coming to find her. But the halls were oddly quiet and then she remembered it was time for general assembly. She crept out, leaving the lamp under the bed, and ran to the back-hallway staircase and scampered up the six flights of stairs as fast as she could go. She carefully laid down on her bed, careful to place her hurt arm on top.

Just as her heart was settling down, she heard footsteps pounding up the staircase and, convinced it was Mrs. Rogers pursuing her like a harpy in a fairy tale, she launched herself off the bed and rolled underneath it, yanking the pale chenille spread down low enough to hide her.

Gertrude stomped into the room and dragged her suitcase from under her bed. Just as Cornelia was thinking of rolling out and letting her know that she was there, she heard another set of footsteps, slower and measured, and she saw Gertrude freeze and go up on tiptoe as if she were about to run.

A male voice called out, "Gertrude?"

"Hall Hamden," Gertrude whispered.

"I know you're in there. I followed you out of the dining room. I think we need to have a little talk. Horace and I are not at all pleased with your performance."

Gertrude gasped, then softly said, "Come in."

Cornelia could see his highly polished oxford shoes standing way too close to Gertrude's cowboy boots. His voice was like a dog growling at a stranger. "First of all, you come into Horace's dining smelling sweaty and wearing pants that are far too tight. What were you thinking? You know Horace says ladies must dress modestly so as not to inspire lust in the hearts of men."

"I took Cornelia riding."

"That's no excuse. It shows a lack of care and grooming. Horace himself has asked me to talk to you, to instill in you just how disappointed he is." His voice rose to a bark. "Your lack of attention to detail. After we brought you into the fold. Provided you with so much opportunity. And how do you repay us?"

He stamped his foot. "Not a good thing. Showing up dressed in an impure manner. I could *smell* you. Then, spilling soup and running away when you're taken to task. This is *not* how we behave when we live by Absolute Moral standards."

"I'm sorry," she wailed, "I've been trying. I really have."

There was a long silence. "Be honest, Gertrude, you have impure thoughts about me, don't you? *Don't you?*" His voice lowered to a snarl.

"Yes," she whispered and looked down, "I'm so ashamed."

Cornelia could hear Hall Hamden breathing as hard as if he had been running. He walked to the door and Cornelia thought he was leaving until she heard the lock click into place. His footsteps were slow in coming back, but measured and heavy, and his breathing grew ragged. "You want it, don't you, you're just a little bitch in heat, aren't you now?"

Gertrude moaned.

From her vantage point from under the bed, Cornelia could see their shoes were very close together now. "This is what you wanted, isn't it? You knew I'd come after you, didn't you? I could smell you. Just like a bitch in heat! Admit it. This is what you wanted isn't it?"

"Yes," she whimpered.

His breathing grew even more ragged. "What, did you think I didn't notice? Swinging those hips. Leaning over when you know I'm coming into the kitchen. Staring at me with those lustful eyes. I know what you want. I saw it the moment I laid eyes on you." And with that Cornelia heard a resounding smack of flesh against flesh and she thought maybe he was beating her as some villagers did their dogs and young children.

And then Cornelia heard the yank of a zipper, a yelp from Gertrude, and then more smacking of flesh. The cries no longer sounded like pain but how the nanny goats grunted when the Billy goats climb on top of them. Then suddenly the room fell quiet and there was a groan from Hall Hamden. Cornelia heard Gertrude gasping for air like a fish out of water, and she could only see his feet on the floor. Then she heard Hall Hamden hissing, "Say something and I'll kill you, bitch. I swear I will. You know I will."

Then in a flash, he was gone, and Cornelia stayed under the bed, confused about what had happened and too frightened to move.

Chapter 3

An hour later, Cornelia crawled out from under the bed, sensing by Gertrude's even breathing that she was asleep. Gertrude lay splayed out, her mouth hanging open, her face scrunched down to one side. Her jeans were down around her knees. As Cornelia tiptoed past, she spotted a row of crescent shaped bites all along her shoulder muscle below her rucked-up shirt. Cornelia shuddered. She had once watched a child get bitten by a dog. These had the same ugly look to them, but they were the shape of a human mouth.

She yanked off her riding clothes with her good hand and threw them under the bed, then pulled on the faded dress she'd worn on her first day there, not caring that she couldn't close the buttons in the back with only one hand. Then she tugged off the rubber bands that had held her tightly braided hair, done that morning by Gertrude, and raked her fingers through to let it unfurl like a flag across her back and shoulders. Then she tiptoed across the room and out the door. She flew down the stairs, out across the giant entrance hall, and back to the front desk.

It was the same pinched young man who had waved her off earlier. He looked up, a frown crossing his face. She stamped her foot. "This time you will pay attention to me. I need you to find my father. Now!"

"Hold your horses," snapped the young man.

"That's just the problem," she raged, "I didn't know how to hold my horse. That's how I got hurt. And now someone else is hurt. And no one will listen to me." She wailed, turned and ran blindly away from him down the long hall, slamming into someone before she could stop. A chuckle surprised her. She looked up to see Hadji, the teenage East Indian boy who had spoken in the meeting. "What's the all fire rush? Your hair is flying up all around you like golden silk threads in a sudden breeze." He spoke in this wonderful singsong accent. It had the fluty tones of the English, but with more of a rollicking cadence. After a quick glimpse at him she looked down but didn't try to squirm away. Something about the way he cupped her shoulders was reassuring. He had big shining eyes and his mouth tugged up at the corners when he smiled.

"I'm just trying to find my father."

"And what has kept you from doing so?" he asked.

"My daddy never even told me what room he was in, and I don't know where Nathan is. He's my brother, and he's on a totally different schedule than me. And I hate it. What's wrong with everybody? Why is everyone here so awful? Why does everyone think they're behaving so absolutely wonderful when actually they're just creepy." She finished, knowing she must sound whiny and awful. "And this one?" She nodded back toward the man at the reception desk, "He just won't help me at all."

"Come now, let's see if he won't tell us now where we can find your father." He kindly led her back toward the desk, tipping his head to one side and speaking ever so politely but imperatively. He was very tall and held himself as if he were used to getting answers. His profile had the perfection of the Persian miniatures in her fairy tale books. Apparently Hadji had some clout where she had none.

"What's that name did you say?" The young man smiled and rubbed his hands together, with a nervous look at an imperious man in African robes who stood behind them, ostentatiously clearing his throat.

"Cornelius. Worthington. Woodstock." Cornelia managed to say his name but then, to her humiliation, she whimpered. Hadji patted her on the back.

The young man at the desk thumbed through an index card file box. "Okay, okay, let me see. Here it is!" He pulled out the index card, holding it up as if it were a winning lottery ticket. "Let's see. He's in room 2023, and let's see, on dining room duty right now, setting up for dinner."

She turned to run away but Hadji stopped her again, kneeling down and touching her arm in the sling. "What's this?" he said kindly, "Did you hurt yourself?"

Before she could answer his hands went without hesitation to where it hurt most. His brow was furrowed. As he looked down, she noticed that his thick eyelashes were so long that they kissed the top of his cheeks. Absurdly, she wondered whether his cheeks were as soft as they looked. He cupped her wrist with both his warm brown hands, then slipped one hand down over hers and pressed his thumb down into the center of her palm and gently massaged.

She gasped. The pain radiated out from her wrist and down into the palm. "This needs to be taken care of," He said quietly, "You're hurt!" He continued his gentle massage of her palm and it both magnified yet eased the pain.

Her throat swelled. Carefully pulling her arm away from him, she didn't stop to say thank you, but wheeled around and ran off, her golden hair flying out behind her, back down the hall toward the long dining rooms that looked out over the lake.

The huge dining room was half the length of the building, built to serve five hundred at a time, with fifty tables in rows, each table seating ten. At the far end of the dining room, Cornelia spied her very tall and skinny father leaning down over a tray full of glasses. He had on a long dark apron over his grey flannel trousers and pressed white shirt; the tiny bow in the back made her furious. Why was her father being treated like a servant while a beast like Hall Hamden was considered practically a prince? The injustice of it struck her like a blow and she slowed from a flat-out run to a walk while she considered how best to approach her father.

Finally, she stood next to him for a while before he noticed that she was there. She watched his hands tremble as he tried to fold the napkins into pretty shapes like the sample one set out in front of him. When he turned to fetch more napkins, he startled as if she were a ghost and not his own daughter.

"I hate that they make you wear an apron."

"I am happy to serve."

"We have to leave here. Something really bad just happened."

As he stared at her, she could sense worry fluttering across his broad forehead like ripples across sand flats. "You know I have committed myself to staying," he chided, holding up one finger, shaking it at her. "Just because you want to leave doesn't mean it will happen. This is *not* about you getting your way, Cornelia. I think Mrs. Rogers is right, you are a classic case of self-will run riot."

"That's not what this is about." She stamped her foot and planted her hands on her hips.

"Did you think I wouldn't find out?" He looked down at her with disapproval.

"You know?" She stammered, relieved that he already knew about Hall Hamden and how bad he was.

"Mrs. Rogers told me all about it. She was most disappointed that you tried to hide the evidence."

She looked up at him in astonishment and then, with a sick feeling of disappointment, she remembered. "The lamp?"

His lips drew into one tight line and he nodded his head, "I'm afraid so. And making up stories about a hurt arm to get out of chores. You have much work to do before blaming others. Don't forget that when you point your finger at someone there are always two fingers pointing back at you."

"This is so unfair." The tears that she had been holding back all day long burst out, and she howled. Terror, frustration, and homesickness all combined into a horrible morass of emotions, roiling into sobs, until she no longer knew what was bothering her, only that she was miserable and alone and very scared.

"You will *not* make a spectacle of yourself here in this public place." He grabbed her by her good arm, hauled her through the dining room, out into the hall, and then opened a door to a tiny room with stiff couches and several writing desks in a row under the windows. "Here!" And he thrust her to a wooden seat. He handed her pen and paper. "We *will* have guidance. Now."

Gradually her sobs settled into gentle hiccups. She drew a deep shuddering breath and looked out to the lake. The sun was hidden by the steep hill behind the conference center, and long purple shadows in the shape of the four towers and the giant teepee crept out across the waters. For a moment, her brain felt scrambled, but as she relaxed, a clear clarion voice came zinging into her head, ringing around and around as if a silver arrow had penetrated her thoughts.

"*Stay calm. Tell him. Tell him now.* She tried to ignore the voice, but it hounded her, spinning in her brain until she felt compelled to speak.

As she told about the horses and the fall, he scowled and would not look at her. But when she finally spoke of Hall Hamden and Gertrude, his eyes popped open and he met her gaze with a deep penetrating one of his own. She came to a faltering stop. "Are you still mad at me?"

He looked at her arm still in its homemade sling, back up to her face, and then to the words in the opened black book in his lap. "Listen to her," he read aloud. "She speaks the absolute truth." He stood up, "We must go see Horace." And with that, he led her out of the tiny reading room and down the hall toward Horace's special VIP dining room to which she had never been invited. The dining room was fancy with carved wooden walls, six tables of eight each, set for dinner with shining crystal and silver. On the far side of the room was an oak door with a silver knocker shaped like a star. Her father reached up and gave it one sharp rap.

A young man opened the door and frowned. "Horace is resting now," he said, "he's not receiving callers."

"Tell him Cornelius Woodstock and his daughter Cornelia are here to see him."

The young man rocked back on his heels and stammered, "I'll see what I can do." He retreated across the room and returned with a surprised look on his face. "He'll see you now. And I'm to go fetch you some tea and cookies and chocolates! He'll be with you in a minute."

They sat down side by side on the small tufted couch placed along one wall. Cornelia thought her mummy would have called it a charming room. It was full of warmth from the dancing fire crackling below a marble hearth. Large fragrant bouquets of flowers decorated every table. All the chairs looked formal and upright but had thick stuffed cushions plumped up for comfort.

The door to the bedroom opened and Horace walked out, wearing a brocade dressing gown with a tied sash, leaning heavily on a wooden cane with a carved dog head on which he kept his hands tightly curled. His bald head gleamed in the firelight. He sank down into the chair across from them, his eyes glittering as if with fever, his face wreathed with welcoming smiles. "I've been expecting you," he sighed, "God has been clamoring in my head about you all day long!"

Horace settled himself down into the chair then leaned in toward them. He reached out to pat Cornelia's good hand. His other hand remained curled around the ornate walking stick. Those fingers were atrophied, turned inward like a claw. Seeing the direction of her gaze, he whispered. "Do not fear. There is nothing to fear here. God protects those he loves."

She dared to look up into his eyes. His gaze was penetrating and bore down into her very innards. He was quiet for a long moment, as was she. He nodded his head as if he could divine her very thoughts.

"Mrs. Rogers believes she's too used to getting her own way," said C.W. "Too smart for her own good, she said, a perfect example of a child whose self-will has run rough shod on all those around her. She feels she has been malingering to get out of her duty time." C.W. fell silent.

Cornelia wanted to protest. Didn't they understand that she was used to hard work? In the islands her farm chores took up hours of every day. She wondered whether Mrs. Rogers thought she was spoiled because C.W. was rich. But before she could say anything, to her surprise, Horace came to her defense.

Horace waved his fingers. "Mrs. Rogers is nothing but a dried-up prune of a bitter old woman! She has her moments, but she forgets what it is to be young."

"I don't know about that," C.W. faltered. "It's just that Cornelia is now telling this story about Hall. If she's been lying and malingering with Mrs. Rogers, then how am I to believe this new tale? And yet my guidance was to listen to her."

Without letting go of Cornelia's hand, Horace gave C.W. one penetrating look. "Good. It's *time* you listened to her. You came to the right place. It's clear to me this child is in pain. And *very* hungry. It's about time for you to understand, C.W., no matter what she has done, no matter what she has to tell us, she's just a *child*." This last was thundered. "Something you know, my good friend, very little about."

A sob threatened to break out of the wedge in Cornelia's throat. Instead she took a deep shuddering breath. Horace tightened his grip on her good hand and leaned back in toward her. "We're going to get you some tea and cookies. And chocolates. You'd like that, wouldn't you?"

She couldn't remember the last time she had eaten. Horace nodded his head, then let go of her hand and slumped back into his seat. His jaw hung slack for a moment. His eyes were glassy.

"Horace!" C.W. sprang to his feet.

Horace waved his hand at him. "Sit back down!" He barked. Then came a knock on the door and a young man came in carrying a silver tray with a pot of steaming tea and a plateful of oatmeal cookies. He set the tray down carefully on the table, leaving it slightly askew.

Horace frowned at him, "Straighten it up. Don't be sloppy." The young man blushed and straightened the tray until its lines were parallel to the table.

"Now, isn't that better?" smiled Horace. "Absolute love is all about getting it just right, Jesus knew that." The young man blushed again and turned to leave. "Send for the doctor!" Horace called out to him just before the door closed. For a long moment, the only sounds were the crackle of the fire and the gentle ticking of the clock, then Horace chuckled.

"Just Exactly Suits Us Sinners!" crowed Horace. "Get it?" he questioned me. "J.E.S.U.S." Horace smiled, "Eat. Eat. Enjoy."

Cornelia reached for a cookie, took one nibble then, as the sugar and butter melted in her mouth, jammed the whole cookie in and reached for another.

"Cornelia," her father chided.

"C.W., I told you. *Let the child be.* Stop trying to control her. For God's sake let her be a child. Something no one ever allowed you to be, I might add."

For several minutes Cornelia was almost senseless with pleasure, jamming cookie after cookie into her mouth until her stomach rebelled and she had to stop. She was out of breath and panting.

"That a girl," chuckled Horace. He leaned over the table and with his one good hand tremblingly poured a cup of tea, then added a lot of cream and sugar and nodded at her. She smiled at him and nodded back, picking up the teacup and drinking huge drafts as fast as she could. She emptied the cup and held it out for more. "More, please!"

And Horace poured her more. Then he handed her a box of chocolates and she took one.

After Horace poured her a third cup of tea, he nodded as if pleased with her behavior then settled back down into his plumped-up chair, curled both hands around the head of his cane, sighed once, then began to talk.

"Let me tell you a story of a man I once knew. He was a tight man. A greedy man. A man who knew nothing about giving. Just taking. Yet the more he took, the more he wanted. And he became convinced that others were taking advantage of him. He blamed them for the fact that he wasn't richer then he was. No one could fetch his dinner fast enough. No one could polish his shoes bright enough. In fact, no one could please him at all. He was a bitter, unhappy man, convinced that the whole world was taking advantage of him."

"Like Scrooge," she whispered.

Horace pointed one finger at her and smiled, 'Exactly right. Except this man lived here in this country somewhere to the south of here in a city you may know called Philadelphia. Your father will take you there sometime. It's a wonderful city, full of history and splendid walks. Anyway, I met this man at a dinner given by friends. And he dominated the conversation the entire time. Everyone was silent because he was so important, you see, so used to everyone paying attention that he no longer knew how to listen to anyone else. And there was a child there, a rather young boy, unsure of his place at the table and I began to watch him rather than his father. I saw the pain in this child who had likely been silenced since birth by this father sucking the very oxygen out of the room until there was none left for this child to breathe."

C.W. leaned forward, his bony knees spread wide apart, his large hands folded into each other, kneading themselves as if wringing out laundry, and tears began streaming down his face, his mouth held wide open in silent grief. The hair on the back of Cornelia's neck rose up. She didn't know that her father could ever cry.

"Sounds familiar, doesn't it, C.W.?" Horace's voice was tight.

C.W. nodded, his large skull wobbled above his thin neck.

"You see child," Horace looked back at her and there was kindness in his eyes, "That young boy was your father. It was many years ago.

But I remember. I remember. I swore to myself that night that one day I would save that child from his pain. And now he has a chance at a new life. Here. With us. And you would want that for him, wouldn't you?" Horace's head snapped back toward her and his eyes were beady and penetrating, as if he were a hawk staring at a small mouse beneath a tree.

She nodded. A honey-colored haze fell over the room. The fire still crackled; the light outside was a lovely cobalt blue. C.W. gradually collected himself. He exhaled so deeply that Cornelia felt sure he was deflating. But then he would suck in the air just as deeply. And that cycle went on for quite a while.

Horace appeared to be catnapping, his head was down, and his eyes closed. In a sugar daze, Cornelia looked out the window where the lake was all violet in the evening. She wondered why sunsets lasted so long in this icy north. In the islands, night fell over the world like a black cloak. Here, the light faded away to dark after many long hours of blue.

A knock came, and like a turtle coming out of its shell. Horace lifted his head up, blinking his eyes, and called out shrilly, "Come in! Come in! Whomever you are!"

A shiny pate poked its way around the opening door and a portly elderly man tiptoed in carrying a black leather doctor's bag.

"Ahh! Good, good, good!" He banged his cane on the floor. Here's the good Doctor Jones. No, no, it's not for me. That can wait. Take a look at the girl's left arm, looks a bit swollen and painful to me and I should know!" He waved his curled-up hand around, making fun of his own disability. And then he burst into a great gurgling belly laugh that was entirely contagious.

Cornelia snorted. She was glad Nevin wasn't around to chastise her for making such an unladylike sound. She dared a peek at her father and, to her delight, his eyes crinkled with pleasure. She could see spasms rolling up out of his chest, and, for the first time in her life, she heard her father laugh. Twice in the last few minutes she had seen her father in a different light. First, he had cried and now he laughed. It made him seem much more human, less wooden, and more like a real person and not just a disciplinarian. She found herself wishing she had known him as child. Maybe she would have even liked him. She tucked that thought away, as if it were a cookie she was saving for later.

The doctor examined her arm, twisting and turning and probing, until she gasped with pain. "Hmmm, let's see." He tapped her elbow; patted her wrist gently. "You'll be fine. It's a bad sprain, which, by the way, I'm sure hurts like the dickens."

Cornelia nodded her head. She liked the way he was assumed she could understand. "It's possible," he continued, stroking her arm, "That you have a hairline fracture. Keep your arm in the sling. I don't have to tell you to be cautious."

"Tell Mrs. Rogers that," she blurted out.

Horace barked with laughter and rolled his eyes at her.

"And you should have an x-ray when you get back to the mainland," continued the doctor. "But you're young and green and you bend just like a twig..."

"Not like us old oaks who crack with every wind." Again, Horace barked with laughter. For a few seconds, they all rocked with laughter. For Cornelia, it was a wonderful release from all the sadness she had been feeling ever since she had arrived at the island.

Finally, Horace banged his cane for silence. "That's enough of that. My good doctor, please come back a bit later for me, if you will. In the meantime, we still have things to settle here, yes indeed, tales to tell, and secrets to divulge." And with that, the good doctor bowed himself out and left the three of them alone.

By this time, the fire had died down to a glowing bed of coals. The light outside had turned an inky black. A golden clock whirled and clicked beneath a glass dome on the marble mantel above the fire. The firelight cast deep shadows on Horace's face, carving scythes next to his cheeks, and highlighting the beaky curve of his nose. As her father leaned forward and lowered his head, his prominent brows cast shadows down over his cheeks, until he looked almost like a skull. Fear flickered back through her. The friendly laughter was forgotten. The stern father had returned.

"Now child, it is time for you to be Absolutely Honest!" And with that Horace stopped and waited for her to talk.

She looked down at her shoes, scuffed mossy green from her fall, and she flashed back to Hall Hamden's shiny black oxfords standing too close to Gertrude's saddle shoes. And she told them what she had heard from beneath the bed. When she said the words "bitch in heat" out loud, her father flinched, but Horace remained as still as water before a storm. "Go on." He nodded.

And so, she did. When finished, Horace gave her a quick look and said, "Is that it? Is that everything?"

She nodded. He looked away and out the window to the dark night.

"Yes, yes, yes," he said, as if he were ticking off thoughts in his head, "This is troubling. This is troubling indeed. I know Hall Hamden to be a man of passion. I had hoped he had learned to let his impurities fuel, not his lust, but a wildfire that could galvanize the globe. But it seems impurity has raised its ugly head once again." And then so suddenly that her heart lurched, he banged his cane on the floor, and shouted, "*This must stop* if we are going to change the world. Change starts here. *With us*. In this room." He turned to her, his eyes narrowed, and he leaned in toward her, grabbing her good hand again, but this time in his claw hand and his long nails probed her flesh. His eyes bored deep into her soul. "But you do speak the truth, I sense that about you. My child, be *absolutely* honest now, you didn't actually *see* what happened, did you now? We don't know for sure whether what happened was forced or consensual, do we?"

"Consensual?" whispered Cornelia, "What does that mean?"

"It means," his tone was kind, "They both wanted 'it' to happen."

Her heart hammered, and fear galloped through her veins. Her thoughts were muddled, and she could not speak.

Horace's gaze bore down into her. "If something bad happened here, then you could go home now, couldn't you? Instead of staying here with your father, where the almighty may want you to be." His voice began to hammer. "Perhaps the Devil put it in your mind as to how you could best manipulate the circumstances to get your own way. You want to go home to your mother, don't you?"

She gulped and nodded.

"You would do anything?" he shouted, "Anything at all to get what you want, wouldn't you?"

He peered down at her and she felt skewered and confused. She thought about when she slammed doors to get attention, about how one day she had exaggerated her cold symptoms to get out of chores, of how she would sometimes tattle on her brother to look better in her mother's eyes. She hung her head in shame. "I'm sorry," She whispered.

"Ask and you shall be forgiven," he muttered. And then, as if his anger had burnt up all his energy, Horace slumped back down, his chin settling down onto his chest. But then, just as it seemed he might fall asleep, his head came back up, and his eyes snapped back toward her, one lid closed in a wink, and he smiled a gentle smile, holding his finger up to his lips. "Hush. You can go back to your mother. All that you have said is between us. And the guy upstairs." He waved his finger at the three of them, then pointed up toward the ceiling. Then his eyes fixed upward, and his jaw hung slack and he looked as if his spirit had gone absent.

It seemed a very long moment until his head came back down, then he slowly focused, sighed deeply and waved his hand, his face sagged with fatigue. "You are special to me, C.W.," he continued, "I am not finished with you. Nor is God finished with you. But for now, take this child away from here. Nothing must happen to cast shame on this first international conference. *Nothing* must come in the way of that. Take this child back to her mother. Then return to us. But go, *go now*." This last was shouted and they scrambled to their feet and obeyed him.

Out in the hall, two men waited, as if they had already been given orders, and shuffled them down to the front hall where their suitcases, already packed, were waiting for them. Down the steps they went to the waiting carriage where a black horse stamped its foot, and snorted steam into the now dark air.

Nathan waited for them inside the carriage. "What's going on?" He asked. But C.W. silenced him with a frown.

"More will be revealed," he said. The bells jingled on the harnesses as they dashed down the hill. Cornelia turned back once and saw the Absolute Standard banners, high above the giant edifice, no longer snapping with life from a breeze, but hanging limp in the night, drooping down around their flagpoles.

Down at the dock, several men rolled empty barrels down the ramp onto the ferry. Lights from the boat streamed out across the waters, shining down on the black surface. Iridescent oil stains swirled outside the churning wake. They walked up the gangplank and into the main cabin.

Just as the boat was about to pull away from the dock, a cluster of young women stumbled up the gangplank toward them. Two from the housekeeping crew stood on either side of a third girl whose face was so swollen from crying that it was only after a second that Cornelia realized it was Gertrude.

Cornelia threw up her chin and stared straight ahead, never once looking back in their direction. But she knew for sure now, no matter how Horace explained it, that Hall Hamden had indeed done something bad. And that there was something horribly wrong with Gertrude being banished in shame. She could only hope and believe that Hall Hamden would be treated the same way.

C.W. had retreated back into his frozen silence. She could hardly believe that just an hour before, this living statue had been laughing and crying. She wanted to cherish those moments, save them in her heart as a reminder of the time she glimpsed into her father's soul.

That night they were whisked off onto an overnight train to Detroit. Cornelia never saw Gertrude again. Nor heard what happened to her. But, as resilient children will, she gave Gertrude little thought because she and Nathan were together again, and on their way back home, going back to her flighty but loving mother, to their stepfather's stern but grounding ways, back to the wind and waters of her island life, and suddenly nothing else seemed very important.

Part II

ABSOLUTE UNSELFISHNESS

Chapter 4

Over the next few years, postcards from C.W. trickled into the island post office. Colorful stamps from places like Deutschland, Finland, Peru and Indonesia proclaimed his presence in various countries where he was travelling with the Moral Absolutes. Though Nevin encouraged them to look up the countries in their Atlas, she and Ray made fun of the name.

"The Morally Absolutlies," quipped Ray.

"And I'm sure we must be the '*Absolutely* beyond the pale and definitely not worth saving' bunch," said Nevin.

"Mummy, stop, I'm trying to read Daddy's handwriting."

"Read it aloud," said Nathan, "I can't read his writing at all."

They were seated around a simple pine table whacked together by Ray in an hour. A Bunsen burner lantern swung above them. No matter that the glass-less windows were shuttered, the trade wind breezes whistled through the cracks in the thin wood walls. Timed to the sway of the lantern, Cornelia read aloud.

"Dear Cornelia and Nathan, our force is housed above the Arctic Circle where reindeer and Laplanders live. We're finding that change knows no boundaries. All is well, Daddy." Cornelia looked up at all of them. Her scowl was fierce. "He always says that. 'All is well.' Why does he always say that? Doesn't he know I had bronchitis for five weeks and couldn't stop coughing? Doesn't he know, Mummy, that made you go to bed for five days, sick with an ulcer because the nearest doctor is 25 miles away?"

"Cornelia, why do you always have to focus on the negative? Didn't we just have a wonderful time hunting for treasure last week?

And aren't we saving up to get a boat so Nathan can go fishing whenever he wants?"

But Cornelia wouldn't let up. "What does your letter say, Mummy?" Her letters came in thin blue envelopes, typed on onionskin paper with such force that they read like inverted braille on Cornelia's fingertips.

"Do you really want to hear it?" said Nevin.

"Of course," said Cornelia.

"Is that wise?" said Ray.

"I want them to know just what kind of father they have."

"May I be excused?" said Nathan and, even though it was long after dark, ran off to join his friends. It was the time for masquerading and every night the village boys ran wild through the dirt streets wearing homemade masks and terrorizing the younger children. So Cornelia was happy to stay behind.

Nevin sighed, and then read out loud.

"Dear Nevin, I know you must wonder about my continued absence from the children's lives. But Horace and others have helped me see that there are greater needs in the world beyond one's own children."

Nevin threw down the letter as if its very touch was distasteful. "Honestly, what's wrong with him? Imagine saying that about your own children!"

"Mummy, stop making comments. Just go on!"

"Are you sure you want to hear this?" Nevin's face crumpled dramatically. "It may be just too awful and hurtful." But when Cornelia nodded, she looked pleased somehow to continue.

"The decision to live apart from them has been difficult, but it is God's will that matters more than the petty desires of one man. My course is clear. Though it may take me away from the children, the way ahead is clear to me. I must join the forces of good to set a world of change on fire. I don't expect you to understand...."

Nevin looked up from the letter at Cornelia and Ray, "No, in fact, I don't understand. I think he's just *awful*. Here we are struggling to get by while he's gallivanting all over the world as if he had no responsibility toward his own children at all."

"But he's our daddy," protested Cornelia, "No one forced you to go live on a desert island where we have to wait weeks for books to come in by boat and where we never have medicine and where they whip us in school when we get bad..."

Nevin flinched as if she'd been struck.

"That's enough, Cornelia," said Ray, "If you don't have anything good to say, better to say nothing at all. You know your mother takes everything personal."

Nevin's eyes flared round with hurt. "I just can't understand how you can still care about him. After all I've done for you, you just don't seem to understand the sacrifices I've made to give you children a wonderful simple life here in the islands."

"No one asked you to do that."

Nevin cringed as if she'd been struck. "You're giving me that black, disapproving look again. I don't know what I've done to deserve such treatment."

"Go to your room if you can't stop badgering your mother," said Ray.

"Fine, I'd be happy to go to my room. Just give me the letter," Cornelia lips were held in one tight line; her black eyes flashed. She held out her hand for the letter.

Nevin held it to her chest

Ray clenched his mouth and pointed to her room.

Cornelia stood up, snatched the letter from Nevin and stomped off to her tiny room tucked beneath the stairs to the attic where Ray and Nevin slept, slamming the door behind her. Their house was a tiny cottage made of thin pine walls providing little privacy. With her legs crossed beneath her, she curled up in the nook below the stairs.

"...I don't expect you to understand," wrote C.W., "God moves in mysterious ways. Maybe one day, the children will come to understand that I must stay the course.

I cannot, at this time, deviate from God's plan for me. Horace tells us that men are hungry, not just for bread but for an ideology that matters. We will not stop until there is enough for everyone's need, not everyone's greed."

"Are you through with your tantrum?" Nevin opened her door without knocking.

Cornelia scowled. "I didn't have a tantrum."

"Oh," said Nevin, holding her belly as if she'd been kicked. "You can just stay in your room then."

Cornelia sat quietly, trying to sort out her feelings. C.W. had forgotten all about Nathan's twelfth birthday and now her tenth was soon to come, and there was no mention of that either. She steeled herself not to care. It wasn't as if it was news that he cared only for his God and for Horace and for the other Moral Absolutes. She took the letter and postcard and jammed it back into the bottom of a drawer where the others lay in a massive jumble.

A part of her was relieved at his continued absence from their lives. Certainly, her time on the Moral Absolute Island had frightened her. It was just that sometimes she had all these concerns about good and evil that no one else seemed to have. Or that she felt drawn, at times, to go sit under the windows outside the village church and listen to the preachers. Her father had given her a Bible to read. The stories in it confused her. There was Jacob's nightlong struggle with an angel. A prophet, who conjured up a bear to eat up a bunch of teasing children, and Jesus who walked on water, cast out demons, and had the devil whispering in his ear. There were times, late at night, when she had to chant prayers to still the voices whispering in her own head. She wanted to talk to her father about these quiet voices. She sensed that they had much in common. If she did ever get to see him again, she vowed to ask him questions despite his rigid demeanor. The Moral Absolutes scared her, but as with a horror story, she was intrigued.

Her relationship with Nevin was also complicated. When she was little, they had been very close. She had always felt like she might die if they were separated. But in the last year or so, everything Nevin did seemed to irritate Cornelia, and vice versa. Though Nevin said she was proud of Cornelia for reading so well, she worried and complained that she spent far too much time with her head buried in books. She expressed far more approval of Nathan's constant need to move. "He's just like me," Nevin bragged, "Full of energy. Cornelia's more bookish, like her father." And Cornelia knew that was not a compliment.

* * *

A few months later, another letter came from C.W. As had become custom, Nevin read the letter to the family. In it, C.W. wrote that Horace had fallen ill and needed a good long rest. C.W. had received guidance to offer his family's mansion near Philadelphia as a place for Horace to recover. He requested that Nathan and Cornelia come spend a few weeks there during the summer. There would be plenty of people to take care of them, promised C.W., because Horace's entire staff of cooks and doctors and helpmates would be coming to stay with him as well. Besides, wrote C.W., Great Uncle Stanley and Great Aunt Janice still lived in the old family mansion, in case Nevin was concerned that the children would only be in the care of strangers."

"As if they could make a difference," snorted Nevin, "Aunt Janice is as batty as a fruitcake. And Uncle Stanley cares only about golf."

"Golf?" said Nathan, "That doesn't sound so bad.

Nevin's voice was shrill as she read more of the letter out-loud, "My lawyers advise me that I'm due visitation rights so, Nevin, if you want the child support checks to keep coming, don't fight this. It is in God's plan!"

That summer, they took the overnight mailboat to Nassau, and a plane to Miami.

"I'm going to miss you," said Nevin at the airport gate as Nathan looked on. Out on the tarmac, a graceful silver Constellation awaited passengers. Nevin tugged hard at Cornelia's dress trying to get it below her knees. Though all her hems had been let out, the smocking of Cornelia's dresses rode high up along her breastbone and hitched most of her skirts way above her knees.

"I know, I know," Cornelia said readjusting her clothes, "I'm as skinny as a bean pole. My hair is all flyaway and full of boogeyman tangles. And my brains are a waste cause boys don't like girls who're smart mouths. Heavens on earth, how shall I ever get along?"

To Cornelia's relief, Nevin giggled and hugged her close, "But I loves you anyway, you ragamuffin girl!"

A smartly uniformed stewardess with a tiny cap perched on her glossy hair leaned down toward Cornelia. "Ready to board?"

And suddenly Cornelia felt frightened. "Why can't Nathan come with me? I don't want to go alone."

"You know I promised your father you'd come first. He said you're going to stay in a splendid hotel and go to museums and everything. And Nathan will be there in just three days and then you'll be together again."

"It's not fair, Nathan gets to stay here in Miami with you and go to Seaquarium! You just like Nathan better than me."

Nevin quailed, "That's not true and you know it."

"Tis so," snarled Cornelia, "You don't love me at all. Maybe I'd be better off with Daddy after all."

Nevin nudged Cornelia away from her. "What's wrong with you?" She flounced off a few feet. With her back turned to them, they saw her shoulders slump and sobs shudder through her.

"Oh boy, now you've done it. You never know when to keep your mouth shut, do you?" said Nathan, "And I *still* think it's not fair that *you* get time alone with Father."

"I'm sorry, Mummy, please come say good-bye."

When Nevin stayed turned away, Cornelia ran at her and clung to her middle, thrusting her face down into her belly where it was softest. "I'm sorry, please don't send me away." She sobbed.

"That's it!" Nevin plucked Cornelia's hands off her. Her face twisted as if she had something sour in her mouth. "I've had just about enough. You're ten years old. You're too big to have tantrums. You have to go and that's all there is to it. He's your father after all. Maybe he can handle you. I certainly can't." And with that she pushed Cornelia away from her.

The stewardess took her hand and whispered in her ear, "It'll be alright. You'll get pilot wings and maybe even get to go up into the cockpit, you'd like that wouldn't you?"

With one last shuddering breath, Cornelia squared her shoulders and let the stewardess lead her across the tarmac to the waiting Constellation and up the stairs and to a seat. The doors slammed shut, the engines roared, the plane rolled faster and soon they were up in the clouds. The plane bucked and rolled, and she held on tight.

* * *

The young girl, a princess it seemed, by the richness of her clothes, stood in the middle of an opulent palace room. Satin drapes swooped down behind her like the outspread wings of a hawk. Light from a far-off window illuminated one side of her face, highlighting her strong jaw. Her hair was pulled back tightly off her high forehead. Her silk brocade skirt ballooned stiffly out below her tightly cinched waist; her arms stuck out for balance, as if even one tiny step in her costume might send her stumbling.

Cornelia thought of how she and Nathan ran along the beach after school, tumbling off the dock into high tide waves, their hair streaming behind them as they ducked under one tumbling wave to catch another. This poor princess in a painting was frozen in time and would never know the joys of running free. Or swimming in high tide waves.

As promised, they were staying in a splendid hotel. Cornelia had her own room with a huge bed. She was even wearing one of the two dresses that Horace had sent to her room, a blood-red merino wool with a dropped waist and a bow in the back. When she first put it on, she twirled in front of the dressing room mirror, liking the way the red made her hair look like polished brass, and her skin glow like ivory, not sallow at all. "I think it's absolutely divine," she smiled, unconsciously mimicking her mother.

"What do you see?" C.W. quietly asked. They were in a grand museum, a vast edifice with long flights of marble steps leading to massive halls filled with gleaming paintings, all with ornate golden frames.

During dinner last night and breakfast that morning, C.W. had barely spoken. She expected that it would be awkward at first, but hearing his voice brought back the warm feelings she had been conjuring in her mind over the past few years without him. She twirled her new dress just a little, and found that, by not looking at him, it was easier to speak. "Well," she said, "It makes me thankful to be free. She seems sad."

"That's good to be grateful. But what makes you say she's sad?"

"Well, look at her," Cornelia said, "She's a princess but she can't move. She's stiff. And everything's coming down around her like she's trapped. Look at the lines of the curtains. She's surrounded. And there's no window or door in sight. She's a beautiful prisoner stuck in time."

"Indeed." He clucked with approval. "Imagine you seeing that."

Encouraged, she continued. "And her eyes. She wants to speak to me, I just know. But she can't. After all, she's in a painting and she's been trapped there for over a hundred years."

"But that's just it!" His tone was excited, "Don't you see? That's the point. She is still speaking to you even though it was so long ago. That's the magic of art! It can speak to us after hundreds of years. The message is eternal and everlasting." She snuck a look at him out of the corner of her eye; his foot was tapping, his arms clasped together in front of his waist and his face alive and excited. "She was a Hapsburg. And in fact, this was painted well over *three* hundred years ago. And it's quite acute of you to see that she's trapped. Diego Hernandez was a Spanish court painter and many people believe he felt sorry for this little princess and tried to show how limited her existence was. It's the power of the artist to illuminate other people's lives, even things they may not see themselves. Look at the placard below the painting," he said.

She drew closer to look at the brass plaque. *Diego Hernandez: 1622* was in large carved letters and below that in a smaller font was: *On gracious loan from the Cornelius Woodstock family.* "Does this mean we own it?"

"Shh!" he said with a finger held up to his mouth, his eyes darting around with mischievous humor, "Don't tell anyone we're Woodstocks!"

"Oh, I won't!" She whispered. And then she giggled. And, before she could stop the impulse, she skipped across the hall and slid three feet to a stop across the shining marble floor. To her delight, he hopped across and slid to a stop by her side. They both collapsed into giggles, drawing a censorious look from the stern museum guard.

"Come!" he said, "I have so much more to show you!" He took her into a hall where huge paintings by a man called Turner captured the luminescent skies of London in winter and of Venice shrouded in a golden fog. She told him of how the cumulus clouds marched along the horizon over the ocean near her village, and of how she loved the way their reflections swirled in the shallows, merging and melding, until everything glowed with color. He nodded seriously, seemingly understanding something that she had never dared express to anyone before.

"I've counted thirty-three shades of color in the waters around the village."

"Have you now? What are some of them?"

"Well, there's turquoise of course, that's obvious, but there's Prussian blue in the deep, and lime green in the shallows, and violet where the sea grass lies."

"Where did you learn all these colors?" he asked with genuine interest.

"My Crayola box has 48 colors and I've memorized them all. My favorites this month are magenta and gold. And before that Cerulean blue and vermilion."

"Ah hah," he said, "That sounds as if you're finding out about how opposites work! Next time you draw a face with your pink crayon, try shadowing it lightly with green just where the shadows fall, and you'll see what I mean. Come, let's go look at Monet."

And so, they moved from Turner to Monet.

As they looked at a painting of a haystack, "See how he takes the light and divides it into dots of all different colors?"

"How do you know all this?" She looked at her father with interest. He still evaded looking at her directly.

"I studied art in Paris. I wanted to be a painter, but I didn't have the staying power." He looked down at his feet.

"Maybe you didn't work hard enough? Mummy says the Woodstocks are effete, that none of you in this generation did a lick of work."

He looked sad, "Did she now? Well, maybe she's right. But now I have a different calling. Anyone can put paint to canvas, but not everyone can harvest souls. That's what Horace tells me."

"Harvest? That sounds like you're eating souls." She wanted him to laugh but he did not.

"No," he said, and his look was stern, "Horace says it's more like a gathering circle of souls. There is power in the group. No one person should have to stand alone."

For some reason, that made Cornelia smile.

Chapter 5

Nathan shot down the steps of the airplane then galloped across the tarmac toward where C.W. and Cornelia waited. He had grown almost a foot in the last year. After a bout with ringworm, Nevin had had his blond hair buzzed so short that his round skull showed through. But his freckles and buck-toothed grin were so familiar to Cornelia that she felt relief. Though she had experienced a few wonderful moments with C.W., her effort to be on her best behavior had exhausted her.

"Does he always have to move so fast?" murmured C.W.

She shot C.W. a black look, then ran out from under the overhang to skip along next to Nathan.

"Did you love the Seaquarium?" she asked.

"Oh boy, did I. The killer whales came up out of water like this, whoosh," he threw his hands way up in the air, "And then they came down, crash, bang, shazam!" The explosive noises puffed his cheeks out. He came to a sudden halt, his cheeks deflating as he spotted C.W.'s tight mouth and awkwardly shook his hand.

"Welcome, son. I assume those *noises* will stay to yourself from now on."

When C.W. turned and stalked off, Nathan rolled his eyes at Cornelia. She shrugged her shoulders and made a moue. "It hasn't been so bad," she whispered.

In the car, C.W. sat in front next to the young man who was driving. Nathan and Cornelia piled into the back seat where they giggled and tickled and roughhoused.

C.W. spoke only once. About an hour into the trip, he leaned back over his seat and said, "You're nothing but a couple of wild things."

They hooted with laughter and Nathan saluted. But then they realized he wasn't joking. Nathan popped his eyes and grimaced when their father turned back around and faced forward.

Nathan jabbed her in the ribs and she giggled.

Without turning back around, C.W. said, "Nathan, you're far too big to still be playing the fool."

Cornelia saw the words slap her brother. He turned to stare out the window, blinking hard, his lower lip swelling out.

For hours the car drove up US 1, passing endless suburbs, stop lights and strip-malls, then turned to the left onto a smaller highway that meandered through a small stone village interspersed with fields and forest. After several hours, the road narrowed to one lane. Behind stonewalls covered with mustard yellow lichen, dark green woods loomed. Finally, the car turned through an open wrought iron gate. Emblazoned at the center of the arch, faded gilt lettering spelled out GREENDELL.

"Have we ever been here before?" Cornelia asked.

"You don't remember?" C.W. turned to look at them.

Cornelia shook her head. "I was only four when you left."

"I remember," muttered Nathan, "I remember everything." But he wouldn't look at C.W.

C.W. waited, but when nothing further came from Nathan, with a shrug of the shoulders he turned back to the front.

A sad feeling bloomed inside Cornelia. She wanted Nathan to experience the gentler version of their father, but somehow, that man had disappeared. This man was grim.

Giant oaks arched up and met over the middle of the driveway, forming a grand alley. Just beyond, on a huge spreading lawn, a herd of deer grazed down by the woods. They lifted their heads, frozen for a moment, then bolted off into the woods; their white tails snapped a warning. The gravel crunched as the car turned into a circle that swept around to the front of the grand stone house.

A long flight of marble steps led up to a portico under which Horace Baker waited to greet them. He was surrounded by a group of smiling young adults. Cornelia remembered those plastered-on smiles and shuddered.

Horace Baker was more hunched over than he had been three years previously, his hands still clutched at his dog-head walking stick, and his eyes were still piercing above his goofy smile. As they got out of the car and walked up the stairs toward him, he called out. "Welcome to Greendell. Welcome to what is now a house of our heavenly father."

Cornelia stopped in mid-stride. "Don't you mean *my* father's house."

Nathan jabbed her with his elbow as an awkward silence fell. Horace's mouth opened in that slack and almost absent way that she remembered, then, as if a bolt of electricity shot through him, his eyes snapped back alive, and he chuckled, "Yes, I forgot about this child. The child who speaks the Absolute Truth, doesn't she now?"

He leaned down toward her and she felt as if the oxygen had been sucked out of her and that she was falling. Those mesmerizing eyes were once again drilling deep down inside of her. "I was speaking metaphorically, my child. Of course, it is *your* father's *house*. But it is *his* generous hospitality that shelters us from the storms of life." He pointed his finger up to the sky. And he looked around at the welcoming crew for approval.

"Amen," said C.W. and the others parroted the blessing.

There was a long silence as everyone looked at Nathan and Cornelia. Though a part of her wrestled with this demanding voice inside her, she could not resist speaking. "And just how does one know that it is *he*? Why not *she*? Why is it *always* he?"

All eyes swung toward her. Nathan coughed and looked down at his scuffed shoes, which twitched as he struggled to stand still.

She continued, "And where are Uncle Stanley and Great-Aunt Janice? Mummy said some of our *real* family would be here to look after us."

Horace laughed. "My dear child, I hear hurt and anger in your voice. Accusing others will get you nowhere in life. You must work on forgiveness, my child. Forgiveness means letting go of the hurt."

She felt stung by his words. The first set of words she had spoken to him had come from a good place but both angels and demons lived in her soul and, she knew he was right. The second set of words had been meant to hurt. It seemed she had not yet forgiven Horace for having swept her story about Hall Hamden under the rug. She looked up at him. "I may work on forgiveness," she said, "But I do not forget."

His eyes narrowed, and he chuckled, "You will come to see that your *real* family is where you find it. All in good time. Come." Horace lifted his cane up then banged it back down. "Take them to their rooms!"

The huge hand-carved wooden door slammed shut, startling Cornelia almost off her feet. They stood in a massive three-story high entrance, with a curving staircase rising delicately on both sides of the hall, meeting at the top at a wide balcony, then spiraling farther up and out of sight to the third floor. The black balustrades were carved dragons with gaping mouths at the bottom, their sinewy bodies curling up around the banister.

As they walked up the first staircase, trailing behind the young man carrying their small suitcases, Cornelia looked down between the curving dragons to see C.W. in conference with Horace. She trotted to catch up with Nathan who was taking the stairs in leaps of three. Much to her relief he stopped to wait for her.

She breathed. "I'll never get grownups. If Daddy is so rich, why is Mummy always worrying about money?"

His mouth turned down on one side and he rolled his shoulders. "Who knows? That's Great Uncle Stanley when he was young," Nathan nodded to a dark portrait hanging on the wall. The man was dressed in an old-fashioned high collared suit. He was carrying a shotgun and behind him were glowing clouds, green rolling hills, and a marble gazebo with a river beyond. "You'll see that river later," promised Nathan. "Come on, slow poke!" He started leapfrogging up the stairs again.

"Who's this?" Cornelia said, stopping in front of portrait of a woman with a brimmed hat trimmed with feathers. A diamond necklace glittered on the bodice of her velvet dress.

"Come on." Nathan bounded down and yanked her up the stairs.

"But who is it?" She wailed, looking back over her shoulder at the elegant lady.

"Great Aunt Janice, of course. Silly, don't you remember anything?"

"No," She shook her head, "Nothing!"

Nathan bolted up to the third floor, hitched one foot up and over the bannister and swooped down toward her at a high speed.

"Whoeeeeee," he yelled, sliding off onto the landing below her with a great thump.

"You okay?"

"Of course!" he snorted, bounding to his feet. A door opened in the nearby hall and footsteps marched rounded the corner. A man glared down at them, hands on hips. His voice honked. "Sliding down the bannister is *not* allowed."

"Who says?" said Nathan, "Mummy always used to let me."

"Well, Mummy is not with us, now is she? And *I* say that is *not* allowed. No sliding down the bannisters. Ever again. Got it?"

Nathan glared right back but the tremble in his voice told Cornelia that he was not as confident as he pretended. "And who are you?"

"My name is Jay Burden. And I suppose you must be the Woodstock children."

"I am Nathan Woodstock, and this is my sister Cornelia." Nathan stood his ground.

"Well, you might as well get this straight right now, so we'll have no further problem. I am in charge of the well-being of Horace Baker. He used every bit of energy he had to come greet you. And now he must rest. He needs total peace and quiet, and I will see to it that he gets it. Are we understood? There will be no running in the halls, no sliding down the bannister." The folds in his face wobbled as he shook his finger at them.

Nathan stood still for a moment, but then his face flushed, and he ran to the end of the balcony, swung his leg up over the bannister and down he went, back down toward the main hall where they had entered. "Whee!" He squealed in as high pitched a voice as he could muster.

Cornelia stood still, with her hands clasped behind her back as Jay Burden strode toward her, then reached down and grabbed the top of her ear. He lowered his face so close to hers that when he spoke spittle sprayed all over her face. "Listen to me and listen good. Get that brother of yours in line or else. You hear me?" And he pinched her ear until she gasped in pain.

She nodded and swallowed hard. She lurched away from him and ran toward Nathan, who was thundering up the stairs toward her. "Say you're sorry," she whispered into his ear.

"No way!"

"Do it!" she said, kicking him hard in the shin.

He hung his head and shuffled his feet, "Sorry," he managed to say, but his tone was sullen.

Jay Burden slapped his hands together in a dismissive gesture, "That's better. Get along now. Go." And he pointed up the stairs. They scrambled past him as fast as they could, running up the last flight of stairs and when they reached the top landing they were panting. They rounded the corner and saw the young man with their suitcases standing down at the end of the corridor under a high window that was pitched open with a giant iron hook.

"What did you have to kick me for?" Nathan scowled at Cornelia, "Aren't we allowed to have any fun?"

She pointed up at her ear which was red and swollen.

"He did that? I'll get him." His hands clenched into fists.

"No, you won't," she said, "We'll just stay out of his way, that's all."

And with that they ran down the hall toward the young man who was tapping his foot. "Come along now," he said, "Here's your room, Nathan."

He opened the door. It was a small narrow room with a very high ceiling and a tiny window all the way up near the top. A narrow bed lined one wall covered with rough-looking sheets and an old, stained wool blanket folded at its foot.

"This isn't my room," said Nathan.

"It most certainly is," said the young man.

"Where's Cornelia staying?" Nathan demanded.

"Down the hall at the other end."

"Yup, that's it." Nathan grabbed his suitcase away from the man, took Cornelia's with his other hand, and said, "Come on, Nee, let's go." He stomped off down the hallway all the way to the other end where he opened a door and marched in as if he owned it. Cornelia trotted behind.

"There'll be trouble about this!" called out the young man as he loped down the staircase.

When Cornelia followed Nathan into the room, memories came flooding back. There was the late afternoon sun flickering down through the green leaves of a large spreading oak, flooding in through the bank of windows, and falling in a lace like pattern onto the blue and cream Chinese carpet below. Just below the ceiling, there was a parade of Winnie the Pooh figures on the wallpaper.

She spun around the room in delight. She remembered lying in the four-poster bed that was still in the center of the room, watching the late afternoon sun play on the patterned carpet. She remembered Mummy tucking her in, and Nana letting her play with her button box. She bounded over to the bed and climbed up onto it. It still had the twirling mahogany posts, and the starched white lace running along the brass rods that canopied over the top, made "especially" for her great-grandmother by craftsmen in the islands of the West Indies. In the corner was a sleigh bed with curling maple scrolls on either end, where Nathan was jumping up and down with glee. She enjoyed seeing her brother act like a kid, even though he was almost a teenager.

"We're home," he yelled, bouncing down to land on his bottom, then wriggling from side to side.

Cornelia jumped off the bed and ran over to the window where bookcases were tucked under a long window seat. There was *Mother Goose*, and *Treasure Island* by Robert Louis Stevenson, with Maxfield Parrish illustrations.

"Remember?" yelled Nathan.

"I do. Except Mummy's not here."

Nathan shot her a quick look, his mouth pulled down at the corners. "Look, let's put our clothes away so they can't blame us for making a mess. But let's be fast about it. I want to show you the gardens where we used to play."

Down at the bottom of her suitcase Cornelia found her little black book. She held it up to show Nathan. "Has Daddy given you one yet?"

Nathan's lips tightened into a straight line and he shook his head.

"You mean *Father*, don't you? 'Member I don't get to call him 'Daddy.' Only you do."

Her days alone with C.W. had clearly rankled Nathan. "Come on," he said impatiently, "Let's go."

They bolted down the three staircases, out the back door, across a vast bowed stone patio, then down a long flight of granite steps to the wide lawns that rolled down to the tree lined river, glittering in the afternoon sun.

Shrieking, they winged out their arms and flew down the hill. Nathan tumbled first, whirling like a top all the way down to a flat plateau. Cornelia followed, though, as always, more carefully, lying down, tucking in her arms and letting gravity roll her into a wild spin. She landed at the bottom, out of breath. They lay, arms outstretched, looking up at small puffy clouds scudding across the blue sky. The grass was moist and cool beneath them. Even though it was summer, there was a crispness to the air and a slant to the sunshine that was always missing in the Bahamas.

"I've been thinking," said Nathan.

"That's unusual."

He poked her in the ribs. "Listen to me. This guidance thing..."

"Yeah? What about it?"

"How about if both of us ask for the same thing? And *pretend* it's our guidance."

"I don't know, like what?" The thought of being dishonest made her uncomfortable. She got the feeling Horace would know, plus she had planned to take it seriously to please her father but having Nathan around changed the dynamic.

"Like that God wants us to go swimming. Or to the circus. Or something. Whatever we decide."

Cornelia was silent, gathering her thoughts. "I don't know how smart that is."

He sighed.

"I'll go along with anything you want. You know I will. I always do." She took a deep breath for courage. "But here's the thing. Sometimes I really *do* get guidance. Sometimes it's like there's this voice in my head telling me what to do. I can't control that."

"Really? You actually get guidance? Come on."

There was a long silence. Nathan looked up at the sky. Finally he asked. "Are you becoming one of them?"

"I don't know."

"Come on, enough talking, let's go." Nathan leapt to his feet and ran down towards the riverbank. Cornelia was used to these abrupt changes of pace. And he knew she would always run after him. That was a given.

About a hundred yards wide, the brown river shimmered in the afternoon sun. Across the way there were no other houses in sight, just a bank of green trees and a thickly wooded hill rising in the distance.

Nathan ran down to the edge, ducked under a row of weeping willows and vanished from sight. Cornelia followed. Inside the shelter of the branches, there was a perfect swimming hole. The water in the river was the color of clear coffee. The bottom, a sandy gold, sparkled with flecks of mica. Scattered by the lowering branches, the sunshine laced the top of the water with lavender shadows.

Nathan scrambled out onto a limb of a tree, which arched out over the water. He paused for a moment, pulled off his pants and tee shirt, threw them back to the land, then plunged up and out into the air in a half dive, half cannonball that landed him way out, deep into the swift current of the river. A swirling row of bubbles marked his passage underwater. He surfaced almost at Cornelia's feet, water streaming off him, and grinning wide.

"Come on."

"I don't have my bathing suit."

"Who cares?"

She pulled her dress off over her head and, wearing nothing but a pair of white cotton panties, climbed out onto the tree branch and plunged off the end just as he had.

The water was cold but underneath the surface such a clear amber that the whole world glowed. She frog-swam underwater, breaking out of the shelter of the willow trees and heading upstream, parallel to the shore, feeling the tug of the swift current around her body. She loved being in the underwater world. Long green grasses swayed. Her hair streamed out behind her just like the mermaids in Hans Christian Anderson, she thought.

She surfaced with a gasp. A chuckle startled her. She looked around her but saw no one. She shook her head, thinking maybe the chuckling sound had only been the gurgle of the waters swirling around several large nearby boulders. She somersaulted back underwater, then popped to the surface, planning the track of her swift underwater trajectory back to the sheltering trees.

"Hello," said a clipped singsong voice.

Her gulp of air turned into a choking cough. She looked at the young man, sitting on a bench in the shadow of a nearby tree, overlooking the river, holding a little black book in his lap.

"Hadji?" she asked.

He smiled at her, his teeth large and white against his caramel skin.

"Don't be alarmed. You looked lovely there. Swimming underwater like you did."

She disappeared, letting the current swoop her back under the sheltering willows. She kicked sideways and swung into shore where she lay, half in and half out of the water. Peeking sideways, making sure there was no gap in the branches, she quickly ran to her clothes, pulling the dress on over her sopping-wet body and finger-combing her long hair into a semblance of order. She sat down to pull on her socks and shoes. She was not yet old enough to have anything but a flat chest, but recently her nipples had begun to chafe and swell a bit, turning round and pink like rose hips. And she was suddenly ashamed of her nakedness, something she had never felt before.

"Hey," called Nathan from the end of the tree, getting ready for another dive. "What's the matter with you? Come back in."

She gestured sideways and rolled her eyes. He rolled his eyes right back, signaling to her, so what? He launched himself up and out into a perfectly executed jackknife dive. When he came back up there was clapping from the other side of the tree and a whistle to boot.

"I'd call that a cracking good ten," Hadji called out.

As she came through the willow branches, Nathan was lying in the shallows, looking up at Hadji with a broad grin. He yelled out to her. "Guess what Haj says? He says that we reminded him of his childhood in Maha..." he trailed off.

"Maharashtra." Hadji smiled. Cornelia had forgotten how white his teeth were. "We used to jump off the trees into the river during the monsoon season when the waters were very high. My grandfather used to say we were like tadpoles in the water." He laughed, throwing his head back, the shank of his black hair shining bright. "We always used to swim right after playing cricket. When we were all hot and sweaty."

"You play cricket?" Nathan's eyes were round.

"Yes, indeed I do. How about you?"

Nathan shook his head.

"Would you like to learn?"

"Could we do it right now?" Nathan asked.

"Right now?" asked Hadji with a breathless little laugh. He waggled his head, as if his skull was balanced and wobbling on top of the stick of his spine.

Nathan nodded his head vigorously. "Yes, now."

And again Hadji laughed. "Don't you think it might be a good idea to get your clothes on first?"

As Nathan disappeared back underwater, Cornelia stood, holding her hands behind her, digging the toe of her shoe into the ground.

"You're the girl who ran slam bang into me at Tall Pine Island, are you not? I remember you were all eyes and with hair as soft and shiny as the gold silk threads that used to fly off my grandmother's loom."

His words so fascinated her that she forgot to be shy and was able to look at him. His hands clasped one knee and he leaned back and rocked slightly, looking out over the river, his face friendly and relaxed.

"Your grandmother spun gold? I thought that happened only in fairy tales."

"It happens all the time in India. You must come visit sometime and see for yourself."

"I would like to."

"Then you must."

"Tell me more."

"Well, I would always go visit her after tiffin."

"What's tiffin?"

"Tiffin is something that children have in India to break up the school day. You have tea and biscuits during tiffin. So I would go to have tiffin at my grandmother's factory down at the bottom of the garden next to the river."

"A factory?"

"A factory in India is nothing like a factory here. It is a simple shed just large enough for eight women, for spinning and weaving, and the silk fluff would fly off the shuttles and out into the corridors between those snapping looms. Those threads would catch the sunshine drifting in the window and just explode with color. Like golden fireflies all around."

He paused for a moment, to see if she were still listening. She was enthralled. No one had ever talked to her like this before. She nodded for him to go on.

"And so when you ran into me pell-mell that time and I saw your golden hair floating all around you, it helped me overcome a sad moment of homesickness. It was your hair that helped me remember the luminescence of those silken threads in my grandmother's factory. And just now, seeing your hair streaming out behind you underwater, reminded me of all of it."

She gasped and turned to run away.

"No! Don't go just yet. I'm glad for this opportunity. I've thought of you often in the years since." His face no longer crinkled with pleasure, but was sober, still his eyes shone and his tone was gentle.

"You have?" Her voice was hardly audible.

"Yes," he nodded. Grasping his knees and rocking back in the bench, he looked out over the whirling waters. In profile, his nose was larger than she remembered, long and curving, his chin more determined than it had been as a teen-ager, and he wore tortoise shell glasses now, glasses that perched on the high bridge of his nose and left red indentations on either side when he took them off. She realized he was no longer in any way a boy, in fact he was a serious young man, but one with a musical laugh, and a magic way of talking about color.

"Yes, I often wondered what became of you. I never saw you after that encounter. How is your wrist?"

Without thinking she held up both her arms; the injury had healed well but had left one wrist slightly larger than the other.

"Ah hah, healed but remembered."

She nodded.

"You were taken away?" he asked gently.

"Yes, whisked off into the night like Kai."

"Hans Christian Anderson? *The Snow Queen?*"

She nodded.

He chuckled, "But hopefully your heart did not freeze like his did."

"Well maybe it did in a different way." She thought of how she had resisted all those postcards and letters from her father. And of how she was often mean to her own mother.

"Well, I hope you are well on the way to letting the warmth and sunshine back in."

Nathan exploded out of the willow tree branches, singing, "All dressed. I'm ready to play cricket."

Hadji's laugh rang out. "I can see that you are definitely almighty ready."

"Almighty ready." Nathan parroted Nathan's sing song accent in a way Cornelia hoped Hadji would understand was in jest. She trusted the power of Nathan's smiles, which were as irresistible to her as the sun rising after days of rain.

"That's decided then. Actually, right now, I'll go get my cricket gear." Hadji clapped his hands on his thighs, tucking his black book into a small leather bag that was slung over his all-white tunic. He was so tall when he stood that Cornelia was intimidated and looked down. She noticed that his white leggings bagged slightly over polished brown shoes, and that he wore a tweed woolen vest even in the heat of this summer day.

"I'll be back directly," he said. With a cheery wave and smile, he strode like a long-legged stork up the hill.

"He's nice," said Nathan, "I like him."

"Me too." Cornelia nodded.

As they ran back up the hill toward the stone mansion, Nathan veered left, cutting catty corner across the lawn toward a clump of sky high bamboo, its feathery tufts swaying in the afternoon breeze. As he turned to go into a narrow pathway between the bamboo clumps, Cornelia came to an abrupt halt. Fifty feet above them on the slope, tucked under the trees, a girl perched on a stonewall.

"Nathan!" Cornelia hissed. He wheeled around and scowled. "It's that girl Rudy," she murmured, "'Member the only other girl on the island? Her parents were in Africa. And she was pudgy and bossy and awful."

"You mean, Rudy pudgy, piggy and pie?" he chanted.

"I heard that!" Rudy called out, "I remember you two. You," she said pointing her finger at Cornelia, "used to lie to get out of housekeeping duty."

"Did not," shouted Cornelia.

And you," Rudy's finger moved toward Nathan, "used to hide in the freezer so you wouldn't have to have guidance."

Nathan ran at her; and, of course, Cornelia followed. As they charged toward Rudy, her eyes opened wide. Cornelia remembered how pretty those blue eyes were, how large and round and thickly fringed with black lashes. And she was no longer pudgy. She had grown out of her baked-potato shape into a sturdy, slim girl. And to her credit, she held her ground rather than fleeing from them.

Nathan wheeled to a stop in front of her, suddenly realizing, as Cornelia had, that Rudy was quite attractive.

Rudy cocked her head at him and wound her tanned little arms around her shiny smooth legs. "I see you're all wet. You must have just been swimming. But where are your bathing suits? Don't tell me you went skinny-dipping? That kind of thing is just not allowed here, don't you know." And she blinked her eyes and Nathan squirmed.

Hadji called out from the stone patio far above them and, with one last wild roll of the eyes, Nathan bolted. Cornelia ran after him.

They heard Rudy calling out. "I'm going to tell about the skinny dipping."

As they neared where Hadji waited, holding two cricket bats and balls, Nathan came to a halt. "*You* can go up to the secret garden," Nathan said. "It's off to the left of the house, up there." He gestured with his head. "I'm sure you'll understand that I want Hadji to teach me cricket alone first."

"Not fair," she said. "Why do you always have to take away the few friends I make?"

Nathan's jaw dropped, "I don't do that."

"You do too. People like me until they meet you. Then they drop me like a hot potato. Oh, Nathan," she cooed an imitation of the village girls calling after Nathan as he ran away from them.

He frowned, his lower lip curled out in a pout. "You know how long it takes for you to learn new things."

"I can't help it if I don't play sports as well as you," she hung her head.

"That's just it," he snatched at her confession. "How about if I learn cricket first then I'll teach it you?"

"That's not the point."

"What is the point?"

"Never mind, just go." She couldn't tell him just yet how much she yearned to keep Hadji all to herself, like a favorite doll. She waved Nathan off.

He flashed a grateful smile and ran off to play.

Cornelia trudged up the long hill toward the house, veering off to the left toward what Nathan had called the secret garden. There she found an arched doorway cut into a moss-covered wall.

As soon as she entered the enclosed garden she felt at peace. Inside there was a miniature maze of fragrant boxwood. Tall rose bushes bloomed in an array of colors from vermilion to velvety violet. Butterflies and bumble bees flittered above a bed of lavender and catmint along one wall. Another high garden wall was smothered with climbing roses.

As she walked in, a breeze snuck in behind her, ruffling her skirts, and plucking petals out of the rose blooms, puffing the pale coral petals up into the air from where they spiraled lazily back down to the ground to form a soft carpet along the worn brick paths. A mossy fountain gurgled at the very center and Cornelia trotted over to sit on its side. A small green frog plopped down into the crystal-clear waters, swam over to one side, then twirled to stare at her, its bulbous eyes just popping up above the surface. She giggled, wondering if that was what she'd looked like to Hadji when he had so surprised her in the water.

"Who's that in my garden?" a voice quavered. Cornelia whirled around. A tiny old lady sat on a bench cut into one of the garden walls. She was all in white, her dress so thin and fine in texture that the sun shone through the folds, lifted in little flapping furls when the breeze wandered by. Diamonds glittered on her necklace as it swung and sparkled in the air. Her skin was wrinkled, and both her hands and face were flecked with brown spots. "Come here child," she beckoned with one crooked little finger. She looked to be no taller than Cornelia but about a hundred years older. Holding her hands clasped behind her Cornelia walked cautiously toward her.

As Cornelia drew closer, the woman's features became more familiar, in pieces at first like a jigsaw puzzle that was suddenly complete. "Great Aunt Janice," she breathed. She had heard all about her from Nevin. The stories were legendary. She was rumored to have a closet full of a thousand shoes, from the satin pearl encrusted slippers of her youth, to the platform strappy sandals of the forties. Today, she wore embroidered flats with purple dragons whose eyes were emeralds. "I like your shoes," she said.

"Do you now?" the old lady snapped. "Are you going to be like that nasty little girl who keeps asking if she can have a pair?"

"Not me," she protested, "My mummy would never let me ask for something that belonged to someone else. Not in a million gazillion years. That must have been Rudy."

The old lady coughed. Her shoulders shook, and Cornelia realized the cough was a strangled chuckle. "A million gazillion years, eh? That's a long time. And who might your mummy be?"

"Her name is Elizabeth Nevin Smith Woodstock Bradbury. But she goes by Nevin. Her mother was already Elizabeth, so she uses her middle name."

Her gaze sharpened and again she crooked her finger, "Come closer, child!" Her eyes were milky blue. "I seem to remember Nevin was a silly girl from a quite good old Baltimore family. She certainly turned young Woodstock's head. And I took a liking to her because she admired my shoe collection. Have you seen my shoes? I have a wonderful collection of shoes, don't you know. So are you *really* Nevin's little girl? She fancied herself quite the beauty, don't you know. Funny, you don't *look* like her at all."

"I know." She sighed.

"Well," Great Aunt Janice grunted, "it's probably just as well. She was the most restless creature I ever met in my life. Always running off to do something else."

"Sounds like my brother."

"You're probably better off with the ability to sit still and listen. I like that in a child. Come," she patted the stone seat next to her. "Come sit with me awhile and we'll talk of cabbages and kings."

"The walrus and the carpenter," Cornelia laughed out loud, "But I hope I'm no little oyster for you to eat up."

"No indeed," the old lady wheezed with laughter, "I won't do that. I could no more eat an oyster now than fly to the moon. I'd choke trying to swallow it. No, I'm afraid I can only eat baby food now. Such slop you never saw. And they make me eat it upstairs all by myself." And her tone turned cranky and she went into a tirade that Cornelia could hardly follow. She talked about how there were too many *strangers* in the house now, people who followed her everywhere and of how she wasn't allowed downstairs in the dining hall anymore because she disturbed the other guests, they said, with her slobbering and slurping over her meals.

"I'm sorry," said Cornelia.

"Are you?" The rheumy eyes narrowed, "Why would you be sorry? Never apologize, don't you know. They'll catch you out then."

"Horace Baker says we always have to say we're sorry."

Aunt Janice snorted, "He's just a horrible, common little man. I can't imagine why Woodstock has so taken to him. Imagine. Quite a come down for the daughter of a man who dined with kings now forced to eat all by her lonesome. Not that these awful 'Absolute people' are very good dinner companions. They keep asking me whether I have impure thoughts. Imagine that." She tinkled with laughter, and her tiny face disappeared into a hundred wrinkly folds. "At my age having impure thoughts! I was finished with all of that a long time ago. Finished." Her splotched hands made a wave of dismissal.

Cornelia noticed that the ruby and emerald rings on her fingers were cloudy with dirt. "They ask me that too," said Cornelia. "I never know what to say."

But Aunt Janice wasn't listened. "Just who do they think they are? Coming into *my* house and asking me whether I have impure thoughts. Honestly, it's quite, *quite* awful. I can tell you that right now." And then she cranked to a halt, like an ancient wind-up Victrola that had started off at high speed then sputtered to a standstill.

Her chin slumped down onto her bony little chest where as her necklace glittered in the sunshine. She waved her hand at Cornelia. "Go now," she said, "I've had enough of you." And then she began to mutter about people stealing her shoes. "You didn't take them, did you now? Did you steal my golden slippers? You know! The ones I wore to the ball with Prince Romaneski?"

As Cornelia shook her head, Great-Aunt Janice slumped back down, beginning the accounting of her shoes on her crooked little fingers, laden down with scratched sapphires and grimy rubies. "There are the purple ones with crimson soles, don't you know, and the yellow ones with the gold buckles, and the lavender ones all made of moiré silk..."

Cornelia inched away from her, trying hard not to make any quick movement to alarm her. At first, she hardly seemed to care that Cornelia was leaving, continuing to mumble, her lower lip flapping. But just as Cornelia was about to slip out of the garden, Aunt Janice snapped. "Enough of my shoes, *what* do you think of my garden?"

At that very moment, hearing another voice, the hair on the back of Cornelia's neck rose up. The charming garden turned black, the fragrant boxwoods morphed into a musty stench. She shuddered. Floating down from the stone patio above, she heard the cadenced boom of a familiar voice. It was Hall Hamden. A phrase from a book drifted into her brain, and she murmured aloud, "Dank gardens cry aloud for murder."

"What's that you say? Murder?" Aunt Janice's voice was querulous as she peered at Cornelia. "Tell me, are *you* the one who took my baby? What have you done with my baby?"

Chapter 6

Cornelia fled the garden. Vaulting above the pounding of her heart and the boom of Hall Hamden's voice, she heard whoops of delight from the lawns below. She almost ran back down toward Hadji and Nathan, but she was afraid that Hall Hamden would see her and she couldn't risk that.

A row of granite steps led up to the large stone patio that ran alongside the backside of the mansion. She tiptoed up the flight of steps, hid behind a pillar and peeked around. She darted back down and slipped around the base of the pillar where a small crevice provided a hiding place. Off to the side, Hall Hamden sat at a round table with three other men. The cadence of his mechanical voice was as ingrained in her memory as words carved in stone.

In all her wildest dreams, she had never thought she would once again hear *that* voice. She had always assumed that Hall Hamden would have been whisked off into the night, as she and Gertrude had been, banished from the Absolute domain. In fact, it seemed, the opposite was true. From her viewpoint, he appeared to still be in a position of power.

His cadence was rapid fire. "The old lady is a liability for sure. From what I've managed to glean from C.W., the bulk of the trust does *not* come his way until her death. Too bad that can't happen sooner rather than later. Hahahaha." His laugh sounded like a machine gun.

"Hahaha," The other men joined in.

"There's no telling how long she'll hang in there," said Hall Hamden. "But when she goes, whoop de doo, Hollywood here we come. That money should be enough to vault us to the next level. Enough to fund several movies and world tours at least. Put us back on the map. With Horace getting old, we've got to have a plan. Without him, it'll be twice as hard to convince people to sign over their inheritance. I'm telling you, it's hard work keeping the flow of cash coming in. So, for now it's an imperative to keep Horace alive. We all know, don't we, that C.W. and others are tied into the Absolute cause because of him?"

Several men murmured agreement. Hall Hamden continued. "And we can never lose sight of that. We must be ever ready to take over the helm of the cause. But we're not there yet, not there yet."

"But C.W. has agreed to give us what he has for now, right?" asked one of the men, who sounded to Cornelia like the guide who had tried to put Nathan in the wrong bedroom.

"Yes, he has," said Hall Hamden, "We'll make an announcement about that at dinner. And then we'll segue into gratitude so there's no misunderstanding how much we all value C.W. and his contributions."

There was a murmur of agreement.

"Frank, you in?" Hall Hamden snapped. "I don't hear anything from you."

"It seems clear to me that God has provided us with C.W. for a reason," said Frank. "We must be careful to cherish the goose that lays the golden egg. Lest it run off and find another master."

"Ah yes, our thoughtful Frank. To remind us we're surrounded with nothing but a flock of ineffective doves and one lone goose. We here at this table are the ones who must dare to lead. All the others just flap their wings when the fox comes into the chicken yard. We indeed must be as wise as serpents but as vigilant as the proverbial watchdog."

Then he abruptly clapped his hands in dismissal, and Cornelia heard a scuffling of feet and a scraping of chairs. She turned to flee back down the stairs and out across the lawn to the cricket game.

For the next hour, she watched Hadji and Nathan. Hadji had signaled for her to join them, but she shook her head and sat down under a tree, arms wrapped around her knees, and stared steadfastly out over the shimmering river waters.

As if a fog was lifting, long-obscured memories suddenly glared.

She shuddered. She might not have been so willing to come visit her father if she had known how even the sound of Hall Hamden's voice would so frighten her. She wondered why it was that only he, of all the Absolute leaders, demanded everyone call him by his full name. Its hammered cadence reminded her of a military march. She was confused by everything she had just overheard. All the talk of foxes and snakes and watchdogs scared her. An image of her father's head clenched between snapping jaws sent her heart skittering. She grabbed her knees tighter. Should she tell Hadji and Nathan? She knew she could trust Nathan. Despite her warm feelings toward Hadji, she had once seen him sitting on a stage next to Hall Hamden. She rocked back and forth, trying to comfort herself.

Finally, Hadji called it quits, "I'm done in!" He waggled his head, then held up his hands in surrender. "Righto, I'll see you later!" He twirled his hand in a mock bow toward Cornelia, ruffled Nathan's buzz cut, then loped back up toward the house.

Nathan ran over and threw himself down beside her, "Hadji is first rate!"

"First rate!" She teased him but was actually thrilled that he liked Hadji as much as she did. Well, maybe not as much. She doubted whether he wondered whether Hadji's cheeks were as soft as they looked, or whether his hair was as glossy as a raven's wing or glossier, no she doubted very much that Nathan wondered about such stuff.

Nathan fidgeted and rolled, then blurted out. "What happened?"

She shook her head, "Nothing happened."

"Yes, it did," he insisted, "I know you. Tell me. I know something's bothering you. You get that squally look on your forehead and your eyes go all black and scary." And so she took a shuddering breath and told him. It all tumbled out. Not just about the horseback ride and the broken lamp, but now about the hiding under the bed, and Hall Hamden's shoes too close to Gertrude's, then the click of the lock, the slap of the flesh, the ugly words, the bite marks along her shoulder. And how she thought Hall Hamden would have been banished. "Instead he's here. He's *here*. And I heard him saying horrible things about our father."

Even Nathan's legs stopped twitching. He was sober, silent for a very long time. "Why didn't you tell me all this before?"

She hung her head down between her knees. It was easier to talk if she was looking at the ground. "I'm not sure. I was scared. Hall Hamden said he'd kill her if she told. And then Horace told me not to tell. Besides, he made me wonder whether I was even telling the truth."

"But you don't lie."

"I try not to."

"And so, you told Horace Baker? Anyone else?"

She nodded. "Daddy."

For a long time, Nathan was as still as he ever got. "Really. And then what happened?"

"What do you mean?"

"What happened after you told? Certainly, something must have happened." He sounded irritated. He didn't like it when people did bad things and then didn't get punished. Their stepfather Ray had made them both believe in consequences for actions.

"Well," she said, "Nothing seems to have happened to *him*. And now I didn't like the way he was talking about Daddy and Aunt Janice."

"What was he saying?"

"He called Daddy a goose and said Aunt Janice had to die before the big money came in. And he likened himself to a snake. It was scary. What are we going to do? Daddy's in trouble."

Nathan grabbed his knees and rocked back and forth. "I don't know yet. We'll think of something."

Finally, as the shadows lengthened, they snuck up along the edges of the lawn, crept up the stairs as if they were evading predators, and then, when the coast was clear, raced across the patio, in through the open French doors and charged up the stairs, two at a time. As they reached the third floor, they ran full speed down toward their old nursery. Nathan reached down and snatched three cookies off a tea tray left in the hallway. They slammed the door of their nursery and sat down on the window bench, wolfing down the sweet treats.

At that moment, there was a knock on the door. "Who is it?" Cornelia called.

"It's your father!" C.W. came in and stood, looking down at them, as he always did, as if they were wild animals of whom he was slightly scared. "It's time for you to get dressed for dinner," he said. "Horace has worked hard planning a special dinner for you. That's quite an honor, I can tell you. They've pulled out all the stops."

"Will Hall Hamden be there?" asked Nathan.

"Yes, of course he will. Why wouldn't he?" And a stubborn look came over C.W., the petulant look of a child who has been told something is not good for him, but who is determined, despite the consequences, to try it anyway. "He's a *very* important part of our team."

"Course he is," Cornelia said, "So important that you..." But she couldn't finish. A horrible feeling of betrayal flooded her. Why was it that grown-ups so belittled the stories children told? Had they not believed she was telling the Absolute Truth? Did they really think Hall Hamden hadn't done anything wrong? Then she remembered Horace holding up his finger to his lips and saying, "Shush, it's our secret. For us and the guy upstairs." So maybe, just maybe, no one else had ever told on Hall Hamden. She felt confused and frightened and very glad Nathan was by her side.

The ceiling of the grand dining room was an inverted carved bowl, with recessed lighting running all the way around the huge oval wood paneled room. C.W. ushered the children in, waved at all the portraits of many ancestors from centuries past, then took them around the room and introduced them to their ancestors one by one.

There was a wigged man who had fought in the Revolutionary War. There was Colonel Woodstock of the Union Army holding up a ceremonial sword on a horse frozen in a feeble rear. Cornelia's favorite: their great-grandmother who had been painted by none other than Sargent, her eyes shone dark and soulful. Cornelia wondered if that's where she got her own black eyes. Certainly, she did not have the same wavy dark hair.

Cornelia was wearing her hair down in what some called a flyaway mess. She decided that it was actually a nimbus of silky gold. She smoothed her hands down over the new dropped waist dress, trying to press out wrinkles from the suitcase. She snuck a quick look at herself in the long golden mirror hanging at an angle to reflect the table. She sighed. Her face was still all sharp angles, not at all the soft oval that Nevin hoped for.

On the table, starched and ironed napkins with the family's initials were on prominent display at the center of each gold bordered plate.

Hanging above the table was a barrel-shaped glass chandelier, all golden and purple with curving wisteria vines. C.W. told them it was Tiffany glass.

"Is it worth a lot?" asked Nathan.

"It's rude to ask how much something is worth," an older woman hissed as she scurried into the room. Cornelia's stomach lurched.

It was Mrs. Rogers from housekeeping, that "dried up prune of a woman" as Horace Baker had called her. A smile twisted the bottom of her face as she spotted Cornelia. "My, my, my, if it isn't Cornelia Woodstock. My dear, how are you, how's your mother? Still living the high life in the islands, is she now?" Her tightly permed hair was still held in check under a net. Her thick face powder clumped in the wrinkly cracks above her mouth. "Now children," she clapped her hands, "Make yourself useful. Here's a seating plan and some place cards." She thrust both at Cornelia.

"Can't I sit next to Nathan?" said Cornelia.

"No, you cannot." Mrs. Rogers' face scrunched up. "It's all been decided. We've had guidance on it. And Hall has approved the seating arrangements. And that's that!"

"Where's Horace Baker sitting? And why isn't Daddy at the head of the table?"

"Horace doesn't come to meals, my dear," she said with weary patience. "He's not well. But he *has* been consulted. And so has our divine savior who speaks directly to us all if we stand *still* long enough to listen," she wheeled around toward Nathan who was bouncing back and forth from one foot to another, hammering down on each fourth step until all the crystal goblets on the table danced to life. "Be careful," she snapped, "That's Waterford crystal. C.W.!" She clicked her fingers. "They'd like a word with you upstairs."

C.W. shrugged his shoulders, but dutifully followed Mrs. Rogers.

Nathan grabbed the list from Cornelia. "Let me see that. They've got Hall Hamden at the head of the table. Where Father should be. This is his house after all." An ugly flush reared up into his face and his jaw thrust out in a stubborn under-bite that Cornelia knew meant trouble. "I think we can fix that."

They left most of the seating arrangements intact but moved C.W. to one end of the table, put Rudy between Jay Burden and Hall Hamden on one side, then put Cornelia next to C.W., Nathan next to her and Hadji next to him. She thought about asking for Hadji to sit next to her, but she wasn't quite ready for that, plus she wanted to have Nathan by her side.

They stood, looking as guileless as possible, holding onto the backs of their chairs as they waited for the other dinner guests. Several tall young men and women came in and found their seats across from them. A friendly looking man with a shiny pate nodded from across the table.

Nathan grinned. "Hi, Uncle Stanley. I remember you. You taught me how to putt when I was little."

"Did I really?" Great Uncle Stanley looked puzzled. "Hmmm, imagine that." He peered across at Nathan, "Might have an extra mashie or two lying about. How 'bout having a bash in the morning?"

Nathan grinned.

C.W. came in and found his name card at the head of the table. A bemused smile crossed his face. As he placed his large hands on the back of the chair, Mrs. Rogers barked, "That's not your place, C.W."

"Surely," he waved at the place card below him.

"You *know* that's where Hall Hamden sits. You know he *must* sit next to our visiting dignitary. We discussed *that* this morning after Quiet Time." When C.W. shuffled his feet and looked chagrined, she snorted. "Do I have to do everything?" She sighed deeply then sailed around the table, gathering speed as she went. She snatched Hall Hamden's card and motioned to C.W., "This is where you're sitting."

Nathan and Cornelia froze as she rounded back up toward them. But she swished past, apparently under such full sail that she couldn't be bothered with them. It was then that Cornelia realized with a lurch of her stomach that she was now sitting next to Hall Hamden instead of her father.

"Quick!" said Nathan, switching places.

Her throat swelled with love for Nathan. When the chips were down she could always count on him. She could not imagine how unsafe life would feel if he were not by her side. She was so full of gratitude that she was hardly aware of Hadji until he leaned over and whispered, "There's all that lovely silken hair again." And she blushed and looked down at her feet.

Hall Hamden swept into the room, flanked by two young men; all three of them dressed in white shirts and ties pulled tight under baggy grey flannel suits. They wheeled around, almost in formation and bowed slightly as a very tall and imposing black man walked in after them. He had on a tight-cut brightly patterned tunic with a starched collar, thick black glasses, and a leopard-skinned cap shaped like a football. The two young men leapt to pull out his chair, which was next to Hall Hamden but on the opposite side of the table to the children. As everyone sat down, Hall Hamden opened his napkin with a snap.

"Let us pray!" he said and lowered his head. After gratitude for service given, Hall Hamden signaled for the food to be delivered. Several young women leapt to their feet, disappeared through a swinging door and came back bearing huge wooden trays covered with steaming bowls of soup.

As Hall Hamden talked intensely with the black man to his right, it gave Cornelia a chance to covertly study him. He still had glib good looks, though his small eyes, too close together, had a beady intensity that scared her. There was a dark shadow of hair along his chin line that gleamed with sweat when he talked. Occasionally he would take out a large linen handkerchief and mop around his neck and under his eyes.

Becoming aware of her scrutiny, his large head turned in her direction. She quickly looked down at her soup as if it fascinated her. Unfortunately, the steam off the broth was unpleasantly fishy and chunks of meat glistened with skin. Her stomach churned.

Over the sound of clinking spoons, Hall Hamden nodded toward the black man on his right and said, "Mobutu has come all the way from the Congo in the great continent of Africa. He is visiting Washington and is finding his way around the influential rooms of that great city. We are honored that he is here with us this weekend. He has shared with me that he wants to learn more about our war against evil. Let us welcome him to our midst."

"Hear! Hear!" came a chorus from many around the table, including C.W.

Mobutu nodded his head and launched into a speech, "Yes indeed, yes indeed, thank you for being so gracious." His eyes wandered around the room. "My wife and I can only *hope* someday to live in such splendor."

A low murmur filled the room. Mobutu held up his broad hands for silence, "Yes indeed, Hall Hamden here shares my mistrust and hatred of politicians. Politicians by their very nature are bound to go where the wind blows and unfortunately our country, which has been for so long under neo-classical colonial rule, is now being threatened by those politicians who would like to welcome the communists into their midst. But I say, to those politicians," he hammered his fist onto the table, making Cornelia jump and two young women titter. "That we shall not fall under the rule of another plutocrat but will rise up from under our cloak of shame! We must root out those pro-communist factions and chase them under the bushes where we will annihilate them!"

There was a stunned pause. But Hall Hamden did not hesitate long. "Hear. Hear." he said.

Another chorus of hurrahs from around the table dutifully followed.

Hadji cleared his throat and spoke directly to Mobutu. "One can only hope you don't actually mean annihilate. Perhaps you are only using it as a metaphor? Certainly, you can't possibly mean to kill off all your enemies?"

Hall Hamden nodded his head toward Hadji. "Our friend here comes from India. His grandfather was a famous pacifist. He doesn't always understand that sometimes meaningful change comes from aggressive actions."

"Kill?" whispered Nathan. "You would really kill all your enemies?"

Mobutu winked at Nathan, but his large thumb jammed down in a rotating motion that mimicked squashing a bug. He threw back his large head and roared when Nathan's eyes bugged out. "Young man, I am only joking."

C.W. cleared his throat, then tentatively proffered an opinion. "Horace says to keep your friends close, but your enemies closer. To kill your enemy is to kill a part of yourself."

Cornelia wondered whether her father knew Hall Hamden was an enemy. Her enemy.

"Exactly right, C.W.," Hadji waggled his head in approval. Next to him, Nathan worked on perfecting the head waggle.

Hall Hamden ignored them. "Let me change the subject, if I may. Let me introduce you to our other special guests today, Nathan and Cornelia, the children of our very good host Cornelius Woodstock. Because I happen to know their mother does not approve of us, and I suspect the children concur, they perhaps are enemies in the making. Am I right, children?" As Hall Hamden swung his head in their direction, his beady eyes glittered, and his toothy smiled flashed.

Mobutu stared at each of them in turn, with such serious calculation that it made Cornelia uneasy. She wanted to shout that she was not a pro-communist whatever that was. There was a brute force to the man that made her uneasy. He had a thick neck and hands as large as smoked hams. Combined with being so physically close to Hall Hamden, she began to feel a queasy rumbling in her belly.

"Ah hah," said Mobutu, "The children of capitalists."

Before she had time to stop them, the words popped out. "Let's hope that's better than pro-communist. Lest we be crushed."

Mobutu stared at her, his mouth fell open, then he reared back to say, "Well spoken, well spoken," and roared with laughter.

"Children," warned Mrs. Rogers from the foot of the table, "Eat your soup."

Cornelia took a few more sips of broth, then forked a piece of fish meat and took a nibble, but the slippery flesh and slimy skin made her gag and she quickly brought her napkin up to her mouth, spat the piece of meat out into the napkin, then jammed it back under the soup bowl. She tried not to listen to the great slurps coming from Mobutu across the table. At least someone was enjoying the broth.

When the women stood up to clear the soup plates, Hall Hamden said, "I gather you didn't like the soup?"

"Oh yes," Cornelia said as convincingly as possible, "It was just absolutely delicious."

Hall Hamden leaned over past Nathan, picked up her soup bowl, exposing the hidden piece of meat and speared it with his fork. He held it up for all to see. "Ah hah," he said, "Not exactly absolutely truthful, are we now?" He laughed and they all laughed with him and Mobutu roared the loudest and she hated them both with all her heart. But she also blushed with shame.

"Some of us," said Hall Hamden, "Did not grow up with privilege. We were glad for every scrap of food on our plates. I for one am grateful for my working-class background. My father was a coal miner. He would come home black with soot. No matter how hard he scrubbed, the cracks in his skin stayed black. I was raised to think the mines awaited me. But that prospect put a fire in my belly. And look at what God has given me." He waved his hand around the room as if it was all his. "Perhaps those who have been given so much," he nodded at C.W. and his children, "Cannot appreciate God's munificence as much as those of us who were raised without."

Mobutu roared with laughter. "The sons of princes grow weak in their palaces. Easy pickings for those of us who are lions."

Cornelia flushed with anger. She too had fire in her belly. She had it right now at the thought of Hall Hamden lording over her own father.

The main course arrived. Cornelia's stomach turned at the sight of a too thick, too raw slice of roast beef oozing clear red and a huge gooey clump of mashed potatoes. Hadji leaned over. "Never mind the meat. I'm not going to eat it either! As a Hindu, I eschew meat." She smiled.

Across the table, Mobutu cut off huge chunks and shoveled them into his mouth. The muscles in his cheeks were large and she shuddered at the thought of being crushed by this man's bite, which reminded her of Gertrude's shoulder so long ago.

Hall Hamden tapped his silver dessert spoon against the wine goblet filled with grape juice. The crystalline ting quieted all conversation. Hall Hamden spoke into the silence.

Cornelia let his words drone on as she poked at her roast beef. She had cut it into tiny little bits, managed to swallow two mouthfuls before jamming the rest into the pile of mashed potatoes. She hoped Hall Hamden would not call attention to her plate again. The more she thought about how he had humiliated her about the soup, the angrier she grew.

Nathan stiffened then gave her a sharp swift kick under the table. "Pay attention. He's talking about Father."

Hall Hamden darted a sharp look at Nathan and cleared his throat. "As I was saying, our good friend C.W. here, in an effort to make amends for *his* family having so much when so many have so little, has welcomed us, unselfishly and lovingly, into his ancestral family home. He has made monies available for elevators to be installed, food to be purchased, clothes to be bought for all those in need...."

Nathan whispered out of the corner of his mouth, "What about us?"

Hall tapped his fingers on the table and waited for complete silence before continuing. "In fact, Cornelius Woodstock has made it possible for us to continue in all our endeavors this year. To fight the good fight. And now...." He waved his hand as if it were a baton. "He has an announcement to make." He clapped his hands, "C.W.?"

All eyes were on C.W. who squirmed, his shoulders bowed, his hands thrust under his legs. His head hung low; his eyes peeped out from under his bulging brow, looking round the table. He focused on his children for a moment and then looked away. "Well," he said, "I've had guidance. We've all had guidance. Everyone has helped me to see that by giving out my money in dribbles and drabbles, well, in fact, that has been a kind of control. A kind of selfishness if you will. So, God has given me the guidance that I must make a grand gesture, something that shows that my heart and mind and soul are committed to this cause. I may not be a fierce warrior on the front lines, but from behind the scenes I can offer the monies that have been entrusted to me." He smiled sheepishly but said nothing more.

Hall Hamden picked up the ball and ran with it. "In fact," and he waved his pointer finger in the cadence of his words, "In fact...." he paused, building up the drama, "He is withdrawing the loan of a family-owned painting from the National Gallery in Washington, D.C. It is to be put up to auction by none other than Sotheby's. And the proceeds from the sale are to go directly to the Moral Absolute cause."

"Hear, hear!" chorused the minions.

Nausea slammed into Cornelia's stomach. Painful tears spurted into the corners of her eyes. "Daddy, not the little princess!"

C.W. nodded and shrugged his shoulders. His hands splayed out in apology.

She stood up, her chair falling behind her with a crash. "Not the little princess!" She stamped her foot.

"Who's the little princess?" said Nathan.

"It seems we have more than one little princess to deal with." Hall Hamden said. "The fact that you are troubled by your father's donation to the cause concerns *me*. Please be open to a fearless and searching inventory of your soul. Know this, child, the better good of many, the need of money for the sake of a higher cause *always* trumps the childish desires of a few." He finished on a roll, his voice reaching up into the domed ceiling.

Cornelia stood her ground. Her chest was tight. But she could not contain her fury. "I'm *not* a little princess. None of you have any idea how Nathan and I live. We have gone to bed hungry plenty of nights."

Hall Hamden laughed. "Surely you don't expect us to believe you actually go to bed hungry?"

Her breathing quickened. "I *know* your father had black in the cracks of his fingers. I *get* it. But *what* about when a rage blows in so big that the mailboat sails on by? Which means our pork and beans run out? And when Daddy's child support check doesn't come, Mummy takes to her bed with worry. And Mr. Stanley at the grocery store cuts off our credit because there's no money to pay the bill. And after six hours of cutting brush in the jungle to feed the goats, Ray feels really bad. And he wants a little rum. But there isn't any. So he drinks Bay Rum, which is supposed to be for shaving. And he goes kind of crazy and he grabs Mummy by the hair and she starts screaming. And Nathan runs out the door to go shark hunting. And I go to my room. Then Nathan and I open up the last can of corned beef hash for dinner. Does this sound like the life of a princess? Does it?" She panted. Her hands gripped the table for support. She looked wildly around the table.

Hadji stared at her.

Nathan whispered. "Mummy said you weren't supposed to say anything."

Mobutu's jaw hung open. Mrs. Rogers frowned. C.W. looked bludgeoned. Only Hall Hamden smiled. He held up his hands. "Now, now, that's quite enough, young lady. Exaggeration is a form of dishonesty and I am sure no one here really believes what you're saying is the *absolute* truth."

She swung on him, her brows so rigid that her nostrils flared, her eyes met his and clashed. "How dare you? When you're just waiting for Aunt Janice to die! How absolutely loving is *that*?"

Suddenly the adrenaline-fueled rage faded and the room began to spin. Her head pounded, and fields of red narrowed her vision to a black tunnel that grew smaller and smaller. Vomit spasmed up from her stomach, hitting her throat with noxious bile, then vaulted up and out of her mouth and onto her plate, coating the mashed potatoes with slime.

She pushed back from the table and ran out of the room, crossed the grand entryway, then bolted up the three flights of stairs and down the hall to the nursery where she threw herself onto her bed and sobbed.

Half an hour later, Nathan came in without knocking. He flung himself down onto the window seat where he rolled around two or three times before saying, "Is your tantrum all done?"

She nodded.

"That was quite a show you put on. I thought we had agreed not to say anything about Mummy and Ray."

"I know. I'm sorry. I couldn't help it. Hall Hamden just makes me so angry. Did I make a fool out of myself?"

"I don't know about that. But you missed a good dessert. Chocolate pie. Now tell me. Who is the little princess?"

She told him about the painting and of how sad the little princess was, of how imprisoned she appeared to be, of how she lived under the thrall of a royal life in which she had no power. "And besides," she continued, "when we were standing in front of the little princess, it was maybe the first time *ever* I actually really talked to Daddy. How could he not care about that?"

"At least you got to talk to him. I *never* do. Anyway, how much do you think she's worth?" Nathan asked. "That big guy from Africa wanted to know."

"I don't know. Maybe hundreds of thousands. Maybe millions. I don't know. She was painted by an old master. Aren't old masters worth a lot?" She rolled over onto her back and looked at the ceiling. Now that it was evening, the tiny stars painted onto the ceiling glowed gold against the cerulean blue. "Did Mummy do that?" She pointed up.

He nodded. "Doesn't our father care about us at all?"

"I don't know," She sighed.

"I just don't understand. How can he be giving so much away and yet be so stingy with Mummy and us? It doesn't make sense." Beneath his freckles, Nathan paled.

"Do grownups ever make sense?"

"Not much I guess. Do you think we can ask him not to do this? That we need the money instead?"

"I don't think so. I think they'd say we were just being selfish. Don't you know we're supposed to be Absolutely Unselfish?" Her tone was bitter.

There was a gentle knock on the door. Nathan and Cornelia quickly looked at each other. "Maybe it's Father." Nathan jumped to his feet and ran to the door. To their surprise, it was Hadji. Cornelia quickly swung her feet to one side and sat primly on the edge of the bed.

"Feeling better, I hope?" he asked, and she nodded. "I hesitate to interfere," he continued, "But I am concerned for your welfare." His brow creased with worry.

Nathan waved at him to come in.

"No, no, I must not come in," his head waggled. "Indeed, it would not be proper, but I thought you should know there is a big brouhaha going on downstairs right now. Quite frankly, it smacks of a witch-hunt. It concerns me that your good father is being taken to task for the imagined transgressions of his children. Forgive me if I have overstepped my boundaries, but I took it upon myself to go and consult with Horace and he too is troubled. He told me to warn you to be ready to face the forces gathering downstairs."

He turned to look at Cornelia. "I don't think I even have to ask, but did you tell the truth about Hall Hamden just waiting for Aunt Janice to die?"

She nodded. "I heard him."

"I told Horace that. We are both troubled by this."

"Can't you do anything to stop them?" She cried out. "I *hate* Hall Hamden! I especially hate that we always use his full name! Horace doesn't make us do that."

"No, he doesn't. Horace does not believe in interfering; he watches and lets people learn from their mistakes. He believes there is a lesson to be learned here. He has shared with me that there are winds of change coming. And not all will be good. As with a hurricane, there will be much destruction before there is rebuilding."

His expression softened, "And please do remember, dear girl, hate can only harm *you*, not Hall Hamden—er, Hall. I believe him to be a man tortured by his own demons. Perhaps he lives in his own hell for all we know."

"Thank you for saying it, but I'm *not* a dear girl. I'm ungrateful. And selfish. Or at least that's what he would like everyone to think."

"But it's *not* what everyone thinks. Certainly not me. Nor Horace. And I do hope and believe that your father will not be long swayed into so thinking."

Cornelia sobbed, "I don't want Daddy to think I'm awful. Why does he listen to them?"

"Remember, it is not always the man with the obvious power who matters. There is a divine force that governs us all. And what people do with the power they have is what matters. My grandfather, the Mahatma, also believed that doing nothing was sometimes more powerful than taking action."

"I don't understand," she shook her head.

"You will one day," he said kindly.

"No, now *you* don't understand. I *do* get it. But that doesn't make what's happening right."

"No, it doesn't," Hadji shook his head.

"And what about our father?" asked Nathan, "Doesn't he care about us at all?"

"Certainly, he does. And never forget that he is a good man. A *very* good man. He means so well that people take advantage of that good will. I have seen that many times in many places. Good men being used by men with other motives."

"Like Jesus and the Pharisees?"

"Maybe," Hadji stared her, "You are a wise little girl. You constantly surprise me."

She blushed. "Mummy says it's not good to be so smart. In her day, women hid their brains from the men."

"I for one think she's wrong about that."

"What about Daddy? Does he really think we're awful?"

"I do believe that for now, the forces that be have convinced him of that, but I think he will come around. In the meantime, please, I come to fetch you to Horace."

"Right now?"

"Yes, he is waiting. Will you come?" And he waggled his head in the way they both liked.

"Come on," she said to Nathan and hopped down off the high bed.

"Let's go talk to Horace. Maybe he can help us make sense of this."

Chapter 7

Horace's room was on the second floor down at the far end of the building. The room was large and overheated for a summer's eve. Firelight danced all along the *chinoiserie* wallpaper. The air was thick and fragrant from the huge bouquets of roses. Sweat popped out on Cornelia's brow. She lifted her hair up off her neck. A beautiful, clear dark-blue light spilled into the room, the dusk of a summer evening in the North, so different than the abrupt sunsets in the islands. A small fire crackled beneath a white marble mantel.

Her eyes drifted up to the portrait of a beautiful young woman lying on what looked like the same window seats that were still in the room. She was dressed all in glossy cream satin, her dark brown hair curling up off her face, a half smile turning up the corners of her scarlet mouth. Her eyelids drooped down over shining green eyes in a vague expression. Was it sadness or sleepiness or some form of wanting dreaminess that she could not name? Regardless, her profile was perfection. "Mummy," Cornelia said.

"Ah hah," said Horace from his perch on a very high four-poster bed, propped up by a plethora of pillows. "That is indeed your mother. It was painted by your good father just after they married. I've spent many an hour looking at her trying to figure out what she wanted from life." He waved his hand at her. "Come child, draw closer. My eyes aren't as good as they once were, and I want to study you."

She walked slowly toward the bed. He lay smothered beneath a satin comforter. He seemed tinier than she remembered, as if he had shriveled. But his eyes still shone with that same strange intensity.

"Excuse me for greeting you from my bed, but my legs just don't seem to obey me much anymore. Used up all my energy getting down to greet you earlier. Darn things." And he slapped at his legs and laughed. Then he extended his claw hand toward Cornelia. The tips of his fingers were smooth and cold, in alarming contrast to the steamy air in the room.

"How does that work?" asked Nathan, from behind her, "Your legs? They just don't obey you anymore?"

"Ah hah, the son. Come stand in the light next to your sister so I can see you both. Couldn't see you very well earlier. My eyes are not much better than my legs."

With a gentle push by Hadji, Nathan came forward into the light of a lamp on a bedside table.

Though he didn't let go of his grip on Cornelia, Horace's gaze probed Nathan and he leaned as far forward as he could. Nathan fidgeted and then settled down, almost as if mesmerized. "Yes indeed, I see that there is anger inside you. Resentment that you believe your father has abandoned you. But he has not. Take it from me, he has not. And I also see that you have a deep need to know how things work."

Nathan's eyebrows danced, a sure sign he was pleased.

"That's true, Nathan," Cornelia exclaimed, "Like that time you cut the baby sharks out of the mummy's belly just to see how it worked. And then they all swam away. You saved their lives."

"Did you really do that?" Horace dropped her hand and clapped his hands together, though one of them stayed curled up as if it clutched something inside its fist. "How absolutely wonderful." He threw back his head and laughed. It was infectious and they all laughed with him. Cornelia was filled with awe that a man who seemed quite diminished still had a sense of humor. Joy, she realized, was a contagious emotion. And despite his health issues, this man had an abundance of joy.

Cornelia spoke, "The bible says where there is darkness, light. And where there is sadness, joy."

"So you've been reading the bible have you?" His gaze bore into her.

When she nodded, Horace gestured to Hadji who waggled his

head, then led Nathan over to a series of pen and ink drawings of cricket games.

Cornelia squirmed but allowed herself to fall under the spell of Horace's penetrating eyes "Ah yes," he smiled, "I am glad to see your spirit survives. You speak truth with the wisdom of an old soul. But you will need more than that. My spy," he pointed toward Hadji, "says that you made quite a marvelous speech tonight at the dinner table. You will need to curb that bravado. You spoke bravely but perhaps not wisely."

His words made her heart skitter. "Why? What makes you say that?"

"Do you not realize that by sharing the story of the chaos in your island home you have opened the door for your father to seek custody?"

"Oh no, is that what I've done?" Her heart pounded so hard it hurt. "I just wanted to make them understand."

"*I* understand. But I fear your brother might not do well in these confinements. What think you?"

"He wouldn't. He hates being cooped up. He goes a little crazy."

"Exactly. Think on that when you are asked to make choices. Consult the man above. Listen to your heart and that little voice inside you. Think about Absolute Unselfishness."

"I'll try." She covered her mouth with her hand and swallowed back tears. "You know about that little voice?"

He winked, "I do, my dear, I fear that some here listen to their own voice and seek to break your spirit. They will always cast doubt on what you say." He waved his hand, pointing at the all the fragrant roses. "See how lovely the fresh picked roses are?" But look at this." His curled fist was opened to expose a dried-up prune. "You must never let bitterness and the need for control turn you into this," he nodded toward the prune. "You must stay positive and trusting no matter what life throws at you. Will you promise me that? God loves children because he knows they are closer to the divine than any grown up will ever be." His kind tone turned suddenly fierce, his beaky nose pointed at her. "Now tell me the truth, did you truly absolutely hear something about Aunt Janice and your father?"

Her heart skipped a beat. She nodded. "I overheard Hall Hamden."

He sighed. "I owe you an apology."

"Why?"

For a long moment, she thought he wouldn't answer. He seemed lost in thought, but nodding, as if he were communicating with someone she could not see, all the while smoothing down the covers around him as if he needed tucking in. Finally, he began to talk. "I chose not to truly believe you once. I could see clearly that you *wanted* Hall to be wrong so that you could get back to your mother. That blinded me to the truth. I have so longed to lay down the load of leadership, to have a worthy son to whom to pass the baton. This selfish desire on my part blinded me to the truth." He winked and pointed up toward the ceiling. "But oh boy has that old guy upstairs given me a hard time about my selfish desire to control. To want to see things happen my way. I am sorry, my dear, I should have listened to you."

He slumped back against the pillows and closed his eyes. "No," he shook himself, "I cannot give into this fatigue. I must speak further. Cornelia, listen to me," he grabbed her hand. "Keep your eyes and ears open. Harness that truth of yours. Learn to be as wise as a serpent. Be careful to whom you speak and perhaps unselfish when it comes to keeping your brother safe. Now, I'm afraid I *must* rest." Once more, he sank back into the pillows, his hands quivering, and his eyes closed. A pained expression appeared to furrow his brow.

The hair on the back of Cornelia's neck prickled. "What does it all mean?" she whispered to Hadji as he came up behind her with Nathan. Hadji cupped both their shoulders and began to ease them both back toward the door. "Perhaps, as Horace often says, more will be revealed as time goes along. Come now, we must let him sleep."

Nathan looked back at the semi-comatose old man. His freckles darkened as they sometimes did when he was frightened. "Is he dying?"

Hadji smiled and ruffled Nathan's buzz cut. "That's nice of you to be concerned. I believe there to be life in him yet. He still has much to teach us. And that fire will keep him alive a bit longer. Maybe many years, who knows?"

Just as they reached the door, a knock came. Hadji turned the knob and C.W. stood there, looking grim. Without a word, he grabbed Nathan and Cornelia by the hand and dragged them down the hall.

"Ouch," said Nathan, "That hurts." And tried to squirm away.

"Be a man," said C.W.

In the grand living room downstairs, a group awaited them: Hall Hamden, his three minions, Jay Burden, Mrs. Rogers and three young women with pale faces and hairnets flanking a smug-looking Rudy. They sat in a circle of overstuffed chairs. In front of the fire in the largest wing-back, Hall Hamden's face was in shadow, his legs were crossed, and his cocked foot swung in a martial rhythm. C.W. plunked the two children down into two straight-backed chairs that faced the inquisitors.

Hall Hamden snapped his black book open and read a list of their transgressions.

"One, not being grateful for the rooms to which they'd been assigned. Two, defiantly sliding down the bannister after being asked to resist. Three, selfishly changing the place cards at dinner to suit themselves. Four, shamelessly swimming in an impure manner in the river. Five, dishonestly hiding good food at the dinner table. Six, Cornelia throwing a tantrum when told of her father's generous donation."

It was, pronounced Hall, an altogether poor showing and a sure sign that their wills were running rough shod over all others, that their own selfish needs were out of control. An intervention was called for, he advised, or else they would be lost forever to a life of immorality and selfishness. "Absolute Love, Absolute Purity, Absolute Honesty, and Absolute Unselfishness, those are the Moral standards you should be reaching for." He thundered to a halt.

There was a long moment of silence. Listed like that, Cornelia had to admit, their transgressions sounded awful. "It didn't happen that way," she wanted to protest, but she reminded herself, to be absolutely honest, that they actually had done all the things he'd listed. Cornelia swung her feet, deliberately not looking up to meet anyone's gaze.

"But of course, I must defer to your father." Hall Hamden cleared his throat, "C.W., will you share *your* guidance about your children?"

C.W. coughed. "At first my thoughts were clouded with shame.

Shame that my children could be behaving in such an ungrateful and willful manner. But then a clear thought came to me that I must love them anyway. That the answer to this out-of-control behavior is unconditional love. That their acting out is a result of having to deal with the evil ways in their mother's home. And that we can offer them a better life here. If they will only open their hearts to change."

Nathan's knees bounced. His fingers drummed on his thighs. Cornelia knew he was agitated. He had never been able to sit still. And doing so just made his anxiety worse. She put her hand on his shoulder.

"We will consider what you have had to say," she said, "But for now, we are going back to our room where we will think on it." She held her shoulders tight, desperately trying not to show how frightened she felt.

"Go if you must," said Hall Hamden, "But say your good-byes to each other. Because as of tonight, I have had very clear guidance that brother and sister should no longer be sharing a room."

Cornelia jumped to her feet. "You can't do this." She stamped her foot. "We've done nothing wrong. We're just kids. It's you who is wrong!" And she pointed her finger at Hall Hamden, only to have the image of Horace Baker showing her how that meant three fingers pointed back at her and an uncomfortable flush spread through her. Confusion and bewilderment dulled her rage and she slumped back into her seat and hugged her knees to her chest. She felt lost and scared, as if a black squall threatened to sweep her into a deadly whirlpool. She gasped and hurtful sobs wrenched themselves up from deep inside.

Nathan patted her on the back, "It's okay."

"It's not okay," she wailed.

"Come on." It was his turn to stand up with as much dignity as he could muster. He leaned over to help her to her feet. "Let's go now, Nee, we'll just leave now. We'll go upstairs and wait for you to come." He looked pointedly at C.W. as they turned and left the room.

Weeping hard, Cornelia stumbled blindly up the stairs. "Are they really going to take you away from me?"

"Shh, let's just get to our room."

They walked quietly down the hall and entered their old nursery, carefully closing the door behind them. Nathan shot the old brass bolt to lock the door. Moonlight filtered in around the leaves fluttering outside the window, falling in an undulating lace-like pattern on the old blue and cream Chinese rug, making the tiny dragons look like they were whirling and squirming.

"How could they?" She moaned, "They made us sound so horrible."

"Yeah they did."

"What's wrong with them?"

"I don't know. We have to have a plan. What are we going to do?" asked Nathan, "We can't stay here. We've got to get home to Mummy. She wouldn't like what they're doing to us."

"No, she wouldn't. But what can we do? We don't have any money. Or anything. And Horace told me they're going to try and keep us here because I told about how bad things were at home. I'm so sorry, it's all my fault."

"Maybe Hadji would help us?" said Nathan.

She thought for a long moment, "I don't think he will. Remember he told us earlier that he has learned from Horace not to interfere. He most likely will let things unfold and watch to see what happens. He said sometimes the power lay in taking no action at all." She curled up on the window seat and looked down where the moonlight glittered on the river, shining as if it were a silver road. "Nathan, come here." She patted the seat beside her. "Look at the moon. See the way it shines down a pathway just for us. When I was at Tall Pine Island, it helped me to remember that this same moon and sun shines down all over the world." She sighed, "So if they do manage to separate us, look out the window wherever you are and remember that I'll be doing the same okay?"

At that moment, there came a knock on the door. Cornelia's heart hammered in her chest. They could hear the doorknob being turned. "Nathan!" shouted C.W. from the hallway, "Open up this door right now." And then their father kept up such a steady hammering that finally, after several long moments, Nathan stood, tears streaming down his cheeks, and walked to the door and unlatched the bolt.

Chapter 8

Later, Cornelia learned that Nathan was hauled down to the narrow room at the other end of the hallway. There, when C.W. told him to stop his blubbering and he did not, C.W. yanked him over his knees and beat him with a yardstick. In between the hard-hitting strikes, C.W. hissed, "You've got to learn to be a man."

That night, determined to find Nathan, Cornelia waited until the house quieted down and owls hooted in the garden. But when she went to her door, it was locked from the outside.

From that day on, they were deliberately kept on different schedules. Nathan was put to work in the garden. In the house, Cornelia chopped onions and cleaned windows. Once she saw, through the window, Nathan ducking behind a wall when Hall Hamden stalked by. His knees jittered, and he gnawed at his cuticles reminding her of a caged animal.

Nathan ate his meals with Great Uncle Stanley in what had once been the servant's dining room. Mrs. Rogers, Cornelia and Rudy ate at a table in the kitchen. While they chattered, Cornelia picked at her food. "Let her sulk," said Mrs. Rogers. "She'll come around."

When Cornelia asked if she could go see Horace Baker again, Mrs. Rogers said that was not allowed. "And Hadji?" she asked.

"He's gone back to India."

On the third day of her isolation, when she was supposed to be resting and having guidance, she snuck down to the second floor and into Great Aunt Janice's room. Aunt Janice lived in a grand suite, stuffed to the ceilings with piles of old fashion magazines and stacks of shoeboxes. She looked up as Cornelia came through the door.

"Did you happen to see my purple shoe? I wore it to the reception at the White House with President Cleveland. I so need to find it. If I could, I'd feel so much better....so much better. I have the one. But not t'other." As her words turned into gibberish, Cornelia drifted over to the bookcases that lined two walls of her rooms. There was Andrew Lang's entire set of fairy tale books. And a set of Dickens. She took *A Tale of Two Cities* and *The Violet Fairy Book*, neither of which she had read. Aunt Janice didn't appear to notice when she slipped back out the door carrying the two books.

Day after day, her virtual isolation continued. It gave her a lot of time to read and think. Some days she felt confused. Other days frightened. If she stayed here would she, like Aunt Janice, turn as nutty as a fruitcake? If she went back to the islands would she be angry and hateful toward her mother and Ray? She knew the village life in the Bahamas wasn't how most of the world lived. But how could she know what was normal? Like Alice in her Looking Glass world, whom could she trust? She felt kinship with the princesses who went on quests through scary forests in her fairy tale books. In those stories, there was often a wise fairy disguised as an ugly old woman. If the princess was kind to her, great gifts were given. If she was mean, she was sometimes turned into a frog. She felt soothed by the thought that perhaps Hadji and Horace were wise guides.

One day, she looked up from her Dickens book and saw Nathan out the window. He had the jumpy stiff-legged walk of a leashed dog snarling at every passerby. A plan began to form.

Finally, her father was allowed to come have tea with her. He spoke to her of how wonderful the group was. Of how Horace gave him wisdom. But it was Hall Hamden who kept him straight. After he finally stopped talking, she asked. "How do you know when your guidance is real?"

C.W. peered up at her from below his beetling brows. "Tell me more," he said.

"I mean, I hear a clear quiet voice inside of me, I do. But how do I know when it's self-serving and when it's true? Can't demons speak to me as well as angels?"

"I try to measure all my guidance against the Four Absolute standards. And if none of them clash, then I think the voice is to be trusted. And here is where we must trust the group to keep us straight. If someone confronts me about being self-serving, they are usually right."

"So, the group may be right about Nathan and me?" She was careful to measure her words. Horace would be proud, she thought, she was being careful. She would keep her enemies close. And, as Hadji had told her, the power lay in waiting to see what would happen.

"Is that what you think?"

"I don't know what to think."

"Would you like to have guidance about it?"

"Now?"

"Yes, of course." And so, they had guidance together and her guidance pleased C.W. very much. Her heart lurched that he was so pleased with her. After so many long lonely days, she basked under his approval like a mistreated animal clamoring for affection. And, in fact, he was so pleased with her that, after consulting with Hall Hamden the very next day, a general meeting was called in which Cornelia was asked to share her guidance publicly.

Nathan shuffled in, flanked by two young men. She tried to meet his eyes, but his head hung down and he looked sullen. His lower lips swelled. His knees jitterbugged. His misery gave her courage to continue with her plan.

Hall Hamden started off the meeting with a sharing about what a wonderful time he had had with Mobutu in Washington the day before and of how grateful he was to have had some small part of influencing the future of deepest, darkest Africa. "A light has been ignited in Mobutu's soul that will never go out, I am sure. But most of all today," he continued, "I wanted you all to listen to some wonderful guidance that comes from our youngest member. It seems change has entered her heart after all. Cornelia, won't you share with us now?"

Cornelia read aloud her carefully written guidance. "It doesn't matter what I need. What matters most is what others need. I have been selfish in thinking only of whether our father loves me. I understand that he needs to love all the little children in the world as much as he does me. I have held anger in my heart towards a God who would take my daddy away from me." She looked up from her notes to see everyone beaming at her. "Maybe there are bigger things in the world than me?"

"Hear, hear," said the group.

"Maybe God wants me to stay here and learn to be good?"

"Hear, hear," said the group.

"How wonderful!" Mrs. Rogers clapped her hands, her face beaming.

Cornelia ducked her head. "I have accepted the evil of my ways. I am willing to stay here and work on accepting change into my heart. But, and Daddy has agreed to this after I begged him, I won't fight you. I'll do whatever you say. But Nathan has to go home. It's not fair for Mummy if she loses both her children."

Nathan looked startled. "Cornelia, what are you saying? What have they done to you? You can't stay here. We talked about it. We have to stick together."

She shook her head. "God wants me to stay here." She needed Nathan to believe in the change of her heart. Or else she knew he wouldn't leave her behind.

Mrs. Rogers shook her head, "Don't listen to him, Cornelia, I'm *very* proud of you. You should never be ashamed of your decision." Her usually prim face was wreathed with smiles.

Using her best grown-up voice, Cornelia chided Nathan. "Nathan, listen to me," she pleaded, "We've been wrong. We could end up batty like Aunt Janice if we don't mend our ways. We've been selfish in thinking only of ourselves. Daddy needs me by his side so that we can fight the good fight." The cadence of her words sang inside her and she liked the way everyone was bobbing their heads in time to her words. A sense of newly discovered power flooded into her. She liked the way this made her feel. And she loved the look of approval shining from C.W.'s face. Nevin had never approved of her that way. Never. She held out her hands to Nathan, "Won't you applaud my decision?"

"You're nuts," snorted Nathan, "What's the matter with you? You sound just like them." After the meeting, Nathan was marched off in one direction and Cornelia was once more taken to her room. She fretted in her room for several hours, then ran to the window when she heard stones crunching as a car drove up around the gravel driveway and came to a stop out front.

On the front steps, her father and a young man led Nathan toward the car. C.W. had him by the wrist, yanking at him. Nathan turned and looked up to the third floor. She ducked behind a curtain.

"Cornelia?" Nathan yelled up to her. When there was no answer, he turned to his father. "You can't do this. I want to see her. I have to say good-bye. I have to know she's okay."

C.W. said nothing at first, but his face was obdurately set. Finally, he said. "It's thought best not."

"What? Who says? Hall Hamden? He's a creep."

"One day you will understand that what I am doing is what God wants. He wants for each of you to be the best you can be. It has been decided that Cornelia's *change* is so new and tender that she must be protected from you."

"That's a horrible thing to say. I always protect her. I do. You just.... You don't care about us at all." His face twisted with anger.

From above, Cornelia could hear every word they were shouting. Nathan turned and yelled up to her window. "Nee! Listen to me. They're forcing me to leave. I don't know what they're telling you, but don't believe them."

"That's enough of that!" C.W. grabbed him by the shoulder and pushed him toward the car.

At that moment, Cornelia turned and ran toward the door. What had she been thinking? Nathan was right. She had to go with him. She turned the knob and yanked, but again it was locked from the outside. "No!" She pounded on the door. "Let me out. I have to go with Nathan."

There was no sound from outside in the corridor. She ran to the window and saw the car speed away down under the curving arch of trees. She slumped down onto the floor and curled up into a ball.

"What have I done?" she whispered, "I should have gone with Nathan. I should have gone." But then her inner voice spoke. "Better you than him. You're stronger. Bide your time. You will survive." She wondered if this was the voice of her guidance. Was she now part of the group and if so, was it so bad? Maybe this was where she belonged, destined to serve alongside her father. Despite these thoughts, a deep wail gathered momentum and she howled, long and loud, like a dog trapped inside an outhouse.

Finally, exhausted, she went over to her bed where the hand painted stars swirled over her and curled up under a satin comforter that had once been her mother's.

Part III

ABSOLUTE PURITY

Chapter 9

With her arms wrapped around her middle, Cornelia stood on the end of the ferry dock at Tall Pine Island, peering out into the murky fog. Nathan was coming in on the ferry and she had not seen him for five years. This year celebrated the first youth conference for the Moral Absolutes. She had written to Nathan and begged him to come.

Over time, Cornelia had grown accustomed to the ways of the group and even learned to embrace her new life. When Nathan was sent away, she initially hoped she would be able to visit her island family on occasion. But Hall Hamden had nixed that. He said her recent conversion to unselfishness was too vulnerable. Gradually, she began to believe her mother when she wrote that Cornelia was better off with her father.

Over time, Cornelia found her place in the Absolutes. While it was far from perfect, she had learned the value of working toward a common goal. Most of all, she had been able to slowly build a relationship with her father and she didn't want to lose that. She also learned to rely on the guidance of her quiet still voice and to curb her tongue, as Horace had advised. She had become adept at watching and waiting. She believed her vigilance had kept Aunt Janice from harm. Just last year, when Cornelia had found her slumped lifeless over a pile of shoes, no foul play was suspected because none of the leadership of the Absolutes was any longer in residence at Greendell. Most days, at the mansion, it was just Cornelia, Rudy (whose parents still saved souls in Africa), Mrs. Rogers and whatever tutor had been hired to govern the girls.

While Cornelia had changed significantly, little was different on Tall Pine Island in the eight years since she had first visited. It was true that the Conference Center for the Absolutes was now bigger, proudly sporting a brand-new movie studio erected just in the last few months. It was paid for with funds from Aunt Janice's estate, which C.W. had proudly arranged. "With the help of my good friend Hall Hamden, I know it is the right thing to do."

She looked up the hill at the conference center and new studio shrouded in an ominous mist. Somewhere up there, Hall Hamden was lurking. She shuddered. Over the years they had learned to be cordial to each other, but her suspicions of him never wavered. He was still very much in control, and she had to make peace with that. Once when Horace was visiting, she asked why Hall Hamden was still in power. He had waved his clawed hand and said, "He's a nuts-and-bolts kind of guy, my dear. He gets things done. We need people like that. As dear as your father is to me, he'll never be a leader like that." He cocked his head at her, "You're cut from the same bolt of cloth as your father, but I wonder often what life will make of you. God only tells me that you are part of his plan and that you are meant to be here."

Just offshore, the fog so clogged the sky that nothing on the water was visible beyond a hundred yards. Only the low flat note of a foghorn, and the jangling of the harness of waiting horses reverberated in the mist wrapped world. Above and behind her, the fog sent wraith-like tendrils far up into the pine-cloaked hills surrounding the harbor. Her stomach felt hollow. She was unbearably excited but equally as anxious to see Nathan. Would she even recognize him? Would he recognize her?

Physically, she had changed a great deal. Because she was no longer playing endlessly in the blasting sun of the tropics, her hair had darkened to a tawny gold. At 15, she had sprouted up to an intimidating 5'11. Her body had morphed from tom-boy slim to a curvy shape much like her mother. Her prominent jaw was often set in a grim line of determination; her cheekbones were high and wedge-like, which came from her father's side of the family. Her eyes still flashed black, with only shining highlights to define the separation of pupil from iris. Her glare had become famous in the Moral Absolute group. If she scowled when someone was sharing their guidance, they were no doubt about to receive a piercing interrogation from her. She was famous for her ability to induct newcomers and bring about "change" in many to ensure they complied with the standards.

As she stood there, restlessly shifting her weight from one foot to the other, she wondered what Nathan would think of her. She knew she had become more like her father, a living statue. Now she was serious and focused, with little time for silliness and anything that distracted from the Absolute mission. Without realizing it, she had become quite formidable.

Her relationship with Rudy had not changed. During meals, Cornelia often read books while Mrs. Rogers and Rudy chattered about frivolous things. The other books she had found on Aunt Janice's shelves after her passing became her salvation, just like when she was growing up in the Bahamas. Regardless of her situation, reading was always crucial to her mental well-being. Austen, Eliot and Dickens had been her most-loyal companions. Once, when Hadji had come for a visit, she found herself talking with the arch banter from those novels. His head had waggled in response, and she blushed. She had smiled so much during his visit that her face ached for days.

Once more the foghorn moaned, yanking Cornelia out of her thoughts and back to the situation at hand. To get ready for the youth conference, Mrs. Rogers had been sent money to buy clothes for the teenagers. After studying back issues of Aunt Janice's *Harper's Bazaar* magazines, Cornelia chose a black sheath that ended just above her knee. Mrs. Rogers thought it entirely too grown up, but Cornelia won by showing her a picture of Audrey Hepburn in the same outfit. In contrast, Mrs. Rogers beamed over Rudy's choice of a full-skirted plaid dress.

Cornelia heard the growl of the ferry motor before she saw it. She shrank back against the wooden wall of the ferry office. Part of her anxiety about seeing Nathan was that she knew he felt he'd gotten the raw end of the deal. He complained Ray made him do endless chores, and Nevin clung to him, saying she had lost one child and she couldn't stand to lose another. Yet he still ran free every chance he got. He fished and hunted shark and swam for miles in the ocean. He was at liberty to do so. It was part of God's plan, she was often told.

She was expected to always stay within the confines of the Moral Absolutes.

When the ferry boat poked its snout through the fog, her heart pounded so hard that her neck pulsed, and she grew so light-headed that it made her scowl. As the first group of girls tumbled off the boat wearing either collared tee shirts tucked into long Bermuda shorts or tea length shirtwaist dresses, Cornelia began to feel self-conscious. Maybe her bold fashion choice had been silly in retrospect. She had a lot to learn about the normal life of an American teenager. The Absolute way of life had kept her totally isolated from the mainstream. The arrival of this fresh batch of newcomers would be her first encounter with teenagers.

In contrast, Rudy was bubbly and sweet. She bounced up the gangplank and greeted the newcomers as if they were long lost relatives. Though she and Cornelia had been seen as effective when recruiting adult members, their styles were completely opposite. Where Cornelia was earnest and direct, Ruby was giddy and eager to please. Much to the pleasure of the leadership, when one approach did not work on a guest, the other often did. Despite their disdain for each other, the two girls made a good team. But it appeared from this first encounter as if Rudy's style might work better with teenagers than Cornelia's more rigid demeanor.

Cornelia's heart thudded even more as she spied a very tall and lanky Nathan bowing his head low so as not to knock it on the exit doorway. She swayed, as if she had been hit, her face felt as if it were trapped in concrete. Before she could force herself to move toward Nathan, Rudy was already there. She sashayed to a stop in front of him and held out both hands. "We must forget all our differences, Nathan. We must promise to be the best of friends." Cornelia had seen this approach from Ruby many times, and she still couldn't understand why it was often effective.

Rudy bubbled on, "I don't know if Cornelia told you, but we've grown *so* close over the last few years. I don't know what I would have done without her, honestly I don't." Her eyes were huge and a liquid blue and rimmed with improbably thick black lashes.

Nathan looked stunned, but his deep blush told her he was pleased. He was well over six feet tall and broad shouldered, with platinum hair that waved down over his forehead. The freckles were practically gone. His lower jaw had been moved back into alignment with the rest of his face and so now he had the perfect sculptured configuration of a Greek statue, with bones in all the right places.

"And look at you, you're all grown up," Rudy giggled. "Not that I know anything about boys, I don't. Spending all my time at either at Greendell or Tall Pine, I don't meet many boys. Now I wish that I did."

He nodded, opening his eyes wide to show both embarrassment and pleasure. Rudy couldn't help casting Cornelia a sideways look to see if she were listening. Nathan followed her gaze and his eyes found Cornelia. But there was no look of recognition, no look of love, not even curiosity, just a blank stare. Her face twisted into what came across as a fierce scowl.

Cornelia wheeled and fled back to the end of the dock where mist still wreathed the posts. She leaned over and looked down into the swirling backwash of the ferry, willing herself not to vomit. A cold sweat broke out on her brow. She took two deep shuddering breaths. When she turned back around, Rudy had Nathan by the hand, leading him down the dock away from her. Just before he stepped up into the waiting carriage, he looked back and raised his hand in a salute. She felt a surge of joy. She tried to smile at him, but he was gone.

When Cornelia checked in at the main reception to get her room assignment, she asked where Nathan Woodstock was staying. "It says he's here in Building A. That's where the important people get housed, you know. You're in C, where most of the kids are housed."

"I know," she said, "I've been here before."

The receptionist quailed, "Oh, dear, Cornelia, I didn't recognize you. You look so grown up with your hair pulled back like that. I'm so sorry. Will you forgive me?"

"Of course," she said.

Protesting that her singing practice would be a bother to any roommate, Rudy had wangled a single in the VIP wing. So, it seemed she and Nathan would be near each other. Cornelia tried not to be angry.

She dragged her suitcase to the large three-story dorm where she had worked housekeeping during the previous three summers. She found her room down at the end of a long undecorated hallway. A scratchy wool blanket, one thin towel and a set of sheets were folded at the bottom of each bed. The communal bathroom was still down the hall.

She threw herself on the bed and rubbed her face against the blanket, feeling humiliated and ashamed. Why hadn't she just pushed Rudy aside and greeted her brother properly? What was wrong with her? Was she getting batty like Aunt Janice? She pulled out her Black Book and had a few quiet minutes of guidance. "Don't be dramatic," said her inner voice. " Stand tall. Make amends to him as soon as you can." The thought of making amends to Nathan calmed her.

As she was making her bed, a young girl poked her head in, smiled cheerfully, and said, "I think I'm your roommate."

From the minute she saw Patty, Cornelia hoped they would be friends. Patty was small and compact with tousled curls, a mouth that turned up and then down when she talked, eyes of bright green, and a nose that was as tilted as a ski jump. "I guess you can tell I'm Irish, what with the nose and the last name of Fitzgerald."

Cornelia immediately noticed that her legs were shapely and muscled; her butt was taut and high; she was virtually hipless but had breasts that were as round and tight as apples under the thin white tee shirt. Cornelia blushed when she realized she wanted to touch them just to see if they were as firm as they looked. Oh my, she thought, I'll have to write down that I've had an impure thought.

"Do you like to read?"

Cornelia nodded.

"Kerouac and Salinger are my favorites. Have you read them?"

When Cornelia shook her head, Patty arched her black eyebrows and shoved two books at her. "Here, you must! I insist. I'm just starting *Franny and Zooey* so you're welcome to them. Honestly! I brought them just to have them here. They're my bibles. At least for this week." She laughed, and Cornelia tried to laugh with her though it came out as more of a snort. "Not too talkative, are you?" Patty asked.

They unpacked, then headed out to the convocation and first general meeting. At the entrance way to the grand lodge pole meeting room, Cornelia left Patty with a wave of her hand and stalked up the aisle to the stage where Rudy was waiting for her, smiling but hissing out of the corner of her mouth, "Where have you been? We've all been kept waiting to start until you got here."

On the dais, Cornelia sat down between Hall Hamden and Rudy, tucked her feet below her knees, lifted her chin, and looked out over the audience. Despite the fact that she had often spoken in Moral Absolute meetings, she was still nervous about public speaking. It flared her nostrils and stretched the skin across her high cheekbones. If she looked like an avenging angel, Gertrude was a pink-cheeked cherub.

Hall Hamden stood and called the meeting to order. His hair now had wings of silver just in front of his ears. His ever-present four o'clock shadow had grizzled. He was thicker in the middle, which emphasized the shortness of his legs. But he still looked wrapped tight and his features had that movie star quality. He pulled the microphone close, then held up one hand to still the smattering of applause. He chuckled, "Thanks for that. Us old guys need to hear applause every now and then." He held up his hand to still the ripple of laughter. But seriously it's not about us old guys anymore. It's the youth that matters now."

Cornelia looked out over the sea of expectant eager faces. The Moral Absolute core group had spent all winter canvassing high schools, visiting church groups, sending out flyers, and encouraging all Moral Absolute followers to recruit every young person they knew. Hall Hamden was convinced that the message of Absolute Moral standards would spark a glow in this optimistic youth that would spread like wildfire around the globe.

In this opening statement, Hall Hamden explained that there were two goals for this summer. One was to get the group fit to be warriors for God. This would be acquired, he assured them, by following a rigid and demanding program of physical fitness and moral strengthening. Everyone would be involved with both sports and spiritual workshops. There would be absolutely no exceptions to these requirements. Unless, of course, he said with a chuckle, they were chosen to be in the wonderful new film to be produced during the summer called: *Youth Warriors*.

"And without further ado, let me introduce, drum roll please!" Hall flapped his fingers and the small orchestra behind the stage answered with an obedient drum roll, "The wonderful writer and director of our very first youth-oriented film, Allan Larches."

A tall and slender man with a mop of unruly hair leapt down the aisle and up onto the stage. His grin was broad and contagious, and his eyes were a startling cobalt blue. He sauntered to the microphone and told them how *wonderful* this new film was going to be and how *fabulous* they all were and how they would all have an *incredible* opportunity to try out for a part in the film. The auditions, he announced, would be at 2 PM the following day. Then with a blithe wave of his hand, he trotted off the stage, waving "Tah! Tah!" over his shoulder.

"And now," Hall Hamden shouted, "let me introduce you to a long-time member of our group, the lovely Miss Rudy Chase."

Rudy bounced to her feet, sashayed up to the microphone, twirling her skirts, and bowing her head low. The stage lights bounced off Rudy's hair; it shone like sunbeams. She looked as wholesome as white bread and butter. "Isn't this something?" She held out her hands. "Aren't we incredible? All of you. The new generation of America. Ready to take on the world!"

As the audience cheered and clapped, she grabbed her guitar, pulling the strap up over her head with a charming toss of her golden curls. "This here is Peggy Sue," she said, patting the guitar. "She's been my best friend through many a long, lonely year."

The audience roared. "This is a little song she helped me write." She strummed a few chords, smiled one last time at them, then vaulted into a song that lifted her pure and sweet voice high up into the rafters.

If you want to change the world
You must clean up all your thoughts
Because...
You can't think dirty
And.... live... straight.

She waved her hand with a flourish encouraging all to join her in the chorus of, "You can't think dirty and live straight!" When the audience burst into wild applause at the finish, she blushed, her dimples curved pleasing lines in her cheeks, and she lowered her black lashes down over her brilliant blue eyes.

Hall Hamden clapped. "Thank you, Rudy. I think a star is born. On a more serious note, Cornelia Woodstock is here to share. She has also been with us a long time. I believe the story of her own personal struggle with demons will touch many of you. Cornelia?" And with that he handed the microphone to Cornelia.

She looked out over the audience. Though she had spoken at many gatherings, none of the audiences had been of her own peers. Her precocity and youth had always touched older people. She was not at all sure what her effect would be on a younger crowd. But as she had always done before, she lifted her chin and spoke honestly, letting the thoughts flow out of some uncharted place inside her. Her guidance that morning had been to talk of change. As she started to speak, she looked down into the crowd and saw Nathan staring up at her. Without thinking, a rare smile crossed her face.

As Cornelia spoke, her face reverted back to its usual guarded demeanor. "How many of us in this room fear the change that looms ahead? We've been children now for many years, but here we are, standing on the brink of becoming responsible young adults. And we will all be faced with a myriad of choices. Will we have sex with our boyfriends or will we save ourselves for marriage?" She had worried this would be too much, but the collective gasp from most of the girls in the audience told her it had been worth the risk. After all, she was often asked to speak because she was able to deliver sensitive messages that older members could not.

"Will we want to keep just the best for ourselves, or will we share our gifts with the world? Horace Baker, our founder, often says there is enough in the world for everyone's need, but not for everyone's greed. I don't know about you," her expression grew rueful and flickered with remorse, "but I've often kept out the last cookie for myself when sharing. Ouch!" She screwed up her face and paused for the laughs. "My guidance tells me that that selfishness comes from thinking this may be the last cookie I'll ever receive. But Jesus teaches us that when we break bread and give to others, there is always more to be had. I hope and pray that love is the same way. That the more we give, the more love there is for everyone."

She scraped her foot, looked down and then back up. Her chin wobbled. "I have been accused of being cold, of being standoffish, of being willful, of wanting things my own way, but you know what? They were right!" A laugh broke out that spread like a ripple all around the hall. "I've been all those things and more. I've slammed doors when I didn't get my way. I've hurt others with angry words that I didn't mean. Hoping that *then* they'd be sorry, then they'd understand how *special* I was...but you know what?" The crowd was silent, hanging on each word. "I'm not special at all. But underneath this skin, underneath this body," she placed a hand over her heart, "we're all the same. We're all special in the eyes of God. What we must nurture is the courage to change the things we can. Until we acknowledge that we all need to change then love cannot come into our hearts and souls."

She bowed her head and thought of the struggles she'd been through to get here; she looked back out at the group with tears in her eyes, shaking ever so slightly with the need to communicate not only her pain but that she saw a way out. She hoped that maybe some would have a shiver of recognition as she spoke.

Silence reigned over the hall. She took a deep shuddering breath, then waved her hands out over their heads. "There is a way that is better, I know that now. My father once told me that the Four Absolutes: Absolute Love, Absolute Unselfishness, Absolute Purity, and Absolute Honesty were like looking at the stars. You could never reach that state of perfection. But if you let those Absolutes guide you, like the navigators of old did when they crossed dark uncharted waters, they would lead the way to letting a great change come into your life. I didn't have to try to change. I just had to ready myself for it. If I am willing to cast off old, uncomfortable behavior despite the difficulties, just like our forebears did, the Moral Absolutes standards will guide me to a better place." Her head bowed low. She turned and sat down again.

"Amen," said Hall Hamden.

Amen said some in the audience. Hallelujah said a few others. Unlike the aftermath of Gertrude's performance, there was no applause, only rustling, and whispers, and a restless stirring in the audience. Before the audience grew too uncomfortable, Hall Hamden led them all in a prayer and then announced that everyone would convene that afternoon down by the lake for their very first Morally Absolute Sporting Games.

As the meeting broke up, several members of the audience ran up onto the stage to tell Cornelia how much her words had meant to them, but she found herself tongue-tied and they quickly moved over to join the throngs assaulting Rudy.

Cornelia tried to catch Nathan's eye again, but Rudy had grabbed him by the hand and was leading him toward the back exit. She thought about following him, but Patty grabbed her by the elbow. "Let's go get some lunch," she said. "I had no idea my roomie was some kind of celebrity."

"Hardly." Cornelia snorted, both thrilled and horrified by Patty's cynical take on things. She had never heard anyone speak the way Patty did.

"What do you bet Miss Rudy gets to be a team captain in the games?" scoffed Patty.

"You're *absolutely* correct about that."

Patty came to a full halt, her jaw dropping open in mock surprise, "Did you just make a joke?"

"Absolutely."

"Oh, come on," she said, "You don't believe all that bullshit you said, do you?"

"Well, actually..."

"What?" snorted Patty, "You can't think dirty and live straight? Are you kidding me? And youth is so wondrous? What the fuck?"

Cornelia actually started at her, but a shameful thrill ran through her as well. She looked around to see if anyone was else was listening. As they entered the dining room and gathered a tray to get food from the cafeteria line, everyone else seemed busy with their own conversations.

"But, omigod, I couldn't believe it!" murmured Patty. "It really *was* Allan Larches? Who would have thought it could be true?"

"Who *is* he?" Cornelia said. "I never heard of him before."

"He's only the most promising young English playwright in decades. He wrote a play when he was at Oxford that got taken up by Pinter." They sat down at a table. Patty drew herself up. "Working with him would be the best. We're going to the auditions tomorrow, right?"

Cornelia nodded and tried to say something as smart and slick as Patty. "He looked like I imagine Puck would look," she sighed, trying to be lighthearted and fey. "I think I'm in love!"

"Not seriously." Patty raised one eyebrow, "That would be a waste of time."

"What do you mean?"

"Well, anyone can see he's a fairy. I guess I probably should have known that."

"A fairy? I don't understand."

"You know," she said, "Guys who fly the other way."

"I don't know what you mean."

"You really don't know?"

"No, I don't."

Patty rolled her eyes, "You're so lame."

"Tell me."

And so, she did. Cornelia was shocked but intrigued. At first, she could hardly believe her, but then Patty told her to stop being so stupid and didn't she know that it was not considered abnormal throughout history, particularly in cultures like ancient Greece, Japan, and England. In fact, famous writers like Oscar Wilde were gay. Cornelia's head swam with all this new information.

The rest of the lunch went by without incident, though Cornelia longed to feel comfortable enough to walk over to where Nathan and Rudy were sitting, surrounded by a throng of admiring girls. It was all she could do to keep from rushing over to him and sharing every detail of the past five years. She wanted their relationship to be like it was, but she was beginning to realize that it would never be the same again.

Chapter 10

Spangles from the lake danced in front of Cornelia's eyes, making it difficult to identifying the faces of anyone silhouetted against the glare of the water. She searched the crowd for Nathan. The Moral Absolute Fitness Games had started some two hours before. Hundreds of teen-agers milled around the sports fields down by the lake; some ran sprints and others fell to the ground for push-ups. Many girls huddled in groups, complaining of the cold. Cornelia didn't blame them. Even in July, the breeze off the icy water cut to the bone. Though the island was gorgeous, the air was such a dark blue, the shadows of the pines so black, the beaches so sharp with rocks instead of soft sand, its icy remote beauty repelled her.

Seeing Nathan again had made her feel keenly homesick for the soft air of the tropics, the warm oranges and reds of the flowers, and the sensual kiss of the setting sun. She shivered, very aware that her white tennis shorts were too skimpy and not at all like those worn by the other girls. As she moved from one event to another, gaining points along the way, she was grateful for Patty, who was dressed in faded jeans. All the other girls seemed to be cutting a wide swath around the two of them, linking arms and averting their eyes. Several girls smiled at Cornelia, but she turned away without smiling back. She was glad for Patty's steady stream of wisecracks, which filled the silence.

"Good speech," grunted one boy, as he passed, his eyes on the ground. She nodded but said nothing. Her years of isolation had left her with no skill for casual banter. As the day wore on, many of the girls begged off because of the cold wind. Hundreds trailed back up the hill. Several dozen more fled the fields when a tiny squall spat cold raindrops down at them. Cornelia stayed to the end because she knew Nathan would. She was suddenly very grateful for the private coaches who had been hired to come to Greendell for training sessions. They had even been taught tennis and golf, which Hall Hamden bragged would make them welcome at any club in the country. In this instance, he was probably right.

Finally, Patty gave up. "I've had it," she said, "you've got stamina, I'll give you that. My team's already out. But guess what, Rudy's team and Nathan's team have the highest other scores. And for some reason your particular score was so high there's going to be some kind of a showdown between you and them. Here, I thought you might want this. I collected your prize for you!" She threw a grey sweatshirt down around Cornelia's shoulders.

The fleece felt like warm water around her. She smiled at Patty. A blast of wind off the lake scattered the few remaining competitors; several groups of girls began to run up the hill, shrieking as they went.

"Thank you for the fleece," she said to Patty. "You're very kind."

"Very kind, huh? Who taught you to talk like that? Where'd you grow up, in a palace or something?"

She laughed, "Something like that.

"So, are you ready to take on the Rudy princess? She sure has a thing for your brother. And from the look of it, he doesn't mind."

"What do you mean?"

"Well, looks to me like a mutual admiration society."

Patty and Cornelia walked over to the stand where the referees were. Turned out that Rudy and Cornelia had the highest scores for the girls. They flipped a coin for a sport of their choice. Rudy won and chose tennis. Cornelia was not surprised. For the last three years, at Greendell, they had taken joint tennis lessons, but they played so differently that the teacher had soon suggested they train separately.

Rudy played a clever patty cake game of drop shot tennis while Cornelia preferred deep baseline shots and had worked on developing a powerful serve. They were taken to a court down right next to the edge of the lake. Cornelia chose a heavy racket that would make her serve hard and fast. She sat down on a bench, Patty beside her. The court belonged to the town of Tall Pine and obviously no money had been spent on it in ages. It was full of cracks and grass was growing up along its edges. But its concrete was familiar to Cornelia who had spent many hours hitting against the backboard next to the garage.

"I don't know if I can play on a fast court," complained Rudy. "I've only ever played on clay. Aren't there any clay courts on the island?" She was dressed all in white, with a pleated skirt, a tee shirt with an alligator on it, and brilliant tennis shoes.

Whether they were in Africa or Asia, her parents always sent her money for new clothes. In contrast, C.W. was stingy about any extra expenses. Cornelia looked down at her own sneakers, which were grey with age. Her big toe poked a hole in the canvas top of her right foot and she knew there were two tiny holes on the bottoms. Shame burning along her cheeks as she stood up and slashed the air with her racket and bounced up and down to get the blood and oxygen running through her body.

Nathan loped down the hill, ignoring Rudy who beckoned to him. He crossed over and sat down on the bench next to the net. "Good luck," he said to Cornelia. At the far end of the bench, Patty studied him. His legs bounced up and down in such a familiar way that Cornelia's heart thumped.

"I'm so sorry about not saying a proper hello at the dock. I don't know what came over me. I guess a terminal case of awkward Woodstockitis."

He snuck a glance at her but didn't laugh as she had hoped he would. "Doesn't matter."

"Yes, it does."

"Well, it swung both ways. I wasn't nice at the dock either. You just looked so different. And you acted like you didn't even know me. And Rudy had me gob-smacked."

"I noticed."

"Nathan," called Rudy from across the court. "Come back over here."

"Speaking of which..." Cornelia raised one eyebrow.

He blushed and called out, "I guess I'll stay with my sister. Looks like you've got enough fans."

Indeed, there were a small group of girls cheering Rudy on. Still, her face flushed with temper in a way that was very familiar to Cornelia. Rudy was used to getting her way. A young man and woman told them the rules. It would be one set, winner take all. Rudy and Cornelia shook hands and spun for the toss. Rudy won and chose to serve first. Cornelia ran to the baseline and danced back and forth, swinging down low as her coach had taught her.

He would yell at her from across the court. "What are you, a little girl? Stay low, hit hard, move in on the ball." And she did. She overwhelmed Rudy's drop serve in the first game, and then blasted her with serves Rudy couldn't return. Rudy flushed and went across to whisper to the referee. A young woman came across to Cornelia.

"Your opponent claims you're aiming for the cracks which makes your serve bounce higher. Says she's not used to the bounce of a fast court. Haven't seen it myself, but...maybe you could aim for the middle of the serve box." The young woman hunched her shoulders and grimaced an apology.

Fury whipped through Cornelia, totally throwing her off, and she lost the next three games in quick succession. Rudy danced and twirled and tossed her curls. Cornelia's vision became more focused. She was *not* going to lose to Rudy in front of Nathan. Never in a thousand years. Cornelia pretended she was playing against her coach and hammered the next serve. After that, she pounded every shot, hitting harder and faster than she ever had. She won the next four games in a row. The score was 5 to 3, 40-Love; she was one point away from winning. She hammered the serve. Rudy tried but failed to connect with the ball.

Instead of conceding defeat, she threw down her racket and stomped off the court. Her girls surrounded her, patting her on the shoulder. As she left, Rudy called out over her shoulder, "Nathan, don't forget we have to work on our songs. If you can bear to tear yourself away from your sister, that is."

He held up one finger, then smiled at Cornelia. "Good game, Nee. Didn't know you could play. Father get you lessons?" he looked down and away; his face twitched as if it hurt him to consider her having tennis lessons. "Golf lessons too?"

"Yup, only the best," she quipped. She was half aware that Patty, from her end of the bench, was intensely following their interchange. It made her uncomfortable.

His tone was bitter. "But guess what, we're up against each other next. Seems we both have the highest scores for the day. Golf all right? Tennis they never bothered to teach me. But at least they arranged for me to caddy. So, I've got golf nailed."

"Nathan, I'm getting cold," called Rudy from across the court. "Are you coming or not?"

"I promised to sing with her later," his face ducked down; his sneaker poked at the dirt.

"Well, what Rudy wants, Rudy usually gets."

"Really?" he grinned but looked pleased at being fought over. "You know Nee, she's not so bad. At least she tries hard to be nice, you know. Something you might try sometime. It wouldn't hurt you."

She was stung, "I don't know what's wrong with me. Just can't be like everyone else, I suppose."

"Us Woodstocks don't quite fit the norm, do we?" He flashed a grin, still looking down at his feet. "I've missed you, you know. Wait here. I'll be right back."

She nodded, not at all sure she could manage a word, but gratitude flooded through her and she watched him walk off the court to follow Rudy up the hill.

Patty moved to her side, "Not bad, Cornelia. Not bad at all. Listen, I've got to go. Are you going to be okay?"

"I'm fine." She shrugged and sat down on the bench to wait for Nathan to come back. She was alone, but she was used to being alone. She watched as Patty ran up the hill to overtake Nathan.

Out over the lake, clouds marched along the horizon, their bellies black with moisture. The breeze freshened and shivered the water. A few minutes later, Nathan came back down the hill carrying two golf bags, one filled with gleaming irons and four woods, the other, for her, had just a putter, three irons and one 3 woods.

"Sorry," he blushed, "It's all we could find. Guess no one thinks ladies play much golf. How about if we just pretend there's a course here? See that tree over there?" He pointed down the way, across the soccer fields to a large oak that stood next to the rocky shore. "Let's see who can get closest, okay?" Then he turned to the two older teens assigned to witness their play. "No need for you guys to stay. We'll keep track of the score ourselves, okay?"

"If you're really okay. You can tell us the score later." They trotted off up the hill.

At first it seemed it was just going to be all about golf. Nathan was as serious as he ever was over any sport. He said he was going to give her a shot per hole since he was bigger and a boy. She accepted. He pounded his first ball well up and away toward the big tree. It took her two hits to get even close to where his ball was. But her third shot smacked the tree and his second shot did the same. Since he was giving her a stroke per hole, they were even.

"Where'd you learn?" she asked.

"Ray struck a deal with the golf pro at the Abaco Country Club. Manure for roses in return for the chief caddy giving me lessons. You know there's lots of paved roads everywhere now. You wouldn't recognize the island."

"Right." Cornelia quickly looked away, knowing her expression would be bereft.

His face twisted. "Why *did* you stay with them, Nee? After we promised never to leave each other."

"I tried to come with you that last day..." She faltered. "The door was locked."

"Father wrote us you didn't want to come home. Not even for Christmas."

"That's not true," she said, "I did want to, I did. But they had guidance that you and Mummy would be a bad influence on me."

"They said that?"

"I'm so sorry," she said, "I never meant to hurt you. In fact, the opposite was true. I meant to save you."

"What do you mean?"

"Well, I had some strange notion that if you stayed with the Absolutes, that it would destroy you. I told Daddy I wouldn't fight him about staying if they let you go. You were like a caged animal with them. I knew they wouldn't be able to get to me in the same way. And then there was Hadji and Horace. They've been teachers for me. And I always hoped to get closer to daddy. But he's not around very much. Still, I never expected it, but I started to feel like I belong. It's kind of comforting when there's always someone telling you how to behave. You know how Mummy never approved of anything I did. Well here, if I do the right thing, they approve." As she talked, his blue eyes pooled with tears and his chin wobbled.

"All this time I thought you didn't care about us." His hands flew to cover his eyes and he slumped to one side against a tree, rocking back and forth. When they were little and slept in bunk beds, he had always rocked himself to sleep; the sound of swaying from the top berth lulled her. Now she took one step forward. Though it had been years since she had touched him, she hugged him, falling into his rocking motion. She didn't know which of them needed it more.

"Well," he said finally, standing up straight, then grinning at her in his old lopsided manner, "guess we'd better get back to playing!"

They spent the next hour lining up shots, playing together as naturally and easily as they used to. It was not about winning, but about hitting the shot, throwing the ball, catching the fish, riding the wave, each daring the other to be better and better until the sheer physical joy of mastering something became the paramount experience of that one moment, that one life. Between each shot, they talked. Loping after the ball, their long legs matching, they were an endangered tribe of two. Their intimate language returned, the words tumbling out of them fast and furiously as they strode after their balls.

He told her about how, once the road came to their village, Ray had started staying out late drinking at local bars. Coming home, his truck sometimes sideswiped the house as he took aim at the driveway. This all made Nevin take her to bed. "Remember how she gets the blues?"

"Oh yeah, I remember." And she told Nathan of how, at Greendell, she was mostly left alone. "After Aunt Janice died," she said, "There was only Rudy and Mrs. Rogers for company. And Mrs. Rogers always preferred Rudy. They were cut from the same cloth, she always said. Mrs. Rogers said she was a born people pleaser while I was just prickly."

"Did you ever try and get along with Rudy?"

"Oil and water, we were told."

"Maybe she's not so bad as you make out," pleaded Nathan. She could see by his forlorn expression that he didn't understand.

"You really like her, don't you?"

"I do," he blushed, "She never had anyone like we once had each other. Can you blame her for wanting that?"

"No. But we don't have each other anymore," Cornelia said. "Now it looks like you have her. And she has you."

"Can't I have you both?" He asked as his chin trembled. "Would that be so bad?"

"Come on, let's play." She turned toward the lake where the late afternoon water had turned a steely grey. "Hit toward that little tree all by itself."

If his shot came closest to the tree, they agreed, she would have to be a good sport about sharing him with Rudy. But if she came closest, he would have to give up Rudy.

With her head down over the ball, she had to hit the best shot of her life. It had to be close enough for him to know that she had given it her best, but not so close that he couldn't get closer. And so, she focused and swung and heard it ping with that sweet soft sound that golf balls only make when they are perfectly hit. As she had planned, his shot was closest.

The following morning, Cornelia awoke early.

"Where are you going?" said Patty from under the covers on her side of the room.

"Going to meet Nathan," she said.

"Again? What am I? A hot potato when something better comes along."

"Not at all, it's just that our father's coming in on the ferry and we agreed to go meet him together."

"Woodstocks," her tone was crabby.

Briefly, Cornelia stood in front of the dresser where a tiny mirror showed a tall girl with a bony face that often flickered. Despite her best intentions, she had yet to learn a way to hide her feelings. She yanked back her hair, spinning it up into a high bun to get it off her face.

When she met Nathan in the front hall of the conference center, he gave her a quick onceover. "Why do you always have to look so different? You never dress like the other girls. Rudy says you're always mooning over *Vogue*. She likes *Seventeen*."

Hurt to the quick, she strode away from him and down the hill. He trotted to catch up, then fell into step beside her, stretching out their long legs to lope down the hill. "Sorry," he muttered. "Of course. How could you possibly know what the others would be wearing? How could I forget?"

"You got it now."

"But do you always have to scowl? It looks like you think you're better than everyone else."

She wheeled around to face him, "Now you sound like Mummy. Are you kidding me? Think I'm better than everyone else?"

He had the grace to look embarrassed, "Well, that's what Rudy says."

"Look, I told you I would try to along with her better and everything. But let me make myself clear. I do *not* think I'm *better* than anyone else. What I do know is that I'm different. No one grew up like me. Like us. No one. Except actually," she paused, "maybe Rudy. You two are the only ones who know how weird everything was. But the thing is, Rudy is running from that. She's all about trying to fit in. And I'm not. That's all. If you can't understand that, then I really don't know what to do. I really don't."

"I get it." He was quiet for a long moment, "The truth is I still don't know how to fit in either. You ought to see me in Nassau. Mummy's got me going to a private school there. It's all the rich kids from Bay Street. They all have boats and cars. And I live over the hill in a shack. I board with a family who has a landscape business. I could give you lessons about not fitting in. Most kids have boats. I shovel manure." He laughed nervously. "Don't you see?" He pleaded with her, "That's where Rudy comes in. She knows just how to fit in. She's good at something we cannot master."

Cornelia sighed, "She does have a knack for saying and doing the right thing."

"Well," he grimaced, "Maybe most of the time she does. But yesterday when you beat her, and she threw down that tennis racket. That wasn't so cool. When I told her that she got really mad at me." He looked bewildered and Cornelia remembered how girls had always puzzled him.

"Really? She did?"

"Yuh, so she's not perfect, that's for sure."

Far out on the lake, the ferry, as small as a toy in the distance, chugged along the surface, trailing a spreading V shape in the calm waters behind it. Clouds towered above; their reflections cast undulating pillars onto the sapphire lake.

"So tell me more things about Father," said Nathan, "How *has* it been with him?"

"Pretty strange. I thought our relationship was going to build, and I guess it has somewhat, but not like I had imagined. He's not around very much. He's still really stiff around me. When we venture out, he will only take me out to eat at the Royal Castle. He likes that the food is so cheap."

They laughed, remembering how often they had talked about how strange it was that their rich father always acted poor. "But he's gone most of the time. They keep him pretty busy. They drag him out at fundraisers, as if being a Woodstock deserves a standing ovation. They're glad to take his money, but they still treat him like a servant."

"That makes me mad."

"Don't tell anyone I said that." Her heart skipped a beat. "Don't tell Rudy I said that, please."

"Why not?"

"I don't know. Things are changing. I got a memo last night from the big HH that I no longer would be needed to speak at meetings. Seems I was a bit too serious to please his highness. But Rudy, she's to be the star of the show. So please?" She mimicked zipping her lips.

"Okay," he promised, "I won't say anything."

They got to the dock just as the ferry was pulling in. At the prow, C.W. stood, as tall and stern as a figurehead. He strode off the boat, pumped Nathan's hand, "Good to see you, son," then awkwardly patted Cornelia on the shoulder and said, "We must talk. I'll take you out to breakfast."

They turned toward the little village where there was a row of souvenir shops and a cafe. Cornelia noticed the cuffs on C.W.'s shirts were frayed and, though they were highly polished, there was a split flapping at the sole of one shoe.

They sat at a table tucked into the front bay window and ordered pancakes with bacon. C.W. stared down at the table, his eyes wide and vacant. Nathan raised his eyebrows at her. "Daddy?" she prompted, "You said we had to talk."

C.W. looked down the street as if demons might be chasing him. "The leadership of the Moral Absolutes has reached an impasse."

"What does that mean?" Worry creased her forehead. Nathan's knees bounced.

Their father poked his finger at the tabletop, straightened the row of sugar packets, sighed deeply then said, "I signed Greendell over to the Moral Absolutes last year."

"What?" cried Cornelia, "That's our family home."

"I know. Hear me out. I found myself a bit short on cash. So, the American team agreed to take it over with the caveat that there would always be a place for the three of us there. But then suddenly just a week ago, I was informed by letter from the Moral Absolute corporate lawyer that they're looking into selling it in order to cover expenses for this upcoming film."

"What? How could they do that?" Outrage surged through her.

"That's what I've spent the last two weeks trying to find out. As you know, the Trust came due after Aunt Janice's death. I had already, in writing, agreed to the proceeds of that going to the cause. Now it seems Hall Hamden and the American contingent have separated themselves off into another LLC and all the funds went with them, including the deed to Greendell."

"I can't believe it. It's not right. Can't you get it back?" Cornelia asked.

"I'm afraid not. I've been advised that's not possible. It was all done legally. Just not very honestly.""

"But what do Horace and Hadji think?" asked Cornelia.

"Well, they knew nothing of this latest maneuver. As you know, the three of us have been spending most of our time overseas. As it turns out, that was probably a mistake."

"I can't believe they're treating you this way," Cornelia blurted out.

"Not everyone, Cornelia, not everyone. The crew in England and Switzerland have been magnificent. And Hadji, of course, in India. They've all come forward and said they'd be happy to have me on their team." A small smile of pride twisted his lips. "I'm not completely without my fans. And speaking of them, they're both flying in this afternoon."

"They are? Oh good, maybe they can straighten things out." She hoped they wouldn't notice her blush.

"I'm afraid it's gone way past that." C.W.'s look was forlorn. "Both of them have been voted off the board."

"Who did that?" Cornelia asked.

"Hall Hamden and his group. To make matters more painful, they sent out letters a few days ago to many of us who have dedicated decades to the Absolute cause and they've told us," he swallowed hard, "that we're not needed anymore. Actually, I'm not even welcome *here*. I've taken a room at the Franklin Hotel up the hill and I'll wait to see what happens when Horace and the others get here. They did manage to find rooms for them up at the center."

Cornelia flushed with anger. "I guess that means I no longer have my room at Greendell."

"You could always go home to Mummy," said Nathan.

"Anyway, not to worry," said C.W., "the powers that be in Europe have assured me that we will always have a place with them. They still have money, don't you see? Money that I gave them many years ago. It's just that my own *personal* well has gone dry. I've given it all away," he said simply and held out his palms.

Nathan shook his head, "Will Mummy's support checks stop? She'll have a fit."

"Can't wring money out of an empty well," C.W. shrugged, then looked at each of them in turn. "You must decide for yourselves what you want to do. I may be leaving here in a few days and you can come with me. Or you may decide to stay here," he trailed off.

Nathan hung his head, "There's the movie," he said flatly. "They want me to be in it."

"What?" Cornelia was shocked, "I thought the auditions were this afternoon."

Nathan looked sheepish; "They came to my room last night and told me I could have this wonderful opportunity to star in the film. Given what you've just told me, maybe it's something I should be grateful for."

"It's not fair," said Cornelia, "It's all because Rudy wants you. Not fair."

"But Nee," he said, "you know it's an opportunity," he said. "Don't ask me to give that up."

"Yes, I can see how you'd see it that way." C.W.'s expression was kind and Nathan looked pleased that he understood. C.W. shook both their hands then walked off up the hill to his hotel. Nathan and Cornelia set back off to the Absolute Conference Center. The first few hundred yards were spent in silence, then Nathan reached out to bump her hip with his.

"That was harsh," he said. "I'm sorry about Greendell. I know it's been your home."

"I can't believe it," she felt bereft. She looked out over the lake to where clouds boiled on the horizon, but their beauty stayed remote and failed to comfort her.

Nathan nodded; words tumbled out of him. "Last night, Hall Hamden told me that a fresh wind of youth is coming. That I could be a part of that. That sometimes the old get set in their ways and have to make room for the youth, like a forest fire burning down the old trees so that the new grass can grow. It's a call to action!" He pumped his fist into the air.

"So, Daddy's just an old tree who's in the way?"

His lower lip swelled. "Well, what else is there for me?" He spread out his hands, "Looks like there won't be any money for college. There's no future for me in the Bahamas unless I want to shovel manure all my life. If I stay and do the film..."

She cut him, "You'll have a chance to make a difference."

He looked startled, "How did you know I'd say that?"

"Because I know the words HH uses to suck people in."

He sucked in his lip. He looked both chagrined and angry. "I guess now I sort of understand why you stayed with them all these years. It makes you feel important, needed, like you belong."

She nodded. "Yup, they're good at that."

"You're coming to the auditions this afternoon, right?" Nathan begged her. "I'm sure there'll be a part for you as well."

"Patty and I will both be there this afternoon. She's a big fan of Allan Larches."

"Oh yeah, Patty. She was awful curious about me yesterday."

"When did you talk to her?"

"By the tennis court."

"Oh yeah, I forgot."

"And then she followed me up the hill when I went to get the golf clubs."

"She did?" As if a cold breeze had blown over her fledgling friendship, an unwelcome intuition made her wonder, for the first time, about the purity of Patty's motives.

"She was a little weird. She wanted to know whether Rudy and I had kissed yet."

"Come on."

"Yeah."

"I don't believe you. I'm going to ask her if it's true."

"Don't you dare," And with that he launched himself at her. They pummeled each other, and she went in for the poke to the ribs that she knew would make him helpless with laughter. He wriggled away from her; she yanked at his shirt.

George, one of Hall's minions, walking down the opposite way called out, "Cornelia, what are you doing? Behave yourself."

As an abashed Nathan tucked in his shirt, Cornelia drew herself up, but the outraged expression on George made her splutter with laughter. "Not to worry, George, this is my brother."

"I'm well aware of who he is, Cornelia. But this kind of behavior will just not do. Engaging in rough horse play with females, even with a sister, is just not up to Absolute Purity standards."

"Yes sir," said Nathan. "I see what you mean, it won't happen again."

"Wait a minute," said Cornelia.

Nathan held up his hand, "Cornelia!" he said fiercely, "Don't make things worse." He charged off without saying good-bye.

The inside of the five-story studio building was a cavernous space whose heights were filled with a bewildering array of lights and wires and backdrops. Cornelia and Patty signed in at a table just next to the door then sank to a seat on the floor where hundreds of other teenage boys and girls waited for their turn to audition for the film.

After a few minutes, the lights lowered, a spotlight snapped on.

Allan Larches sprang up onto the small stage. He shook his copper curls. His voice had the crisp sweetness of a flute. "I know," he said, "We all hate these cattle calls. But what else are we to do?" His tone veered swiftly from sweet to ferocious. "If you're not prepared to get up on this stage and let yourself go, then think hard and long about whether you should be here at all. Maybe this isn't for you. It won't be glamorous. It will be long hours of hard work and a lot of boring downtime in between takes. So please, be my guest, feel free to leave. Right now. Before you make a fool of yourself, *particularly* if you haven't prepared a monologue."

As silence filled the dark corners of the sound stage until the shadows vibrated with tension, a large number stood, including most of the boys. As the three-story high door swung open to let them out, shimmering reflections from the lake flooded in, striking a pathway across the floor to the exit until only forty remained.

"Right," Allan clapped his hands. "That did the trick. Nothing like separating the goats from the sheep. I like goats better myself." And his grin was infectious. "Now let's get to it. Looking forward to this. The results of these auditions will be posted in the hall outside the dining room late this afternoon. We'll go alphabetically, shall we?"

The first girl swung her body from side to side as she stumbled through a poem by Robert Frost.

"Thank you," said Allan, cutting her off before she had finished.

"Baa," said Patty.

The two girls who followed were better, less flat in their affect, but hyperbolic instead. And though they were allowed to finish, Allan said nothing more than, "Thank you! Next?"

Then a few girls showed off their cheerleader jumps. "Not interested," said Allan. Another girl shared that she had played the lead in her high school production of *Our Town*, but she couldn't remember any of her monologue. He dismissed her. Allan indicated that the next boy was not bad, not bad at all, but then said next, in the same clipped manner.

And so it went until Rudy sashayed up onto the platform. She tossed her hair, flashed her teeth and delivered a fast-paced peppy monologue from *Oklahoma*. She was the first one to receive applause, though Allan's bland, "Faultless as usual, Miss Chase," sparked hope in Cornelia.

When Patty's name was called, she slouched up onto the stage. With her head bowed, she seemed less brash than usual.

"Yes?" Allan snapped.

Her gaze slowly fixed on him and, as if she were telling him a story, she spoke to him alone. "I used to go to the soda fountain after school. I spent quite a bit of time there. I mean, I used to talk to anyone who would listen. It was okay for a while. But sometimes I would just go on and on, riffing until it was as if I was hallucinating and I couldn't stop talking. But I could see things. I could see things so clearly. Then just when I thought I was being so clear, everything got very quiet. It was always so quiet. And then someone started a lie about me. And someone told my mother about things I'd said. I couldn't understand why she couldn't see they were lying. It had all been so clear to me. But my mother listened to them and she took me to a doctor. He suggested I might want to visit this very nice hospital that would quiet the voices in my head. I didn't want to go, but they made me. And then they asked me all sorts of questions. And then they told me I had a condition. That they were going to have to do something to my head. Then they took me and did something to my brain. And now I don't talk as much as I used to. But I miss seeing everything so clearly." Patty stopped suddenly and hung her head back down. There was total silence.

Cornelia guessed she was telling her own story, that her mother had given doctors permission to do something to her brain. But Allan understood it in a totally different way. He clapped.

"Well done, well done," said Allan Larches. "Such a clever adaptation of a Pinter monologue. Remarkable to think that it was written for a middle-aged man and you've made it believable for a teenager. I must say I'm quite impressed. Well done. Well done. Next."

Patty poked her hands back into the pockets of her jeans and sauntered off the stage. Eyes were riveted on her, but she slumped down into the seat next to Cornelia.

"That was amazing," Cornelia whispered.

"What do you know about anything?" Patty said.

When Cornelia jerked away from her, Patty's mouth twisted into a smile. She pulled her knees into her chest and jammed her chin down between her knees. Cornelia's lip tightened. She would not let either Patty or Rudy get to her. She needed to stay focused.

When Cornelia's time for her audition finally came, she felt faint with trepidation. She took off her trench coat, smoothed her white cambric nightgown, which she had worn as a costume, and shook out her bun, letting her hair fall down in disheveled waves all the way to her waist.

She walked slowly up the aisle to the stage, her heart pounded, she almost blacked out. As she went up the stairs, she heard Rudy giggle. "She's got on a nightgown."

She swallowed and turned to face the audience. She closed her eyes and remembered the advice Hadji had once given her. "What they think doesn't matter. Let the words take you."

As the words rolled off her tongue, she saw willows flashing silver, sunbeams quivering the water, a cloud-like crown of splashed drops around her dying head. As her cadence slowed, she drifted downstream, fading away, until, face shining with tears, she roused herself from death and finished with a resounding, "This is I, the Lady of Shalott!" And she stood up proud and tall.

She hardly heard the shouts and catcalls, the whistles and jeers. She walked off without looking at anyone, just half hearing Nathan call out, "That's my sister," as he bounded past her up onto the stage.

"That'll be a hard act to follow," he bashfully smiled, and they all laughed.

Cornelia sat back down next to Patty, shivering with cold as she pulled her coat over her sweaty body.

"Nip patrol!" Patty chided.

"What?"

"Your nipples, stupe, they poked through like pencil nibs."

Cornelia was filled with blistering shame. When the catcalls and whistles had come after she finished, she had hoped it was because her performance was good. Until Patty said something, it had not occurred to her to think about the sweat and the lighting making her nightgown almost see-through.

Cornelia couldn't look at Patty; she couldn't focus on Nathan and Rudy singing together. After the last audition, Cornelia pushed out ahead of the others and ran down to the lake where she walked alone for over an hour. The more she stomped along, a strange tingling elation surfaced, an exuberance that caused her to finally gallop along the shores of the lake. An hour later, she ran back up to the conference center, flushed and triumphant, standing tall, *this is I*, she chanted inside, *the absolutely one and only Cornelia Woodstock.*

Two things happened late that afternoon. Horace and Hadji arrived on the island. And both Patty and Cornelia were on the list of callbacks for a possible role in the film. Abandoning her cool for just one moment, Patty jumped up and down. Cornelia felt a surge of excitement as well but contained herself. She noted they were scheduled for cold readings of the script the following afternoon. The only other people on the list were two boys and, of course, the new golden couple Nathan and Rudy. There was a note from Allan thanking everyone for their efforts, reminding everyone that there would be plenty of opportunity for smaller parts at a later time but, for the moment, he was just casting the principals.

"Oh," said Patty, "that sucks."

"What sucks?" Determined to salvage the fledgling friendship, Cornelia had decided to forgive Patty for her earlier nasty comments.

"Are you so clueless, dummy? I guess your cheap half-naked act did the trick."

"I don't understand. We both got callbacks."

"Don't you get it?" Her eyes narrowed, "We're up for the same role."

"What?"

"Yeah, stupe, didn't you see our names down at the bottom? We're both reading for the part of Jocelyn. Rudy is set to get the good girl lead. And oh, look, surprise, surprise, your brother has the male lead. That leaves us in competition for the bad girl who *sees* the light and gets *changed* by the good girl."

"That's awful. I'm sorry. I'll bow out if you want."

"Are you for real? Get with the program. This is not about friendship. This is about who gets the part. I can't afford to like you right now."

Patty stalked off. Cornelia wondered whether she was right. Did she want a part in a movie more than a friend? Her lips turned down into a moue. The truth, if she was being absolutely honest, is that she would like to have both.

Cornelia came out of the main entrance doors just as a grand cavalcade of horse-drawn carriages trotted up the hill. High up on the four towers of the building, the Absolute banners snapped in the late afternoon breeze.

Far out on the sapphire lake, a sailboat keeled way over in a sudden wrinkling of wind. Hooves clopped. Harness jangled. With a snort, the horses halted. When C.W. and Hadji jumped out, and Cornelia's heart skipped a beat. A rare smile bloomed on her face. Hadji grinned as he spotted Cornelia. "Ah hah, my spiritual doppelganger awaits. Your quite lovely welcoming smile, Cornelia," he raised his hand in a salute, "lights up my whole day."

He bounded up the stairs toward her, holding out both hands. She let hers be clasped tight. They never hugged. That was not up to Absolute Moral standards. But they could not hide their pleasure in seeing each other.

His skin glowed a golden chestnut beneath a Nehru cap. Wearing his usual baggy leggings and tunic with a grey flannel vest on top, Cornelia always got the feeling of him as a prince from an unknown land. Around his ears, his hair was close-cropped, and his glasses still pinched the top of his long bony nose. He was definitely a young man now, no longer a teen-age boy in any way. His genuine friendliness and pleasure to see her was obvious. As if she were standing under a hot shower after a bone-chilling swim in a Northern lake, his warm greeting flooded through her body.

Then Cornelia became aware of a number of people streaming out the front door and gathering on the steps to properly greet the incoming guests. George put his hand on her shoulder and firmly pushed her to one side. Hadji let go of her hands with a wink and a head waggle.

Through the crowd, she watched her father. He looked tired and drawn. Wrinkles fanned out from his eyes. His brows threw dark shadows over his eyes. His mouth was a thin, grim line. She realized that she had selfishly thought little of the dilemma he had shared with them that morning. She had been so swept up in her own drama that she forgot how painful this impending split must be for him.

To be so summarily dismissed, cast aside like picked over bones, had to be a grievous injury. She saw Hall Hamden shaking Hadji's hand while turning his back on C.W. as if he didn't even see him. Hall Hamden's gaze went over his head to the next carriage pulling up and his lips drew back, exposing his large yellow teeth in a fake smile.

Several young men bounded out of the second carriage, Horace's doctor followed; they all turned and put up their hands to steady Horace as he struggled to descend from the carriage. He looked like an old ivory figurine, shrunk to miniature size. His spine was so bowed that he stood no higher than four feet. But his eyes snapped with that familiar penetrating light. And his delight at being so grandly greeted was as gleeful as a child seeing the Christmas tree lights go on. He turned his gaze away from Hall Hamden and shifted his focus.

"C.W.! Come! Give me a hand. Let's go have tea together." He called out for all to hear. "Hadji! You too." He ignored Hall Hamden's outstretched hand. But Cornelia could not help noting how Hall Hamden's face purpled with rage.

Horace held out his claw-like hands to greet the two men. He fell into their grasp and was half lifted/half carried up the stairs toward the entrance. Cornelia followed.

They settled Horace into his suite off the dining room. She sat out in the living room as they tucked him into bed. The room was no longer as glossy as it once had been. The crimson silk brocade of the upholstered chairs had faded to a pallid pink. The cloth on the cushioned window seat was frayed. And there were no longer bunches of flowers everywhere. C.W. came back out of the bedroom and stooped to build a fire. His face looked thunderous. "They didn't even have a fire ready for him. Everyone knows Horace likes a fire."

"Is he okay?" Cornelia asked.

"The fire of his spirit burns as bright as ever, but the flesh is weak. We must pray for him." He fell to his knees and held up his hands in the prayer position. "Pray with me, Cornelia, pray with me for God to save his body for one last hurricane of change."

She dropped to her knees beside him while he intoned the Lord's Prayer. Over the sound of his prayer, she could hear bits and pieces of Horace's rant. His voice quavered with anger.

"I could smell sin in the air. They have surrounded themselves with corruption. This will never do. Corrupt trees cannot bear fruit. Casting out the faithful and hiring sodomites. This will never do. We must dig out the sin. We must cast out the rotten fruit. We must smash this ambition. It reeks of hell." Then his railing faded to a murmur.

Beside her, C.W. had moved from the Lord's Prayer to Shakespeare. She been reading Shakespeare out loud to herself the previous winter, but never knew that her father loved the poet as well. He muttered the words and she never knew whether he was referring to himself or Horace, but she knew he wanted her to hear.

I never gave you kingdom, nor call'd you children,
You owe me no subscription. Then let fall
Your horrible pleasure. Here I stand your slave,
A poor, infirm, weak, and despis'd old man.

He fell silent and Cornelia rose up off her knees and balanced awkwardly on the edge of a seat as C.W.'s head stayed bowed. She felt frozen. What was the loving thing to do? Pat him on the back and tell him everything was going to be okay? Or should she run out of the room and leave him alone? She closed her eyes and prayed for guidance. Her thoughts were clear. "Love is a risk, but the person who risks nothing has nothing. Without risk, change cannot enter your heart." She reached out to him and cupped his shoulder. He turned to her, a furrow between his eyes made them droop, and his mouth wobbled.

"It doesn't matter," she said, "love lives on even when we're weak and old. All is well." He nodded, and his large hand moved awkwardly up to cover hers.

A few minutes later Hadji came out of Horace's bedroom looking drawn and ashen. She saw that he had aged some. There were new lines on his forehead. It made her care about him even more, and for the first time she saw him as a person, not just a crush. She could tell he was hardly aware of her presence. He directed his words toward her father who slowly, as if his skull was very heavy, lifted his head up to listen.

"He's close to sleep. We must let him rest to recover his strength. As much as he can. I fear the worst." And then he swung his gaze toward her. "Cornelia, he has asked that you come sit by his bedside for a few minutes. He still calls you 'the one who speaks the truth.'"

Her heart skipped a beat. Over the years, she had always felt scorched by Horace's penetrating gaze. Yet, despite her unease, a part of her also yearned for this trial by fire, as if each time she faced him, she exposed another level of her very essence to examination and thus into her own consciousness. Horace had often told her over the years that nothing was more important than the growth and nurturing of her own soul. Trembling, she stood up and walked into the room. He was tucked under a huge down comforter, his upper body propped up on a pile of soft down pillows.

"Come child, you're not still frightened of this feeble body, are you?" he chuckled.

She perched on the edge of the bed. Her gaze flickered over him, then veered away from his intent regard and out the window to the lake, which lay like beaten copper under the hammer of a glowering sun. She sighed and looked back at him and allowed herself to fall under his enchantment. His contemplation of her continued silently for quite a while. He shook his head, but it was kindly. "I can see your purity is weakening. I can also see that your intentions are good. But if you do not follow God's plan for you my dear, you will be a slave to your own earthly passions. I sense that that has already happened?" He cocked his head to one side, as if he were a curious but sympathetic bird. "Does desire haunt your nights?"

She nodded, keenly aware of her constant struggle at night not to touch herself, and totally humiliated that he had so easily penetrated inside her to see the truth. Was it that obvious to everyone, she thought?

"Take that passion and turn it into a fire for change. You must prepare yourself for battle. I have great hopes for you. Now go, I am tired, send your father in to me if you will. I too must gird my loins for a fight."

Back in the living room, she told C.W. that Horace wanted to see him, then moved to the window, because she was suddenly uncomfortably aware that she was alone in a room with Hadij. That had never happened before. Their conversations usually took place while walking to and from meetings or sharing a cup of tea with others nearby. It was an unspoken rule for the Moral Absolutes that males and females were never to be left alone or else their passions might ignite.

Avoiding his gaze, she stared out at the lake. A great tanker slipped between Tall Pine Island and a smaller isle, dwarfing the straits. A long rooster tail of a wake surged behind the boat. She heard the call of a foghorn and saw the first tendrils of white fog swirling above a row of spiky pines. She turned finally to face Haj. He was standing with his hands fanned out to the fire. He darted his eyes sideways at her then turned his gaze back to the fire and smiled.

"Us Indians have such warm blood. I'll never get used to the chill of your summer."

"Not my summers," she laughed, "Don't forget I used to live in the islands. It was always hot."

His head waggled, and she was happy to see that again. Between visits, she always forgot how beguiling and odd it was. "That's right. I must tell you, I am glad of this opportunity, to tell you how much I have appreciated your father's generous largesse."

"Largesse?" she asked. He looked straight at her then and his gaze shot warmth all through her. A faint sheen of sweat bloomed between her breasts.

His eyes darted down as if he could see through her clothes, then darted back up. He cleared his throat and turned back to the fire before he spoke. "Certainly, he may have told you that the Moral Absolute movement is gaining strength in India. In point of fact, your father's monetary contributions over the years have enabled us to start construction on a center in Chidapunji, that's a hill station up in the foothills of the Maritime mountain range, you must come sometime and see it for yourself, certainly you must." There was a long silence. "Cornelia, please turn and look at me. I need to know you're listening."

She slowly turned, but keep her eyes down, "I'm listening. To every word you say. I always have."

"Have you now?" He spoke gently, "Then why can't you look at me?"

She looked up. His eyes glowed. She fell into his gaze, her pulse picked up and she flushed. "Go on," she said, "Tell me more about my father." She was afraid that if they just kept looking at each other she would melt, and her knees would buckle. Her groin twitched, and she squirmed her legs together. To her humiliation, this just increased the intensity of both her anxiety and desire. The tip of his tongue peeped out from between his teeth and darted over his full lips. She shivered.

"Are you cold? Do you need my jacket?"

"No, no," she backed off, holding up her hands, "Please just go on. I'm fine."

His eyebrows rose at the edge in her voice. He turned toward the window. A huge sigh shuddered through him and she marveled at the thought he might be as nervous as she was. He rocked up onto the toes of his Oxford shoes. Like her father, he kept them at a high gloss. For some odd reason, the thought of him rubbing and brushing his shoes heightened her arousal. "Please keep talking," she urged and looked away from him.

He went back to the fire and paced back and forth in front of it. "Well," he continued, "I am not just speaking of money here, it is the largesse of your father's spirit which touches us in India. He truly gives with no expectation of getting anything in return. To my mind, that makes him a remarkable man."

"He hasn't always been an easy man to love."

"Why is that, do you think?"

She snuck a quick look at him. He was scrutinizing her. When his gaze moved to her lips, she flushed. Then he too blushed and looked back at the fire as if he found it fascinating.

"Well, he's awkward with us." She looked back out over the lake. "Like you and I are with each other."

He swallowed hard, "Why is that, do you think?" His hand shook as he raked his hair back off his forehead.

"I don't know." Her voice held the hint of a moan.

"Perhaps we can change that awkwardness. Horace used to say, be the change that you want to see in others."

"I'm trying," she said.

He was silent for a moment, then quietly continued, "Please look at me again." It took courage, but she did, she fell into the warm glow of his eyes, and her heart beat faster. "My guidance tells me that we will walk side by side in this fight," he said. "Will you join me? Can I count on you to walk gently by my side?"

She could not speak but she nodded yes and the look they shared was filled with such peace and love that Cornelia knew she wanted to walk by his side forever.

C.W. soon joined them. "He's sleeping.

"I'll order some food to be brought from the kitchen and we can eat here in front of the fire," said Hadji.

"But Nathan?" C.W. asked, "I was hoping he could join us."

"Daddy, he sent a message that he couldn't because he was already committed to rehearsing with Rudy and dining with Hall Hamden."

"Oh, I see," said C.W., turning away to look out the window.

Hadji joked, "His loss is my gain."

A tray of Indian food was brought in from the kitchen: puffy puris, vegetable curries, dhal, and a plate of sliced fruit. Hadji chortled to see Cornelia take seconds on everything. He threw one last puri onto her plate, shaking his finger, "Once it touches your plate, you must eat it. Or else you will insult my capacity as a host." He held his hand over his heart and faked a mortal swoon. She laughed out loud.

"Your daughter is beautiful when she laughs," said Hadji.

C.W. looked startled then turned to Cornelia. With his head askance, he studied her. "She might be a beauty after all. Her mother never thought so."

"Mummy always used to say I would have to have character because I certainly would never be the belle of the ball. As she had been." Her face twisted into a self-deprecating moue.

"Well, I for one, declare her wrong, your character just enhances your beauty, not the other way around."

Their evening sparked with laughter. She had never seen C.W. so relaxed and it pleased her that he got along with Hadji.

When Horace called to Hadji from the bedroom, Cornelia said a quick goodnight and ran down the empty halls and out into a star-studded night. She hugged herself. She couldn't remember a night when she had felt so warmly appreciated. She was glad to see her room was empty. The last few days had been such a whirlwind of intensity that she quickly fell into a profound sleep.

The slam of the door startled her awake. A light snapped on.

Strangled sobs filled the room. Patty sat cross-legged on the bed across from her, rocking back and forth. Her face was tortured; tears rolled down over her cheeks and into her wide-open mouth. When Patty's sobs slowed down and her breathing went from gasps to occasional shudders, Cornelia asked. "What's the matter?"

"You really want to know?"

"Of course, I do. You can always be honest with me."

"Omigod," Patty threw her hands up, "Enough with the blarney. You sanctimonious Absolutes make me sick."

Cornelia recoiled as if she'd been slapped. "I'm sorry."

"But worst of all, if you must know, it's you high and mighty Woodstocks that really make me sick. You pretend to be so naïve. But actually, it's how you get your way."

"That's not fair."

"Oh whatever." She waved her hand, "Don't get all self-righteous on me now. I've had enough of that for one night."

"What are you talking about?"

"Your brother made me feel as if I were a whore."

"My brother would never do anything like that." Her face twisted.

"Oh, so now I disgust you? Give me a break!" A squall of rage darkened her face. She spat out her words. "I've seen the way you look at my boobs. You don't fool me."

Cornelia blushed. "I was curious. I haven't been around many people my age. Forgive me for being awkward. And forgive me for looking at your body. That was an impure thing to do."

"Oh, for chrissake, don't be so smarmy. I looked at you too, you know. I thought that's why you hid in the closet when you undressed. You knew I was looking at you."

Cornelia's jaw dropped, "I didn't know."

"That's it. Work that injured innocent bit one more time and I swear—that's what your brother did too. Yeah, don't look so surprised. I just came from his room."

"What?" Cornelia was shocked, "You did that?"

"Of course, I did. Where have you been? Under a rock or something? You want the truth. Well, here it is. I *told* you I wanted that part. That's why I came here after all. My high school drama coach told me the Moral Absolutes were doing a movie and that Allan

Larches was to direct and I knew this was my chance, my chance to be somebody, to make all those lying fools back home understand that I wasn't crazy. I could shine with a brilliance that would stagger them all."

Her face took on a crazed look. Her eyes narrowed. Cornelia felt a shiver of fear. It didn't seem to matter whether Cornelia was listening or not, Patty stormed on. "And so, I came here, and I saw your name on the roster and requested you as a roommate. Oh, I knew just how to work you, yes I did." Cornelia eyes sparked with tears. Patty didn't seem to notice. She was flushed. Her eyes had an odd glint to them. "Yeah, and I thought I could work your brother too. I could kill two birds with one stone. I figured he could help me nail the part *and* take care of my horniness."

Her eyes bored into Cornelia, "You see, that's something else you don't know about me. I'm off my meds now. Ten days and counting. I couldn't stand the old flatness. I didn't feel alive. So, I went off the meds. And the old fires came back and shook me to the core. I had to have sex. It's the only thing I know that takes the edge off. So, after dinner, I waited in the hallway, then followed him into his room and locked the door before he could say or do anything." Harsh laughter barked out of her. "You should have seen his look when I pulled up my shirt." Cornelia gasped.

"Yeah," Patty snarled, "you're not the only one who likes my titties. You can tell when a man likes what he sees. His breathing gets all loud and funny. So, I went and pressed myself against him and it got all hot and heavy. I was close to getting off just by rubbing myself on his thigh when suddenly he pulled back as if I had struck him and said we couldn't do it and that I had to leave."

Cornelia covered her ears with her hands, but Patty didn't seem to notice. Her words were coming so fast now that she was panting. "At first I thought he was kidding. I mean I could see his boner sticking up inside his pants, so I knew he wanted me. I'm no dummy. But he pushed me away again even with this giant hard on."

An involuntary retch burned up through Cornelia's throat, flooding her mouth with foul bile. "Stop. Stop it right now. That's enough. He's my brother."

Instead, Patty leaned over toward Cornelia's bed and fired her words at her. "Oh yeah, act all high and mighty on me now. You know what, I'm sick of you guys from the seaside of town. Oh yeah, you may go to the same school as me. But no one figures we're equals, none of you *ever* forget that my family comes from a long line of firemen. And that you come from a long line of *evil, crooked, stinking tyrants* who stomped all over us Irish every chance they got. Who the hell does he think he is pushing me away like that?"

And then, quickly, as if all the rage had emptied her, Patty crumpled. "I'm just a nothing. And now I've ruined my chances at being in the film. Nathan is sure to tell Rudy what happened, and they'll say I'm impure. That I don't measure up to the Moral Absolutes. And I'll be gone. Poof. Like that." And she snapped her fingers. She cringed down into as small a ball as she could, curling up on her side, facing away from Cornelia.

Without thinking, Cornelia slipped out of bed and went to her, putting her arm around Patty and pulling her close. Patty's head fell down onto Cornelia's knees. As she sobbed, tears soaked through Cornelia's nightgown. As if she were a toddler, Cornelia patted her on the back. "Now, now," she soothed, "Everything's going to be alright. When we try to force solutions, it rarely works out the way we want. Hadji says, 'when in doubt, don't.'"

"Really?" Patty looked up at her and for a moment it seemed she might be comforted, but then shame twisted her face and she wailed, "It's not alright. It'll never be all right. I've made such a mess of things."

A flash went off in Cornelia's brain. As she rubbed Patty's shoulder, it reminded her strongly of how she had taken care of things when her mother took to bed. Patty's unpredictable mood swings were exactly like Nevin's. Another flash of synapses brought back the memory of Gertrude and her bewildering mood fluctuations on the day they had gone horseback riding so many years before.

Her patting slowed down as suspicion crept in. Was Patty's crying manipulative or genuine? Wise as a serpent, she thought. She stood up, went back to her own bed and pulled the covers up over her head and rolled over to go to sleep. Patty was strangely quiet, but Cornelia deliberately did not look at her.

Much later, Cornelia awoke to see moonshine spilling across her pillow, and felt a warm naked body curled into her. A taut round butt pushed into her crotch and a voice murmured, "Let's just cuddle. Just snuggle me now." Patty's bottom kept twirling and a fire flared up inside Cornelia, pulsating in great throbbing surges, and she thought of Hadji and what his body might look like naked, and so, without thinking, she pulled Patty's bottom closer into her. An explosion sent sparks flying behind her eyes, and her groin throbbed in almost painful spasms. Through the pulse pounding in her ears, she heard Patty's snort of disgust as she leapt out of bed.

"What's wrong with you?" Patty crowed. "All I wanted was a cuddle. Yuck." She flounced across the room and bounced back into bed, pulling the covers up over her head.

Cornelia shivered. Her groin still throbbed. What had she done? Her body had betrayed her. The thought of Hadji's naked body and the pressure between her legs had sent her over the edge. What was the matter with her? She must be evil. Impure. She tossed and turned for the rest of the night, praying for guidance that didn't come. Her mind churned with shame. Finally, just as the light turned blue, she fell into a deep sleep.

She awoke an hour later, as Patty banged around the room, throwing her things into a duffle, announcing that she was going to request a room change, that she certainly couldn't room with her now that she knew Cornelia was a pervert lesbo.

At that very moment, C.W. knocked at the door. "Cornelia, come at once, there must be no delay."

She got up and quickly dressed.

Chapter 11

As they loped back toward the main conference center, C.W.'s urgency made Cornelia's heart hammer. "Are Hadji and Nathan okay?"

He darted a quizzical glance at her, but nothing slowed his stride. "No. It's Horace. He's dying."

"But he's been dying for years. He always bounces back."

"Not this time."

"What happened? He seemed so at peace last night when I left."

"He *was*." A frown creased his large flat forehead. "Then Hall Hamden came to see him and I'm afraid they had it out."

"Oh."

"You know how Horace is." He shook his head, as fondly indulgent of Horace as a parent might be of a two-year-old.

"I do," she said simply. She understood. They put up with his occasional tantrums because he dispensed wisdom in the same naïve but authentic way of children.

"Well, Horace confronted Hall, and yes Horace blustered, as is his way when he sees a wrong that must be righted. But, instead of agreeing, Hall got defensive. And then he refused to have guidance with Horace. Denied that he had done anything wrong. In fact, denied everything. Denied asking us full-timers to leave. Denied any covert maneuvers to take over Greendell and the trust money. Denial. Denial. Denial." His tone was bitter.

"Go on, then what happened?"

"Well, Haj and I were in the living room. We heard the argument, but then Hall began to talk, and his voice was like a hammer. He told

Horace he was sick and tired of being bossed around. Tired of having to check in with him about guidance. Did Horace really think that he was the only one that had a direct line to God?"

"Yikes. That was harsh."

C.W.'s face was set in grim lines as he continued. "When we didn't hear any response from Horace, that finally alarmed us. So, we broke in and Hall was standing over his bed, no further than three inches from Horace, and he kept yelling and Horace was flinching as if each word were a nail in his side." He paused.

"We pulled Hall off of him. He left in a fury, but the damage was done. Horace was gasping for air; his chest was convulsing. We ran for the doctor and we've been keeping a vigil all night long. His breaths have been coming and going. Sometimes he doesn't breathe for what seems like minutes at a time. But then it evens out."

He clamped his mouth shut. When he spoke again his tone was quieter. "He finally fell into a restful sleep around 4 AM. But when he awoke a few minutes ago he was very weak, and he called for us all in the room with him to have guidance. Then he said he wanted to say his good-byes and you were one of the people he mentioned. So, come, come, we must hurry, I don't think there's much time left."

They picked up their pace until they were running. When they reached Horace's suite, the living room was full of the old faithful, Mrs. Rogers and Jay Burden and several aging Englishmen. There was a marked absence of Hall Hamden and his sidekicks. Hadji greeted Cornelia with a warm smile and a head waggle, and he gestured for them to go on into the bedroom. As she passed by him, she blushed. She couldn't help but remember how she had climaxed when she had fantasized about his naked body the night before. He stopped her with a gentle hand on her shoulder.

"Is everything okay?" he asked.

At first, she hung her head, then that niggling voice zinged inside, *you must tell him*, nagged the voice, *you must share your shame. Or else it will haunt you*. Miserable at the thought of doing that, she nodded and dared to look directly up into his warm gaze. "Can we talk later?" She blurted before she could change her mind.

"Of course," he cupped her elbow and led her into Horace's bedroom.

The air was hot and fusty as if the rot of death had finally caught its prey. Horace was propped up on pillows, his eyes closed, his jaw hung open. He was so still that Cornelia thought they were too late, and she looked out to the lake where the sun shattered the surface into a thousand bright crystals. She jumped at a sudden gurgling.

"Don't be scared," said Hadji, "I've seen death many times before. It's nothing to fear. His spirit is just moving into another dimension. We must let him go. He'll know you're here. Speak up. Speak loud and clear so that he can hear you."

She was flustered and a little bit scared, but very aware that Hadji would expect her to do her best. She took a deep breath and reminded herself that fear only nested in her if she let it. She reached for his claw hand and held it between her two palms. She leaned down. "It's me," she said, "It's Cornelia. You have always told me I spoke the truth. So, I'll try to be absolutely honest."

To her surprise, she felt a twitch and two of his fingers curled around one of hers. "I haven't always liked you. I thought you took my daddy away from me. I did. And I'm sorry for that. But I know now that my father chose to follow you of his own free will. It's taken me a long time to see that because," she took a huge breath, "you also scared me. It's like you could see inside me. I'm sorry for that as well. Because," she paused, "even though I was scared of you, I loved you. We all did."

He interrupted her with another rattling breath, which shook his frail chest, followed by a gurgle that might have been a chuckle. "Sorry..." he managed, "magic.... Little word.... can change the world." There was a long silence, followed by another shuddering breath, then, quite clearly, two final words, "Hall.... Sorry."

Much to her horror, he vibrated, a horrible rasp came out of his throat, and he arched up, then fell back down. A long hiss of yellow foam bubbled up out of his mouth. The doctor, standing on the other side of the bed, nodded his head, then with great ceremony, leaned over him with a stethoscope and put it to his chest. After a long moment, he looked up and shook his head. Tears silvered his face. C.W.'s face shone as well. But Hadji looked almost beatific. He looked at Cornelia with such pride and love that she throbbed in response. "You did well. You helped him go."

Back in the living room, they shared the news with the others. A shocking keening from Jay Burden made the hairs along her arms rise up. To add to her discomfort, Hall Hamden and his men came in and stood along one wall.

"It was time," said Hall Hamden and crossed his arms.

"What did he say?" wailed Mrs. Rogers. "What were his last words?"

Hadji demurred to Cornelia. "They were meant for her."

She sighed. "He said that 'sorry' was a magic little word. That sorry could change the world. And then," She paused and looked directly at Hall Hamden, "His very last words were 'Hall' and then 'sorry.'" She turned and fled, without saying good-bye to anyone. She ran down the hall and out to the lake where she paced and thought and wept and laughed. What had his last words meant? That he was sorry he hadn't acted on her accusations involving Hall Hamden so many years ago? Or was he trying to say he was sorry to Hall?

She would, of course, never know for sure just what Horace meant by his last words. Nor would anyone else. Finally, she threw some rocks far out into the lake, loving the way they pierced the water and then disappeared beneath the surface. Perhaps, she thought, death is like that. Souls slip from one side to another, spiraling down into another sphere, but somehow, they still exist.

As always, being in nature soothed her, and as she looked out over the lake, smooth as glass, she let her thoughts swirl up to the billowing clouds above. From a distance, she heard Hadji hallooing her as he strode down the hill, his glasses flashing silver in the sun, his mop of black hair flapping sideways. At first, she smiled at the sight of him, then flashed with anxiety, remembering she had asked to speak to him.

He came to an abrupt halt next to her, "I saw pleasure leave your face."

"Am I that easy to read?"

"For me you are. I am afraid to hear what caused the frown."

She wheeled away from him, then was drawn back to face him. "I must share a painful confession with you."

"Oh my," he comically crossed his arms across his chest.

"This is serious," she frowned.

"I'm all ears." He cupped his hands behind his ears and flapped them open.

She laughed and slapped him on the arm.

"It's always good when I can make you laugh. It's so infectious. I lay awake at night trying to devise stratagems to make you laugh."

"You do? That so pleases me." She gulped in air then announced, "I don't know how to say this any other way. Please forgive me, but I must share that I've had impure thoughts about you."

His look was very intent for a moment and then he turned away from her and she felt scorched. Though she was engulfed with embarrassment, she continued. "I had guidance that I needed to share that with you, but I've horrified you, haven't I? Oh, I wish I hadn't said anything. Forget I ever said that." She slashed her hands through the air as if erasing the words.

"You've really had these thoughts?"

She nodded.

He strode down to the edge of the lake, then paced back and forth several times. Finally, he stopped, and his look was so sober she feared he would chastise her. "You're young, you know."

"I'm fifteen," she cried.

"I know," he said quietly, "But I am twenty-three."

"What difference does that make? I can't help the way I feel. I can't help being young. I feel so ashamed. I'm sorry I said anything." She looked away from him out to the lake.

"Cornelia," he said gently, "You always look away from me. Don't be afraid. Look at me now."

As she turned to look he opened his hands up and sadly waggled his head from side to side, "I've had them too."

"What do you mean?"

"If Horace were still alive, he could vouch for me. I often had to share with him my shame that in the last year or so, I have had impure thoughts about you, my dear Cornelia."

Her heart beat so fast she thought he might be able to hear it. Her hands flew to her throat to still the pulse.

"I thought that by sharing them they would go away, but they have not. They have increased to the point that sometimes at night I'm maddened by them." He stepped forward and took hold of her hands and held them to his chest. "Can you feel my heart pounding?"

She nodded.

"Do you know that you are very dear to me?"

Again, she nodded. For a moment they stood still. The air throbbed between them. She grew so giddy that she swayed, and he reached for her to keep her from swooning and pulled her in close. Before she had time to react, he cupped her chin and brought his face down to hers. His lips were so close to hers that she could feel their heat and she could smell the musky cinnamon scent of him. His body radiated heat. Every fiber of him quivered. Through the soft white cotton of his shirt, his skin glowed.

She quivered, relinquishing herself to the magnetic pull. She brought her lips to his, and they were so soft and forgiving that she could not tell where hers ended and his began. For a long moment they kissed, and the universe spiraled down to just the two of them. Then hearts still racing, he gently pushed her away. "My darling Cornelia, indeed we must not go further. Consider this kiss a promise."

He held her away from him, but his eyes burned into her. Her lips felt branded by their kiss. "Here is what I propose," he said, shaking her ever so gently to clear the cloud of passion that fogged her brain. "Listen to me," he whispered, "Pay attention. This is important; I think we both know now how we feel. But we must each go our own way. We must."

"Forever?" Her voice trembled.

He laughed, "No, not forever. But you have some growing up to do. And I? Well, I have some souls to gather. I have the business of gods to conduct."

His hands slipped down from her shoulders to hold her hands clasped tight. Hearing that they were to be separated made her want to run. She tried to squirm away, but he held her fast and waited until she looked at him and every fidget in her body was quieted.

He nodded once to make sure she was listening. "Let us pledge that we will have the slowest, grandest courtship that has ever happened in the history of the world." And with that he turned his face and shouted up into the heavens, "Let the gods know that I cherish this young woman. That I pledge with all my heart and soul that I will protect the absolute purity of this love." And then he threw back his head and crowed.

Cornelia laughed with him, then paused for a minute and said, "Does that mean we can never kiss again?"

He laughed even louder, "No indeed it does not. It just means that they will be few and far between lest we do anything rash that we would regret." And with that he turned and enfolded her into his arms until every part of her arched up against him. She melted and the world slowed down to let them kiss.

Moments later, both giddy with joy, they walked side by side, but not touching in case anyone was watching, back up to the Conference Hall. Telling her he had to go help plan Horace's funeral, Hadji said he would see her later and left her in the main entrance hall where a huge crowd of teen-agers was milling around. Hall Hamden had called a general meeting, mandatory for all youth attendees.

At the apex of the general meeting hall, where the massive lodge pole pines converged to hold up the giant wooden teepee, the atmosphere pulsated with the whispered cadences of hundreds below.

Hall Hamden strode in, surrounded by his usual henchmen, all identical in grey flannel suits buttoned tight over starched white shirts. As the buzzing faded to silence, a cough rang out. So many people jumped that a titter ran through the audience. Hall Hamden bowed his head and spread his fingers wide as he shushed them. Though the crowd was mostly the teenage attendees, Cornelia noted that a group of full-timers, including C.W., stood at the back of the hall.

In the silence, Hall Hamden's words were strong and slowly cadenced. "A great leader..." He paused, "A great *man*...has passed. Horace Baker was taken from us this morning." There was a collective gasp.

Then as Hall Hamden strolled back and forth across the stage, basking in the spotlight, his words picked up speed. "The world will be a lesser place without him. Horace Baker was one in a million. There will *never* be another one like him. Thousands will mourn. Leaders the world over will recognize this great loss. For they know that the force for Good will be diminished by his passing." For a long minute he was silent, then he shouted. "*Opening the door for evil to step right in.*"

Somewhere in the crowd, a young girl screamed.

"Yes!" He thundered. "You are right to cry out at the thought of evil forces gathering strength at his passing. But there is a way to fight that. We will say YES to carrying on the fight. We will say YES to picking up the banner of the Four Absolutes. We will say YES to marching in to fight. We will say YES to bringing change into our hearts and souls first. And YES, to bringing that message out to the world. We have a mission. We are *not* afraid of a fight. We will say YES! YES! YES!" And as his fist pumped the air, hundreds answered that thrust of his fist with a roar. Dozens of young men rose to their feet and pumped their fists in the air.

"YES! YES! YES!"

For a moment, chaos reigned as more and more young people sprang to their feet shouting out their approval. Cornelia stayed seated as the hair on the back of her neck rose up and a shiver ran through her. "What's wrong with you?" chided the girl next to her, "Get up on your feet." But she could not. She waited to hear what else Hall Hamden had to say.

Again, Hall Hamden held out his hands for silence. "Please sit down." The crowd obeyed. Hall Hamden let his face and shoulders sag into a humble expression. "In his last hours, Horace Baker gave me the great honor of passing the baton to me."

Cornelia startled. She wanted to shout out that it was a lie, but the room vibrated with expectation. Many were looking up at Hall Hamden with hopeful anticipation. She quickly shot a look to C.W. who looked slightly angry but mostly stunned. Behind him, just inside the hall, Hadji looked concerned but not impassioned. She recognized his detachment. She knew he believed that taking no action was often the best action. *Bide your time*, whispered her inner voice, *the time has not yet come*.

Hall Hamden continued, "And I agreed to carry that banner. I am honored to carry that banner. To my own death, I will carry those banners of the Four Absolutes. And what are they?" He called out. "Who knows?"

One girl called out something, but her voice was lost in the air. He cupped his ear, "What? I can't hear you. What is that first banner?"

"Absolute honesty!" The girl screamed.

"That's *right*. Sing it *out*.

"Absolute honesty!" roared the crowd.

And, as he shouted out the Moral Absolutes, one by one, the crowd roared ever louder. His face was raw and swollen. His fiery blue eyes sparked. He stamped his foot in time to the cadence of his words. He seemed fanatical, possessed almost, and most of the teenagers seemed spellbound. There was a look of crazed ecstasy on most faces all around her.

The sound of hollering crashed up into the rafters, as loud and overwhelming as if a hurricane whirled around them. Cornelia covered her ears, but even so the mass hysteria tugged at her. She dove under the roar, fighting for sanity, and when she broke back up into a pool of her own rational thinking, she slipped past several people and made her way up the aisle to the exit. Hadji and C.W. were gone.

The next few hours went by in a whirl. She forgot all about lunch and walked down toward the lake as if on automatic pilot, overwhelmed with a bewildering array of emotions. There was sadness at Horace's passing. And trepidation that Hall Hamden seemed to be gaining even more power. And yet, below these troubling thoughts throbbed a deep sensual delight that Hadji had kissed her. Yet, that joyful memory was coupled with the fact that she had responded sexually to Patty's naked body. She thought back to something Horace had said, "It is not having the impure feelings that is a sin. Only when we forgive ourselves can we then freely give back to others." She felt comforted by that thought. Bowing her head in prayer, she both confessed her sin and then let it go, forgiving herself for the transgression.

Far offshore, a breeze ruffled the water. As it approached, pleating the surface in front of it, the slap of turbulent air roiled another muddle in her brain. Nathan was back in her life, which should have been a happy thing, but he seemed embroiled with Rudy and that confused her. And then, much to her relief, her guidance took over. *Talk to Nathan. More will be revealed.* And so, a few minutes later, she showed up at the movie studio for the cold reading of the script, knowing Nathan would be there.

As Cornelia walked in from brilliant sunshine to the cavernous sound stage, she shivered though it wasn't cold. Spotlighted in the center of the sound stage was a long table. Allan Larches sat at the head, Nathan and Rudy on one side, Patty across from them. Cornelia slipped into a chair in the shadows.

Allan cocked his head. "Righto! Thank you all for showing up. I know this is a difficult day for all of us. Horace Baker was much admired in his life. And we shall all miss him I am sure. But the show must go on! Shall we get started? Please turn to page 85. For those of you who haven't had a chance to read the script, this is where Cynthia, played by Miss Rudy." He nodded toward her and she ducked her head with an apparent show of modesty. "Where Cynthia ever so sweetly confronts Jocelyn about her dishonesty and Jocelyn fights back. So Miss Fitzgerald, as you know, you will be reading the part of Jocelyn. As will Miss Woodstock, after you've finished."

Rudy read her pleading speech with a natural ease. Her stage presence was sweet and alluring and seemingly without cunning. Nathan looked enthralled. Cornelia sighed. She could see why he was fascinated.

Patty's speech in response to Rudy was muted and flat, almost as if she were half asleep or drugged.

"Speak up," snapped Allan.

Patty jumped as if she had been jolted by a prod. Her flat delivery morphed into a strident flood of words that were almost indecipherable. When she finished, Allan said, "I don't know where the intelligent and angry girl of yesterday went, but Miss Fitzgerald, I am disappointed by this reading. Nevertheless," he twitched his neck and they all heard a crack, "Perhaps you just can't do cold readings. We shall see. Miss Woodstock, please come to the table."

"Please," Patty burst out, "give me another chance. I can do better. I promise you I can. Please. It means everything to me." And she broke into ugly sobs.

"Control yourself," Allan bit down on his words. "Misplaced histrionics won't get you the part. Miss Woodstock?"

Patty pushed back her chair and swept past Cornelia, shooting her a withering look as she passed. Cornelia came to the table and sat down.

"Let's hope you don't disappoint as well," Allan snipped.

Rudy began the scene again. Cornelia made herself look at her as she spoke the words. Again, she was struck by the apparent sincerity of Rudy's performance, but Cornelia steeled herself against the plea and, as she did so, a mask of rage tightened her face. The words on the page shot out of Cornelia, carrying darts of jealousy and pain. Rudy flinched as she hurled the written words at her. Cornelia was shaking when she finished, and Rudy looked close to tears.

"Wow," said Nathan, "There's the old firecracker I remember. Way to go, Cornelia."

"Indeed," said Allan, "Well, well, well, it seems we have an actress here after all."

Cornelia flushed and looked down at the table, wanting to shout that she wasn't an actress at all, that every hateful word she had spoken was true, that she wanted to squash Miss Rudy and Patty and the rest of them for making her feel small and pathetic. Then she heard her guidance. *Anger is an emotion that only hurts yourself. Don't tilt at windmills. Save your strength for the main fight*. She closed her eyes and swayed. It was true. Rudy was not the demon. Nor was Patty. She stiffened her spine and reminded herself to stay strong.

"Miss Woodstock," said Allan, "I think we can safely say you've got the part. Now, let's move along to the boys' parts."

From the hidden depths of the sound stage, there was a yelp of pain and the thud of running feet. Patty had stayed just long enough to hear the news. Wondering what lay ahead for her, Cornelia sat through the other readings, hardly paying attention except when Nathan read. He was bashful and somewhat stiff but believable as an earnest high school jock.

When the readings were over, Allan announced that there would be rehearsals later in the afternoon and that shooting would start the following day. As everyone began to disperse, Cornelia walked to Nathan, grabbed him by the arm and began to haul him toward the door. She heard Rudy call out to him, but Cornelia was determined. To her relief Nathan allowed himself to be drawn along, calling back over his shoulder to Rudy that he'd see her later.

Once outside Cornelia bolted down the hill toward the lake, knowing he would follow. And indeed, arms pumping, he soon passed her by and they ran down to the water. Down they went, arms wind-milling, almost falling down the steep hill, legs pumping, feet striking out, down and down until, breathless, they reached the stony beach and came to a gasping halt. Nathan laughed, "I forgot how much fun it is to be with you." And he grinned at her and she felt her heart surge with happiness that he remembered. She turned to the water and, without a word, picked up a rock and sent it skipping out across the icy clear water.

"Seven," she called.

He leaned over, picked up a flat rock, and with an expert flick of his wrist, sent it skipping across the gleaming water as if it were a rocket gone to heaven. "Nine." he crowed.

And then, for many silent minutes they did nothing but throw rocks into the water. Finally, when all the tight kinks seemed stretched out of her shoulders and a pleasant exhaustion settled in, she blurted out, "He had yellow foam coming out of his mouth!"

"Who? What?"

"Horace. I was there when he died."

"No way."

"Way."

"Tell me everything."

And so she did. Every detail she could remember from the harsh sound of his breaths to the wrenching contractions of his body and the final awful bilious foam. A gull cried out as it swirled up away from them. Nathan prodded at the rocks with the toe of his sneakers. "Mummy really misses you. She talks about you all the time."

"She does?" Her heart skipped a beat. She had thrust the thought of her mother so far down that the pain had burrowed deep. Over the years, her guidance told her that the time had not yet come to deal with that pain. But an image of Nevin lying alone in a darkened room crept into her consciousness.

"She needs you, you know."

When she didn't answer, his foot kicked the rocks again and a look of petulance flashed across his face. "I want to stay here and do the film."

"I know."

"Ray told me if I didn't get my act together, I was going to end up a worthless entitled misfit just like my father."

"I'm so sorry. You didn't tell me."

"I haven't had a chance."

"Right, you've been spending so much time with Rudy after all."

He stared down at his feet, his face all broody. His heel slammed into the dirt next to the path and he kept bashing it into the soil, not looking at Cornelia, but out over the lake, his foot striking the dirt over and over again.

"Things are really bad at home. Mummy says Ray has a whore over the hill. And when I opened the shutters up to let in some light, there were bruises all up and down her arms."

"No," Cornelia was shocked.

"And she flinches away from him every time he gets close which just makes him madder and he stomps out of the house."

"I'm sorry," she said simply, "That sounds terrible."

"It is terrible." A long silence stretched, then he added, "I don't want to go back. This film is an opportunity for me, you know." His lower lip pouted, "Besides, maybe it's your time to take care of Mummy. I've been doing it alone for years now."

Cornelia nodded and swallowed, trying to keep the pain from making her throat swell up. "I hear you," she said, "Let me think about it."

"You mean have some guidance, don't you?" It was his turn for sounding bitter.

She considered it. "Maybe."

He snorted but said nothing.

Hovering above them, a gull dropped a mussel shell down onto the rocks where it snapped open. The gull wheeled down to pick at the pink flesh.

"Listen," she said, "I know Patty came to your room."

"What?" He twitched. "She told you?

"Yup."

"Damn, I'd hoped she wouldn't say anything."

"Well, that didn't work."

"Guess not."

"Did she tell you I sent her away?"

"Yup. But only after a while."

He blushed and suddenly his freckles reappeared, ghost-like but legible, and he looked the twelve-year-old boy she had loved so much. She prodded him in the ribs where he was most ticklish.

"Careful now," he laughed, "They'll accuse us of inappropriate touching." She moved in to tickle him harder and he bolted off up the hill, laughing as he went. "Bet you can't catch me!"

She ran as hard as she could, then rammed into him as he came to a complete stop. He looked frightened. "Do you think I'll be a useless misfit?"

"Not hardly. Never." They turned and continued their walk up the hill. "Sometimes when I was alone at Greendell," she said, "I used to worry I was going to be a crazy fruitcake just like Aunt Janice."

He peered at her, his brow furrowed, "That will never happen. You're the sanest person I know."

"Really?" She flushed with pleasure. "You mean that?"

"Actually, I really do. Excepting the fact that sometimes you don't know when to keep your mouth shut."

She laughed, "Horace always used to say I was the speaker of the truth."

He looked sad, "I know he did. I just run away from things at home when they get bad. It used to be easier when you were there." He was quiet for a moment, his stride lengthened. "For what it's worth, I think Patty may be a little off."

"It's funny you should say that. Because I thought that she reminded me of Mummy a little bit. The way her moods swing up and down all the time."

"Rudy's not like that," he bragged.

"No," Cornelia sighed, "I don't think she is. And that's a good thing. She's very consistent."

His brow furrowed. "Why don't you like her then?"

She thought about it before answering. She was navigating tricky waters and didn't want to make a wrong turn. "I think maybe she's like us."

"Yup," he nodded.

"Somehow not crazy in the midst of madness."

"Yup."

"She's survived a lot. I give her credit for that. At least you and I had each other when we were little. But," she chose her words carefully, "I think the difference between us is that at the bottom she's out for herself. And as long as you go along with what she wants, all will go well, but cross her will and watch out."

"Really?" He looked troubled.

"Really."

"I hope you're wrong."

"I hope so too. Honestly, I do. I don't want to see you hurt."

"I don't want to see you hurt either." He reached out to put his arm around her shoulder and for one long moment she allowed herself to feel comforted by his touch. But then she looked up and saw one of Hall Hamden's minions watching them from a stone terrace and she sighed and pulled away, jamming her hands deep down into the pockets of her trench coat.

"Daddy will probably try to make me leave with him," Cornelia said. "Things are not good between him and Hall Hamden as you know."

He sighed loudly, "I know." He shook his head, "But I want to do this movie, Cornelia. Can't you stay and do it with me? Come on, Nee, it would be such fun to do this film together."

"We'll see."

His lower lip swelled. "Okay, then." He ran off to find Rudy.

Hunger finally gnawed at Cornelia, so she went on a search for food. The vast dining rooms were empty. Industrial-size coffee brewers stood like tin sentinels next to the swinging doors to the kitchen. Only a handful of dutiful white-coated workers were chopping onions and cabbage for the night's fare. They hardly looked up when she asked if there was anything to eat. There was a dazed atmosphere everywhere, as if Horace's death had stopped the clock. One of them nodded at the wall of huge refrigerators along one wall.

When she looked behind the cold stainless-steel doors, there were only slabs of uncooked beef, veiled white with fat. She bolted out, wandered down the hall, and ended up in Horace's grand dining room. The overhead lighting was dimmed except for one end of the room where, below a huge mural, a coffin lay surrounded by banks of sickly sweet lilies. As heedless as a moth, she walked toward the light and leaned down over the open coffin to see a stiffened Horace lying on a bed of cream satin. There was a smudge of bright yellow pollen sticking to the end of his protuberant nose and his jaw hung slackly open. She felt a hand fall softly onto her shoulder.

Hadji chuckled, "I kept trying to put his chin back in place but it's frozen now, so I just let it be. Can't you hear him laughing at the sight of himself?"

"You're right about that. He would have laughed at the absurdity of it." She beamed up at him. Black dots swirled in her vision and she stumbled.

"Here, here," Hadji gently led her to a chair. "Stay right here." He ordered, "I'll be right back."

As her dizziness subsided, she became aware that there was a group of full-timers scattered around the room. Most of them bowed in prayer. Several sat slumped low, their heads buried in their hands. Her father was at the back of the dining room listening intently to Jay Burden who was gesticulating wildly. She turned back toward the coffin.

The huge newly painted mural gradually came into focus. It was a painting of many people, mostly men. A much younger Horace stood in the midst of a grand gathering of dignitaries, both American and foreign, many of whom Horace liked to say the movement had influenced. She recognized Mobutu, now leader of the Congo, and Conrad Adenauer, the former Chancellor of Germany, and there, off to one side, almost hidden, was an eyeglass-wearing Hadji dressed in his usual white. Hall Hamden was prominently down and to the left. Right above and behind Hall Hamden's head was Mount Rushmore, which seemed to her more than just a little self-aggrandizing. Though there were generals and presidents and people in national costumes from all over the world, C.W. was nowhere in the painting. It reminded her once more of who was the enemy.

Hadji chuckled before he sat down. She quickly peeped up at him and flushed. He had followed her gaze to the mural and his head was waggling in bemusement. "Bit pompous, don't you think? Hall Hamden's idea, I believe. Though Horace couldn't help but be flattered.

He always had that child-like wonder about being the center of attention. Here, I brought you something to eat."

He handed her a plate covered with a row of tea sandwiches: watercress and cream cheese, cucumber and egg, a bunch of grapes alongside, and several cookies. She salivated at the sight of it.

"Horace always said people must be fed first. Feed their bellies, he said, and you'll feed their souls."

She began to gulp the food down, almost choking as she ate. When she finished, she caught her breath and thanked him. "But how did you know I was so hungry?"

His head waggled from side to side and the corners of his mouth turned up in a smile. "I was born in India after all. I recognize that glazed, vacant look. Even those of us who had some land often went hungry. And ever present throughout the country are the sights of hungry children and men pulling rickshaws when they're nothing but sinew and bone. And yet they run as if possessed. All for a bit of bread to give to their children. It humbles you, hunger does."

As he spoke of his country, his face transformed. And she knew two things. One, she loved him. And two, he would always be the kind of man who cared most about everyone else which meant she might have to share him with many others. It was a sobering thought. And, not for the first time, she wondered why nothing about her path seemed easy or normal.

At that moment, Hall Hamden strode into the dining room, flicking a row of light switches as he came in, flooding the dim room with a harsh brilliance. As always, his minions flanked him. C.W. threw his hands up to shield his eyes.

"Look what I have here!" shouted Hall. He held up a sheaf of telegrams and waved them as if he had pulled up a winning lottery ticket. "Telegrams. From all over the world. Nixon. General McArthur. Ludwig Erhard. His highness Mohammed Reza Pahlavi. Emperor Hailie Selassie. Mobutu. It goes on and on. All sending their condolences. And regretting our loss." His bragging blared like a trumpet.

From a corner, a shrill voice rang out. It was Jay Burden, Horace's longtime companion; the man Horace called his little boss, but a man who had dedicated many years of his life to caring for Horace.

Though Cornelia didn't like his persnickety manner, she knew he was self-less and completely dedicated to Horace. "This is a sacrilege. Turn off those lights. Let us pray in peace. Enough of the banner waving." His voice was shaking; he had his arms wrapped tightly around his skinny middle, and his jaw wobbled alarmingly as if it was loose in its socket. C.W. stood next to him, patting his shoulder with one hand and shouting, "Hear! Hear!"

Hall Hamden wheeled back out and left the room but did not turn down the lights. Jay crossed the room and dimmed the lights.

"And so here it starts," murmured Hadji, still standing next to her.

"What?" she whispered.

"The fight for the leadership," he whispered back, "You can bet your bottom dollar that Hall Hamden won't waste any time answering those telegrams, pronouncing himself as the new leader of the Moral Absolutes."

She shuddered at the thought of Hall Hamden having no check on his desire for power, but her pull toward Hadji pushed those thoughts to the side, as she allowed herself to giggle. "Bet your bottom dollar? Where did you get that expression?"

He shrugged his shoulders, "I must have read it in a book. Are you telling me I'm not up with the latest American teen-age vernacular?" His thick black eyebrows shot up in mock surprise.

"And I am?" she joked. "Hardly. What would I know about such things?"

Looking directly at him, she once again found herself overwhelmed with impure thoughts. She wondered if they were so bad, why did this feel so natural and true? His bushy eyebrows made her think of body hair and a sudden flash of golden skin. In her fantasies, he was bare and smooth like a nymph in a fairy tale, but in reality, she knew, they had both matured. With no advance warning, thick dark hairs had sprouted on her ankles and calves and in her crotch. Who knew what hairs were hidden in the folds of grown men's bodies? She flushed sick at the very thought. And yet desire pulsed through her. She looked back up at him and she was sure he could read her mind.

"It's okay," he whispered, leaning down toward her, "we're in this together." And, as always, his delightful head waggle poked fun at himself. "That wonderful fact astonishes and delights me. And for now, I must go. But for *my* sake you must take better care of yourself, Miss Cornelia. Please don't forget to eat. Your body is a sacred temple, don't you know." He shook his finger at her, smiled kindly and then, with his long stride, was off across the room to stand next to C.W., Jay and several other British Absolutes. Cornelia took that opportunity to slide out the door.

She spent a good hour in the nearby library, curled up in a corner chair overlooking the lake. She had found *Pride and Prejudice* on a dusty shelf and dove into its familiarity for about the fifth time, happily escaping into the comforting world of eighteenth-century language and manners. Every once in a while, she would look up at the relentless march of cumulous clouds across the sky, their bulbous shapes casting gloomy shadows on the lake's wrinkled surface.

Later, she walked outside. On a long bank of grass that rolled down toward the lake, Rudy and Nathan sat under an apple tree, the late afternoon sunshine flickering lace shadows on their faces. "Sit down," said Nathan, patting the grass beside him. "We've been waiting for you."

"Yes, do," cooed Rudy. "Please do sit down." Her tone was as welcoming as a duchess to her incoming petitioners. Cornelia sat down with a plunk beside Nathan.

"Isn't Allan just amazing?" purred Rudy. "We've just been talking about what a privilege it is to be working with someone so wonderfully talented. Don't you think he's just so wonderful?"

Cornelia nodded.

"Oh," Rudy simpered, "I'm so glad you think so too. So glad."

And then an awkward silence fell. Finally, Rudy fell into an easy teasing banter with Nathan, talking about things they had done in the last few days, complete with inside jokes that didn't include Cornelia. Once, she had been the only one allowed to tease Nathan. Now, she felt a pang of intense sadness. But having promised him she would make an effort with Rudy, she stayed close to them, even joining them for dinner that night.

Several others joined them, and Cornelia again was struck by how easy it was for Rudy to make small talk. She would put her hand on one girl's arm and commiserate with another about a stomach bug she'd had, or another's painful phone call home. She seemed to be a master of empathy and small talk. All through dinner, Cornelia felt too tall, too awkward, truly immobilized by her inability to chatter with ease.

Halfway through the meal, Patty arrived. Rudy waved her to their table. To Cornelia's infinite relief, Patty sat down at the far end. Her face was tight, and she seemed preoccupied with something other than the table conversation. Rudy chattered on, mainly about how wonderful everything was, and of course, how terribly sad it was that Horace's death had come at such an inopportune time.

Patty turned to Rudy with a horribly twisted expression. "Oh, is the film still on?"

"Of course," trilled Rudy, "He would have wanted to see our film. He would have loved it. I just know it. I was one of his favorites, you know. He would have loved to see me in this film."

Cornelia swung her head toward her but said nothing. Rudy had always avoided Horace like the plague. He made her uncomfortable, she always used to say. And once she had thrown a tantrum to get out of meeting with him.

Several girls cooed that they knew she was right. Horace Baker would have loved to see Rudy's performance. Rudy ducked her head and her mouth turned down in a charming moue. Nathan looked besotted. And Cornelia felt sick.

Oh no, Cornelia sighed to herself, *what's wrong with me that I don't want Nathan to be happy. But didn't it strike anyone else as odd*, Cornelia thought, *that Rudy was speaking of Horace's death with such insouciance, as if he had inconveniently missed a luncheon date?*

After dinner was finally over and they walked out into the hallway, Nathan pulled Cornelia into a quick bear hug and whispered, "Thank you for trying." Then he headed off to Building A.

To Cornelia's surprise, Patty was already in their room when she returned. Patty's eyebrows lifted, "Turns out there was no other room in the Inn." As she shrugged, her cotton nightgown slipped off one shoulder, exposing a row of crescent bruises running up along the ridge of muscle that ran up to her neck. A frisson of true terror bolted through Cornelia's veins. She had a flashback to when she first saw those marks many years ago.

Patty hardly seemed to notice. "Just wait and see. Tomorrow

there's going to be a *new* announcement about the casting. And let me just say, you Woodstocks won't like it one little bit." With that she flounced onto one side, flipped off the light above her bed and snapped, "Us Irish girls need our beauty sleep."

As Cornelia lay sleepless, wild scenarios tossed and turned in her head. Finally, a few hours before dawn, she crept out of the room, carrying her clothes with her, then dressed in the bathroom down the hall. She ran down the hill and for an hour she stalked up and down along the edges of the lake, watching the sky turn from a deep indigo to violet and then become washed with peach and gold. As always, nature settled her down and helped to quell the clamor in her brain.

She had no doubt about the origin of those crescent shaped bruises. This time it would not go unpunished. There must be some way of exposing the evil that lurked beneath the complacent exterior of the self-appointed new leader. But how to do it? Her thoughts were a jumble. *First things first*, zinged that clarion voice. *Feed yourself.* Knowing she could not face the chatter in the dining room, she veered off and headed down a path through the woods that would take her to the village.

After breakfast, she felt more settled but still assaulted by too many different trains of thoughts. She walked back along the shore, past the turn off to the conference center, and then followed a path that veered up through a meadow where cicadas shrieked and bumblebees swayed drunkenly over wild marsh flowers. Beyond the meadow, dark pinewoods formed an impenetrable black backdrop. A thick carpet of pine needles stretched off on every side and there was a stillness that made her shudder. She conjured up the image of her mother lying alone in a darkened room. *Nathan is right*, she thought. *It's my turn to take care of her*. The thought filled her with dread. Yet, she knew it was necessary. Their relationship was unresolved. Horace had been telling her that for years. So, for both her mother's sake and her own growth, she probably needed to go home. At least for a while.

If only she didn't feel so alone. She had been so long with the Moral Absolutes that their patter and way of life had slipped over her like a familiar comforter. But Horace's death was going to rip that cover off. The Moral Absolute leadership was splitting apart. C.W. and Hadji represented the best of the cause, that she knew, but they would most likely withdraw to Europe and India. She shuddered at the thought of what the Moral Absolutes would now be under the full rule of Hall Hamden. He fostered ecstatic unthinking followers, the opposite of her. Worse still, he was a hypocrite. Once he had hurt a young woman and it had been swept under the rug. And now, it seemed, he had hurt another. Given his history, she had no reason to believe he would now be absolutely honest about this impurity. Hadji and her father would most likely advocate detachment. Was she the only one who would dare to confront the truth? And yet, from her own history with the group, speaking the truth would either go unnoticed or be twisted around to suit Hall Hamden's needs. No, the truth was she had to form a plan to ensnare him in his own evil.

This decision further solidified when she broke out of the confining pine woods and back out into the sunny meadow. Striding along, looking down at the lake, she rejoiced at the sight of the sun spangling the morning waters. A brisk breeze slapped her face.

Alongside the lake, she splashed through rain puddles until her leather flats flapped. The sound evoked the slapping of flesh. A vague plan began to form. *Be as wise as a serpent, gentle as a dove,* her guidance spoke. And so, she marched up the hill, filled with resolve.

Chapter 12

Once inside, she slipped into a seat at the back and looked out over the sea of heads to the lit stage where Hall Hamden sat; his legs crossed, his face complacent with victory. There was no sign of Hadji or C.W., though she did see a few elderly full-timers sitting on the far side of the hall.

When Hall Hamden began to talk, he didn't jump to his feet but brought the mike down to his seated level, as if he were conducting the meeting from the comfort of his own living room. This fatherly manner gave her the shivers far more than his usual bombastic approach. As always, his tie seemed pulled too tight, his shirt too white against the blue of his beard shadow.

"How are y'all?" he drawled. A rumble answered him. "Yesterday," he continued, "In honor of a great one who has passed, I asked each and every one of you to perform a fearless inventory of your sins and make every effort to make amends for those transgressions. Some of you, I know," he nodded toward the front rows, "have already done this. It was a long night for many. With much gnashing of teeth and tearing of hair!" He waited for the laugh that came slowly. It struck Cornelia as a nervous, almost canned response.

"I am sad to say," he hung his head and shook it sadly from side to side, "that only *some* of you took this task to heart. Others of you ran from it. Some of you have laid down your sins at Jesus's feet and asked for his forgiveness." He slowly rose to his feet, his eyes narrowed, and his face turned that eggplant purple that so repelled Cornelia. "But some of you," he thundered, "Some of you have failed to examine your sins. Have failed to admit them. You are so mired in impurity that you are blind, blind, blind to the evil inside you."

As always when he spoke, the hackles on the back of her neck raised and goose bumps raced up and down her arms. She was learning that these physical reactions were a manifestation of her intuition. Because she had been fending for herself most of her life, she realized that she was developing a refined awareness of those around her and could detect negative energy quite easily. Now that Horace was gone and her father and Hadji were soon to leave, there was no way she wanted to survive in this mob mentality. Despite her trepidation, a part of her rejoiced that she was beginning to trust her own guidance.

One of the henchmen strode down the aisle; he stood arms akimbo at the exit doors to bar anyone from fleeing. From the front rows, a group of teenagers, the girls in pastel jumpers, the boys in khakis and button-down shirts, bounded up onto the stage.

Rudy stood front and center. The spotlight gleamed her skin, glittered her eyes, and made her teeth shine like moonstones. She almost looked unreal, like a china doll. Behind her, looking somewhat abashed, Nathan had a phony smile pasted on his face.

Over the years, Cornelia had noticed a difference between Horace's converts and those who adhered to Hall Hamden. Horace encouraged people listening to their own inner voices. Hall Hamden encouraged unquestioning obeyance to the rules set down by the elders. The former sometimes looked lost as they sought out their own inner truths. The Hall Hamden followers often sported a pasted-on smile of entitlement.

Patty stood at one end of the group. Her curly hair was wet and combed back off her forehead. Her face held that glazed look of a recently "changed" Moral Absolute. But knowing what a consummate actress Patty was, Cornelia could not help but wonder about her sincerity. While the pastel dress molded pleasingly to Rudy's curves, on Patty it hung like a sack. To Cornelia it smacked unpleasantly of the hospital gowns worn by inmates in an asylum. Patty's arms hung in front of her, as sinewy and taut and pink as a rabbit carcass stripped of its fur. Cornelia shuddered at the sight of her, remembering the bites hidden by the costume.

As the group burst into song, Cornelia's fear grew. Would she be able to stand up to Hall Hamden? Would she able to entrap him? "You are not alone," whispered her inner voice.

"It's up to you!" sang the group, then jumped forward as one and pointed their fingers out at the crowd. Cornelia cringed away from the jabbing motion, as did many others. The drummer pounded, the trumpet blared, the music grew to a maddening crescendo.

The meeting hall descended into a maelstrom of abandon. There were screams. There were wails. There were shrieks of tortured joy. One girl rose to her feet and proclaimed, "I feel the coming of the Holy Spirit, oh lord. I feel him in the air. He is whispering around the rafters. Oh Lord, bring me your rapture. Come down and cleanse my soul!" Her whole body shook with spasms. Several people ran down the aisles toward her. They reached out to the girl and she joyfully threw up her hands as they led her toward the stage. When she stood under the lights, tears streaming down her face, she looked demonic. A part of Cornelia wanted to run out of the room; but her inner voice chided her, "Stay the course, Cornelia, stay the course."

Members of the chorus ran out into the aisles, pulling people out at random. For a while all was confusion. Hall Hamden blessed those who confessed, then sent them back down to their seats. Cornelia slumped further down and looked back over her shoulder at the door, but the minion scowled.

So be it, she thought. A phrase from Horace flashed through her, "Accept that which cannot be changed," followed quickly by, "Act as if and the feelings will follow." So, she relinquished herself to the thought of being trapped. Claustrophobia kicked into gear. A painful flash of heat zigzagged up her legs, fired up into her chest wall and then flared up into her face until she felt like ripping off all her clothes and screaming out loud. She was ready.

Up on the platform, Hall Hamden beckoned to Patty. Looking frail, she stumbled across the stage and into the limelight. Hall Hamden held up his hands and called for silence. Sobs stilled into shudders, shouts to whispers, and then finally silence fell. But it was charged, as if they were all floating in a very still pool of water with a live wire hanging above.

"It has been brought to my attention that this girl...." He paused and waited for the silence to thicken. "This girl has confessed to an abomination. To the kind of evil that corrupts. The kind of evil impurity that not only corrupts.... but corrupts *absolutely*."

And then Hall Hamden let silence fall again and waited until his next words would hold more portent. He nodded, and his words marched with an inexorable cadence. "A *wickedness* has sprung up in these rooms, yeah, even though we turn to God, some turn away, slaves to their own impure desires. Rudy, go get those who have sinned." He pointed out into the audience. A shudder ran through the whole room. Cornelia rocked back and forth slightly. Shouts swirled up into the rafters.

In a dusty old book, Cornelia had read an account of hunting with nomadic Bushmen in Africa. The pygmy bowmen and their barking dogs surrounded a tree. High up, clinging to a branch, a teenage baboon was just out of striking distance of the piercing arrows. If he had only stayed high, he would have been safe. But the taunts of the warriors, the barks of the dogs, the howls of the hungry children maddened him and finally he leapt out from his safe perch. Out into the void he soared and as he did, the chief's arrow plunged into his heart and he plummeted with an awful smack to the sandy floor of the bush below.

She looked up and saw Rudy bounding down the aisle toward her much like the bowmen did the baboon. Cornelia tapped into that intuition and steadfast resolve that Horace had taught her, but also, as a true actress will, gave herself over to the fear and leapt to her feet, bolting for the door, howling in terror as she went. She panted, gulping in air as if it offered some escape.

"See! See! The demon of impurity tries to escape," Hall shouted. "Our evil *will* control us unless we *sear* it with the brands of absolutes."

As the minion barred her way, Rudy confronted her with a sickly smile. "Don't be afraid, darling Cornelia," she purred, "I promise you, you'll feel so much better when you face the truth of your sin."

"No," Cornelia moaned. Her heart was skipping so wildly that stars danced in her vision. The panting had made her dizzy and weak on her feet. They dragged her up onto the stage. Rudy's grip on her upper arm was relentless, but the plastered smile never left her face.

They brought Cornelia to face Patty who held up her arms and began to confess. Her cadence was rough but stirring, with the hypnotic cadence of the old fife and drum corps. "Yes, I admit it. I came here with an impure agenda. I had no purpose in life other than my own selfish desire to succeed. If people got squashed, then that was just too bad for them. I would do whatever it took to get my way. Ambition ruled me. Yes, I have been guilty of leading others into impurity. I would seduce anyone I could. Even, I am ashamed to say, another girl." Her voice wobbled. Out in the audience, a girl shrieked. The sound jolted Patty out of her speech and she fell silent.

"Be at peace child." Hall Hamden rested his large hand on her head. "Those that were higher up in the organization should have led the way to purity. Not succumbed to impurity." Hall Hamden looked straight at Cornelia, "How the mighty have fallen." He shook his head as if truly saddened. "We had such high hopes for you, Cornelia." Then he turned to Patty with an expression of gratitude. "Instead we have a convert. This child came to me yesterday and humbled herself before me. Offered herself to the cause."

Galvanized by his words, Patty's hesitation vanished; her cadence fired back up into a wild gait. "I can no longer sit by and not right the wrongs of the world. I want to live now for something bigger than myself. I want to dedicate my entire life to the Moral Absolutes. Let them rule me."

"Hear! Hear!" shouted Hall Hamden.

"Hear! Hear!" roared the crowd.

As claps and cheers surrounded Patty, she yowled. "There is a fresh breeze blowing. Can you feel it? I can."

"Yes, Lord, feel the wind!" A girl called out.

"Amen!"

"Can you feel it, Cornelia?" Patty turned to her, her eyes wide and scary, "Can you forgive me? Are you willing to let this fresh breeze of purity and forgiveness sweep into those lustful parts of you? The parts that haunt you?"

"Yes indeed," Hall Hamden spoke slowly and deliberately while holding out his hands toward Cornelia. "Are you with us, Cornelia Woodstock? Or against us?"

And suddenly all eyes were riveted on her. Trembling with painful anticipation, Cornelia looked over to Nathan. When they were small, he had coached her on how to survive in a disaster. *If a shark circles you and comes in for a kill, strike him hard in the nose. If you're ejected from an airplane crashing into the sea, make sure your legs are pointed down feet first so that they take the force and break rather than your head splitting open.* But he was no help here. He looked as frozen as a deer in headlights.

Once again, she found herself alone. Then she looked up and saw Hadji standing at the back of the room. His glasses flashed. His expression was inscrutable. She hardened herself to losing him. *What people think of you doesn't matter*, zinged her inner voice. *What matters is keeping your eye on the ball.* She knew this was a defining moment for her. She had to decide to either trust her instincts or go along with the group that had raised her. They were not perfect, but it was all she knew. Over the years, she had come to terms with her initial reservations and actually excelled in many areas. Now she had to make a choice that would decide her future path. Despite the risk of losing everyone's good opinion of her, she decided to trust herself and gamble on the unknown.

To everyone's surprise, she tossed her head, raised her chin, and confessed to impure thoughts about Patty. She even took creative license and made up lascivious thoughts about other girls. She didn't weep. She didn't blame Patty. She announced that it was all her fault. She had engineered the whole thing and she wasn't sorry for anything she had done. "Evil has entered my soul," she stared at Hall Hamden, offering herself up. "I dare you to confront the evil in me. If you are the moral leader you say you are, you will punish me for my sins. And confront the devil that resides inside my blackest soul!" Unwaveringly she held out her arms toward him.

His eyes sparked with an unholy light. He nodded his head toward Frank and another minion, muttering, "Take her to my room. I'll take care of this." The two men took her by the arms and hustled her off the stage. She could not bring herself to look at either Nathan or Hadji. She hoped that one day they would understand what she had done. That is, if it worked the way she hoped it would.

As they charged her up the aisle, girls flinched away from her as if she were a witch. She snarled at them and laughed when they squealed. Once outside the meeting hall, she slumped down a bit. But the two men kept her in a tight arm lock and goose-stepped her down the aisle to Hall Hamden's suite of rooms. They locked the door and took the key.

She had time only to note that his room smelled stale and though the bed was tightly made, the pillow bloomed with yellow stains. His highly polished shoes were laid out in a careful row below a line of starched white shirts. Two grey flannel suits hung next to one blue-black one. The only other sign of the room's inhabitant was a Holy Bible placed in the center of his bedside table.

Within ten minutes, the key turned in the lock. He entered and quickly relocked the door, pocketing the key as he did so. Her heart hammered. He wheeled to face her, his eyes were slits; his face engorged with blood. He staggered toward as if he were in the grip of a powerful drug and grabbed her by the arms.

"This time, little Miss Cornelia, you've gone too far. Self-will run riot is no longer the right description for you. Demonic is more like it."

"So, take me down a peg," she reared back from him, "I no longer have to listen to you. Horace is gone now, and he was the one with the divine connection. Not you," she spat the words out. "You'll never be the man he was."

And just as she knew he would, his anger escalated. "You little bitch," he snarled, and the word reverberated in her ears. She made herself look at him with insolence, but inside she was chanting, *this is for you, Gertrude. And all the others. God knows how many. This is for you.*

"Think you're better than me, don't you?" He lifted her off her feet and shook her. Her head snapped back and forth. Black dots spiraled across her vision. His eyes were glazed and empty of compassion. Horror stabbed her heart. And with that he growled and sank his teeth deep into the muscle of her shoulder. Pain seared her, and she yelped. One hand came over her mouth, and the other grabbed her throat, silencing her totally. He groaned and sank his teeth in for another bite, shaking her as he held fast to her skin. As he reared back, he barked. "You little bitch, if I have to pound the rebellion out of you, I'll do it." And again he groaned and burrowed his teeth in her.

The pain made her wild. She convulsed against him, slam[illegible] against him in an effort to breathe and stop the pain. He pushed her away and growled, "You're just moaning for it, aren't you?" Maintaining his stranglehold with one hand, he reached down and yanked off his belt. The sound of a zipper slashed through her like lightening. Wheeling her around, he pushed her hard down onto her belly, smashing her face down into the pillow. He yanked his hand off her throat and moved it to her back, jamming her deep down into the mattress until two ribs cracked. She screamed, but the pillow muffled it. Willing herself to stay conscious, she scrabbled, kicking, fighting back, writhing and moaning.

"You *will* obey me," he hissed. "I *will* purge the evil out of you. I *will* wrestle you to the ground. You *will* be humiliated in order to be reborn. That's it, you bitch, fight me why don't you?" He yanked her dress up, ripped her panties down. And then, with his belt, he began to whip her, methodically, mechanically, and with each slap of the whip he groaned. Suddenly she felt hot fluid spurt all across her bare ass and lower back. He groaned again and fell down on her, his barrel chest pinning her to the bed. She lay quiet, gulping for air, fighting to keep alert. She sobbed as air came back into her lungs.

His tone turned loving. He stroked her back and cupped her ass. "Oh, pretty baby, are you upset? Did Daddy hurt you? I'll give you the part back. That's what you wanted, isn't it? Just like the other one who came sniveling. You women are all alike. Full of vanity and self-love. It sickens me. Of course, I'll give it back to you. Allan does what I say. And it's you I want. You're the prize. I'll keep you by my side. Just like it's meant to be. You'll help me rule the world."

His words of endearment were harder to bear than the violence. She forced herself to purr. "I *do* want that part. You know I do. I deserve it. After all these years of being good and staying quiet, I deserve it."

"Yes, you do." He petted her, stroking her. She remembered once watching a man beat his dog and then stroking him right afterwards while the dog cringed and wriggled. So she forced herself to whimper, "I'll be good now, I promise. Please don't be mad at me anymore. I hate it."

He rolled his thick body off her. "Go," he said curtly, and snapped his fingers at her. "You're a mess. Get yourself dressed." She twisted away, making sure to keep her shoulders bowed and subservient. He went into the bathroom and left the door open. The sight of the thick stream of yellow splashing down into the toilet bowl made her sick. She yanked her dress down, pulled up her panties and quelled the urge to vomit as the wet from his coming soaked through her clothes.

"You'll publicly apologize at the next meeting," he yelled.

"Of course," she said meekly. She picked up her trench coat, belted it around her soiled clothes and, once outside, ran as fast as she could back to the main entrance hall. The receptionist informed her that some attendees were running sprints down by the lake and that some were rehearsing in the sound stage. She bolted to the sound stage, afraid that at any moment, Hall Hamden's faith in her subservience would fade and that he would be sending minions to pursue her. Pulsing with anxiety, she opened the door and at the far end of the huge cavernous space, cameras were rolling, and Patty and Rudy were filming the scene where Patty confronts the sinful girl. Patty had stepped right into her part.

So be it, thought Cornelia, I have another far more important part to play. Still, she could not help but note with some bitterness that Patty was back to her old flamboyant, insouciant self. But Nathan was nowhere to be seen.

A lump filled up her throat and it hurt to think she might have to leave without saying good-bye. She fled the sound stage, jamming her hands into her trench coat pockets as she ran back toward the main conference hall. Just as she arrived, a black curtained carriage came up the hill, the door opened at the main entryway, and six men came down the steps, carrying the coffin. Two photographers and several reporters were waiting at the bottom of the steps. Cameras flashed.

Hadji, C.W. and Jay Burden bore one side of the coffin on their shoulders while Hall Hamden and two of his minions managed the other. Hall Hamden's hair was carefully combed; his clothes perfectly in place. There was no hint of the struggle from just moments before. He was obviously experienced in covering his dirty deeds. He looked supremely complacent.

Then Hall Hamden called a halt to the downward progression of the coffin so that photos could be taken. Cornelia took that opportunity to bolt up the stairs to stand close to her father and Hadji and then walked with them the rest of the way down the steps. She was hardly aware of cameras flashing.

As coffin was loaded onto the backside of the carriage, where it lay surrounded by a bed of roses and lilies, C.W. turned to her. "I've been looking for you. Hadji and I are leaving. We will accompany Horace to his final resting place in Arkansas where his parents are buried. Maybe it's best that you stay here for now. That's what you want, isn't it? To be with Nathan." He held out his hands to her. She grabbed on, determined not to let him go.

Her heart jigged as she heard heavy footsteps behind her. Hall Hamden's hand landed on her tender shoulder. She flinched, biting her tongue in an effort not to scream. "Yes, of course," he said, "Cornelia must stay with us. She has an important part to play in the movie."

She held tightly onto her father's hands, and said, "No Daddy, I want to go with you and Hadji. Please?"

"Cornelia," Hall Hamden warned squeezing her shoulder again, "that is not what we agreed on."

Hadji turned to face Hall Hamden. "Please take your hands off her, man," His tone was polite but firm.

Hall Hamden's face flushed purple. "No, Cornelia will stay. She has had guidance that I alone can be the recipient of her confessions." Hall Hamden's tone was as calm and convincing as always.

Hadji paused and looked down at her. She quivered, and her eyes opened wide with fear. He turned back to Hall Hamden, a grim line to his lips and a fierce warrior glint in his eyes. "I *said* to take your hands off of her."

"Cornelia's self-will is blinding her to the truth. She must stay here. The Good Lord has spoken. Our work is not yet finished."

She turned to him and forced a smile. "Of course, you're right. We're not finished. Yet. I'm just going to say good-bye to them at the ferry." For the first time in her life, she smiled the Moral Absolute smile.

Then Frank said, "Hall, an altercation would not be welcome at this time." He nodded his head at the newspaper photographers who were still there and snapping away.

Hall Hamden shook slightly and then turned to smile at the reporters, "Forgive us, a recalcitrant sinner needed to be reminded of the path she needs to follow. We will never give up the fight for her soul. And for those of many others. We will not. Horace Baker may be gone, but there are those of us who will continue the good fight." His large yellow teeth flashed.

Hadji took her by the elbow and was ushering her up into a carriage. She bolted up the steps, settled back into the seat and finally sighed with relief when both C.W. and Hadji got into the carriage with her.

"We must go. The ferry leaves in fifteen minutes," said Hadji.

The coachman snapped his whip at the pair of horses, jolting them into a wild downhill trot. At the sound of the leather slapping against their flesh, Cornelia burst into a paroxysm of weeping. Hadji put his arm around her shoulder and pulled her gently close. She yelped.

"You're hurt," he said.

She nodded, blurting out between sobs, "When we get to the mainland, I must go to the police."

"Then, without question, that is exactly what we must do," said Hadji. Anger flickered across his face.

"But why?" said her father, "*We* have important business to conduct."

"C.W., C.W.," Hadji sadly shook his head, "Do you not see that she is in a panic? Something has happened to her. Indeed, her soul and body radiate that she is in mortal danger. And she is injured. But not from what Hall Hamden would have us think. She is not evil, no it's not that at all." And then he looked at her with such sweet sadness. Maybe, she allowed herself one brief consoling thought; maybe she hadn't lost him after all.

Hadji scowled as he looked grimly back toward a receding conference hall. She turned to follow his gaze and saw Hall Hamden and his goons still holding forth to the cluster of reporters and photographers. Then, as she watched, she saw Nathan running full speed down the pathway from the sound stage toward the conference center. Her heart pounded.

"Stop!" She cried. "I must say good-bye."

"You can't," Hadji said. "We must be sure to catch that ferry."

She nodded back to show she understood. She turned forward and never looked back.

Part IV

ABSOLUTE LOVE

Chapter 13

As the plane angled down over the Florida everglades, Cornelia hoped that being home would bring her comfort. The previous twenty-four hours had been harrowing. The assault from Hall Hamden, the anxious flight from the island, followed by a grueling three hours in an Emergency Room where they swabbed her bites, took fluid samples from her clothes, and then, only after an hour long interview from a policeman, allowed her to scour herself raw.

Cornelia wondered if she would even recognize her mother after all this time. Her only reference had been the portrait at Greendell which had cemented the image of a glamorous but aloof beauty in her mind. When the plane landed and she trotted down the stairs, peering into the small crowd waiting at the gate, her glance went right over the woman with a graying bun pulled tautly back off a tired face. Then she heard the unmistakable fluty voice.

"Nee, oh Nee," Nevin waved. "Here I am. Just look at *you*, so tall and bony." Her laugh tinkled, "Just like your father."

Cornelia's gaze swept toward this little stranger. Not only was Nevin inches shorter than Cornelia, but her face drooped into jowls, her mid-section was thickened, and her skin coarse. There were new little pillows of fat below her round eyes. She drew close, embraced Cornelia quickly then pushed her off. "You're scowling. Do I look so awful?"

"Of course not," said Cornelia, "You're as beautiful as usual. I'm just tired from the journey. I'm sorry." She air-kissed her mother's cheeks. The old role of giving her mother needed reassurance slipped over her like a funeral cowl. But, her compliment had not been enough. As she watched, her mother's face crumpled.

"Where *is* he? Where's Nathan? What have you done to him? Why hasn't he come with you?" As Nevin's eyes grew wide with horror, Cornelia was reminded that she was not the chosen one, the golden child. That was reserved for Nathan and likely always would be. It reminded her of one of the reasons she ran off to the Absolutes in the first place.

"What happened?" Nevin's face twisted. "Don't tell me those awful Absolutes have now got their claws into him. Wasn't one of you enough?"

"I'm sorry," she said as if it were her fault. "Mummy, please don't be mad at me." Tears rolled down her cheeks.

"Now, now, don't make a fuss." Nevin linked their elbows and pulled her daughter down the corridor away from the gate. Nevin patted her arm and the old familiar tinkle of her gold bangles eased Cornelia's pain. "Oh darling, honestly now, don't cry, I've got you now, don't I? We'll have to make do with each other, won't we? It won't be so bad." Nevin stopped, turned to Cornelia and looked her up and down. She yanked Cornelia's hair out from behind her ears and fluffed it up, then sighed as it fell back down to lay flat again. "How do you expect to get the attention of boys if you don't cut and curl it?"

"Mummy, please, stop. Besides, I'm not that interested in boys." How could she tell Nevin that the object of her affections was East Indian with cinnamon skin and very much a man not a boy? She squirreled away the memory of Hadji, knowing instinctively that to expose him to Nevin's criticisms would destroy something very precious to her.

"Imagine that. How do you expect to get along in life?"

She didn't bother to answer. She thought back to when she had said good-bye at the Detroit airport, and Hadji had held her hands while C.W. stood off to one side.

"I still feel filthy and a little scared," whispered Cornelia.

Hadji looked concerned. "I truly believe that, in time, that feeling will fade. I can promise you that. There will be scars, but you are strong and determined. That will help you recover."

"You think? I'm not sure I'm strong enough to make it without the group support. It was difficult to do what I did. I still feel a pull to return. Even though I couldn't live under Hall Hamden's aegis anymore. I couldn't." She shook her head, holding off the hysterics. "Will I fall apart without the group telling me what to do? Will I still have my own guidance? Can I trust it?"

"I know, my dear Cornelia, that all of us go through dark times. Times of fear and doubt. You may lose your way for a while that is true. But though I am struggling myself to understand what you have done in this matter, my guidance was clear this morning. I must continue to have faith in you. And you must trust in your own strength and wisdom. You must. Even if you waver for awhile."

Gratitude welled up so strong it hurt her whole upper body. "Thank you," she whispered.

"But I must be honest. My guidance also told me that for this time let us forget any promises that we have made, can we agree upon that?"

Hope flickered and died. "Okay," said Cornelia and turned away from him. She went down the causeway and fought the urge to look back. She knew the only real direction for her now was forward.

As Nevin chattered on about their wonderful new cottage in the islands, Cornelia's hand went up to the row of bites along her shoulder blades. They were still sore, and her cracked ribs hurt when she took a deep breath, but she didn't let on. She wanted to confide in her mother, tell her everything that had happened, how she'd hated it at first, then grown to rely on the group and the regime, only to be attacked by one of the respected leaders. She wished they had the type of relationship where open dialogue was encouraged without judgment, but she knew better. Perhaps in time.

"There, there, that's much better." She patted her, then tucked her arm through Cornelia's and steered her down the concourse to the baggage area. "You're going to *love* our new little house. You know of course that we just *had* to leave the village to move closer to Marsh Harbor. Ray's found a whole new market for his composted dirt. A lot of rich people have built houses out along the new golf course. Ray jokes that rich people always have to have their roses." Her laugh tinkled into broken glass.

"Roses? What happened to the goats?"

"Oh we still have them, not to worry, that's where Ray gets the manure for his compost. And our house is just the sweetest, with flowering vines climbing up all over the front of the house, it's just *sweet*."

Ray picked them up at the Marsh Harbor airport. The bed of his pick-up truck was filled with freshly composted dirt, redolent with the strong musky smell of goats. The scent pricked at Cornelia's eyes. She had forgotten how strong all smells were in the thick humidity. That would take some getting used to. She clambered up into the cab, squeezing in between Ray and Nevin. He didn't hug Cornelia, but his blue eyes sparked at her and he made a laugh that sounded like an engine turning over but not catching. "Tuh, hunh, hunh, well, well, who would have thunk little Cornelia would turn into a beauty?"

"Do you really think so?" Nevin's tone was arch. "I for one think she's a little bony. Pale and peaked to me. Altogether too drawn. Not at *all* attractive. And look at her skirt, way too short. I can't imagine the Absolutes approved of *that*. She yanked at Cornelia's skirt, trying to get it to cover her knees. "I've always thought knees were the most unattractive part of a woman's body."

Cornelia felt the blanket of sleep weigh heavy on her. She nodded off, Nevin's words becoming sludgy and undecipherable. She woke up once, when Ray hopped out of the truck, went inside a concrete shack and came out stinking of rum. She woke again when they pulled up in front of the cottage, just down a street crowded with other pastel colored conch shacks.

In contrast to the rotting cars festooning the house next door, bougainvillea and jasmine climbed up the wooden posts of the tiny front porch. But nothing could hide the concrete pilings that lifted the shack just inches up off the dirt where flocks of chickens scratched for ticks. Nevin showed her to a closet-sized room. The rough pine walls had been freshly bleached clean and the sheer lace eyelet curtains turned the harsh sunshine into a pearly light. "Thank you, Mummy," she whispered and gave her mother a hug.

That night Nevin cooked all of Cornelia's favorite foods: crispy fried chicken with pan gravy, crusty fresh baked biscuits and Cole slaw. Cornelia fell on it as if she hadn't eaten in months. Perhaps things would not be so bad here, she hoped.

"Guess those blue bloods haven't been feeding you too good, tuh-hun-hunh?" said Ray. "Don't know if your mother's told you or not, but some of her lah-di-dah friends were out staying at the golf course a few weeks ago. Course they couldn't stay here, not fancy enough, oh no, nothing but the best for them." He cocked his little finger. "Your mother had to get all decked out just to go have tea with them. You'd think she was going to a ball there was such a to-do. Then she pitched a fit when I brought them over for a surprise visit to our manure mansion. Tuh-huh-huh, she wouldn't even come out of her room."

Cornelia had once found Ray funny. Now, she thought he just seemed mean. She shot a quick look at Nevin. With downcast eyes and rounded shoulders, she was flinching at his every word. Cornelia thought of how their wooden shack must have looked to Nevin's boarding school friends. The backyard stuffed with chicken coops. The goats penned up across the road. The pack of mutts sleeping under the front stoop. It must have been humiliating. She smiled at Nevin to show she understood. But her moment of empathy faded as she saw the martyred bow of her mother's shoulder, the downcast slant of her eyes. She had as much dignity as a cringing dog, wriggling his bottom just after getting a nasty kick. Why didn't she stand up for herself? Things had certainly changed over the years.

"They got out of the truck, don't you know," Ray barked with laughter. "You could see them tiptoeing through the yard, trying to avoid stepping in dog shit. Oh whoops," he clapped his hand over his mouth, his eyes wide open in simulated surprise, "I forgot. Can't use dirty words around the duchess."

"You're being so mean," said Cornelia, "You never used to be like that."

After a long beat of silence, his false teeth flashed white. The smile held no humor. "How do you think it makes me feel when she doesn't talk to me for weeks? When she shrinks away from me like I've hit her? Oh I hear her creeping around the kitchen at night after I'm in bed. Getting food. Just like a mouse. Matter of fact, it took your return to get her out of hiding. This is practically the first time I've seen her in weeks. The grand duchess herself," he twirled his fingers and mock bowed, "deigning us with her presence."

"Stop it," said Cornelia, "Just stop it."

His jaw dropped. His face paled, and for one moment, Cornelia thought he might apologize, but then the blood rushed back in and his bright blue eyes flared. "Well, now, Miss Hoity Toity number two, the stink of manure become a little too much for the likes of you too, has it now?"

Cornelia ignored his taunts.

"Might have known that the blue blood would run cold in you sooner or later." He looked back and forth between the two of them. While Cornelia stuck out her jaw at him, Nevin slumped even lower.

"Well then. Might as well remove myself, since the very sight and smell of me seems to disgust you both." He pushed himself up off the table and only then, when she saw how he used the table for balance, did she realize he was drunk. Something else she had pushed out of her mind. The possibly idyllic return home that she had manufactured in her mind was quickly coming undone.

"It's not that," said Cornelia, "I just can't stand by and watch you humiliate her. It's wrong."

He leaned down toward her. "Wrong, is it? Oh you don't have to say anything. I noticed the way your nose wrinkled when you got into the truck next to me. Your mother's the same way. I tell her, what the hell, I only take a bath every six months or so whether I need it or not. Well here now, here's something for you to clean up." Without warning, he upended the table.

The silver and china went flying, tumbling through the air, and then for one long second, everything paused before the cacophonous clash of silver and china smashing into smithereens sent slivers into the air. The silence returned, but this time tension clouded the room.

As he passed behind Nevin's chair, without even looking at her, he flicked his middle finger with his thumb and snapped her right behind where her neck bowed. She recoiled as if hit. Soon, they heard the truck start.

Nevin sat for a minute, took a deep shuddering inhalation, then pulled herself upright, settled her face into a more presentable demeanor, slapped her thighs and said flatly, "He'll be gone for several days now. He goes to his whore over the hill. Yes, that's right, don't look so surprised. And when he comes back he'll be so sick with the booze that he won't even remember any of this."

"Why do you stay? Why do you put up with this?"

"Where would I go?" She spread out her hands. "Who would have me looking the way I do?" She shook herself and managed a little laugh, "Well, as Ray would say, I made my bed now I have to lie in it." Her mouth curved down with resignation. She stood up and leaned over to begin to clean up the mess. "Well, I'm certainly glad I tucked the Limoges away. And a few nicks on the silver will just add to its patina, don't you know."

Cornelia laughed. "Isn't that ridiculous?"

And then they both laughed. Yet neither could shake the sadness.

The next few days went by at a sluggish pace. It was summer, and the days were so hot and humid that seconds after drying off from a shower Cornelia's body was already slick with sweat. Smells ripened in the thick humidity: the putrid sweetness of chicken manure, the salty stench of unwashed dog. She swam through the days, suffocated with lethargy. It was so hot she found it hard to even think, as if humidity had clogged up all her synapses.

One afternoon, just to get away, she slunk deep into the bush behind the house, skirting around limestone potholes, following winding bush pig trails through the scrubby jungle. Up ahead she could see the patchwork blue of a clearing spotting the livid green of the surrounding brush. She saw a woman squatting, stirring in an aluminum pot perched over smoking embers. A baby was strapped tight to her back; another crawled in the dust. The bound baby mewed. With a quick hitch of her sling, the woman exposed her breast and flipped the baby into a position to latch on. The crawling baby reached up to grab her other tit. Cornelia shrank back into the bush and skittered down a pathway, breaking out of the bush onto their street, where overarching lacy Poinciana trees broke the sunshine into a million points of light.

Just as she was catching her breath, a young man catcalled from across the street, "Where you gwine white ting?" She picked up her pace. "Mmhmm, sure would like to have me sum of that sweetness." He smacked his lips and laughed when she broke into a trot.

She slammed the gate of the front yard behind her and willed her skittering heart to slow down. It took her a moment to hear her mother on the phone in the tiny hall, just off the front porch. "No, we don't know anything about *that*." Nevin's tone was snippy. There was a pause. "No, certainly not. We are definitely *not* going to press charges. That won't happen. Not if I have anything to say about it." Another pause. "That's the most horrible thing I've ever heard. Better to just let it be." She slammed down the phone.

"Who was that?" asked Cornelia.

"Never you mind now." Nevin raised her chin.

"That wasn't the DA's office in Michigan, was it?" Her pulse pounded in her ears. Red blurred the edges of her vision.

Nevin twitched. "What if it was?"

She willed herself to stay calm, but the sound that came out of her was shrill and wailing, "Mummy, that was important. You. Had. No. Right." Her hands trembled.

"In case you hadn't noticed, I'm still your mother. I *won't* have you dragging yourself through some sordid court case. Nosiree."

Cornelia covered her eyes with her hands and slumped over, "No, don't do this to me. You can't do this."

"Oh yes, I can. Don't you forget, you're not yet eighteen. What made you tell people something so shameful?"

"You don't know. You weren't there. He's evil."

"Well, you're not the *only* one who's ever been the victim of an unwanted pass, believe you me. But most of us," Nevin drew herself up, "have the decency to keep it to ourselves. We don't go dragging our dirty laundry out in the streets for everyone to see."

The bites on her shoulder throbbed. Every deep breath stabbed at her ribs. "He hurt me." And then she wailed, as loud and as out of control as a toddler.

"Oh, it's just all so unpleasant. Spare me the details." Nevin covered her ears.

Cornelia could take no more. She ran into her room, slammed the door behind her, and threw herself down onto the mattress, letting the sobs spew up out of her with total abandon. She let her despair run its course. Finally, she lay curled up in a fetal position, her hands tucked between her thighs, her face and eyes all swollen shut. When her shuddering sobs had slowed to an occasional hiccup, the door opened and Nevin came in. She sat at the bottom of the bed.

When she was sure Cornelia was silent, Nevin let her hands fall into her lap where they wrung themselves. "I should think you'd want to just set this behind you. I should think you would be grateful for a mother who doesn't want to see you further humiliated. I should think you would know that the last thing I would want in this whole wide world was to have to show myself in some awful courtroom drama and have everyone looking at us. Laughing at us. 'Oh, how far Nevin has fallen.' I should think you would spare me that. Oh, I'm *sure* he was awful. Most men are, don't you know. I've had men come after me, don't think I haven't. But I *always* had the decency to keep my mouth shut."

Cornelia had no fight left in her. She let the words flow over her as unstoppable as a flood tide. For the next few days, she hardly ate and hated herself for falling into the blues, just like her mother. She began to doubt her once steadfast resolve, and she ached to return to the familiarity of the Moral Absolutes, the very place where she was attacked. It's then that she realized just how they had programmed her, convinced her they were on her side. However, when she needed them most, they turned their back on her and supported the powerful leader. There was no investigation, no acknowledgement of what had happened. It made her sick to think of how many other trusting young women had been abused, like poor Gertrude so many years ago.

As Nevin had predicted, Ray had gone missing. Cornelia couldn't help noticing how much more buoyant Nevin was without him in the house. She even picked roses for the glass vase on the kitchen table. She hummed as she swept the sand off the pine floors and out across the porch and into the front yard. She didn't even complain about their motley pack of dogs that spent most of the day piled up in drowsy heaps, sleeping under the house next to the stone pilings.

Every afternoon, somehow mirroring Cornelia's inner turmoil, the thick humidity of the tropics spawned thunderstorms. Purple-bellied clouds boiled up into the sky, their golden ramparts soaring many thousands of feet up into the blue-black stratosphere. Above them, thunder crashed and then sheets of rain sluiced down in sheets, steaming the pavements, bringing relief from the enveloping heat. And every afternoon, as the rain beat down, Cornelia would sit out on the front porch, idly rocking, temporarily shielded from the constant scrutiny of neighbors eager to get a look at the girl from the cult.

Nevin came out on the porch. "Wouldn't it be wonderful if Nanna really did follow through with her invitation to come visit? We could get out of this awful place. And maybe even Nathan could be persuaded to come home, wouldn't that be wonderful?"

"Did she actually *even* write?" Cornelia asked. She looked at the rain, wondering if she even cared about anything but the mesmerizing raindrops falling down in front of her.

"Well, she didn't actually, but Aunt Fanny did, and she said maybe Mother was finally ready to forgive my marrying so badly." She sighed, "Oh Cornelia, you don't know how much I've suffered being cast aside by my family. I just long for a chance to forget about my troubles." The phone jangled. Nevin jumped as if jolted by a live wire, then leapt to her feet, clapped her hands and trilled, "Maybe it's Nathan." She sprang to answer it, letting the front screen door slam behind her.

"Hello?" Nevin answered, her tone timid. Cornelia watched her mother through the fine mesh of the screen door. It made Nevin's coarsened skin looked younger, offering a brief glimpse into her youth. She still had the visible bone structure of a beauty. That would never completely disappear. And with one hand cocked on her hip, as if the caller could see her, her stance was still upright, her profile on display. "No, no, it isn't. That's my daughter. Yes, yes, I'm her mother, my name is Nevin, and who are you? Oh I see.... No, I didn't... No, I haven't. No, we don't get the *New York Times* down here, we're lucky if we see the *Nassau Guardian* once a week." Her voice cooed like a flute.

Cornelia hated her mother's titter. Why did her mother so irritate her? She longed to have the type of relationship she's heard others talk about—a mother she could share with and learn from and confide in. Through the screen she mouthed, "Is it for me?"

Nevin shook her head and frowned at her. "What's that you say? How tall is she? Why, she's 5'11" I believe. Is that bad? I'm 5'4" myself, I always thought that was the perfect height for a girl. Doesn't limit the dance partners, don't you know." Her tone was lilting. "Oh, what's that? Taller is better. Oh I see. I didn't know that. No, she hasn't. No, she doesn't. Oh, I see. Well, yes, that might be wonderful." To Cornelia, she signaled wide-eyed wonder. Her feet danced a little jig of excitement.

Cornelia shrugged her shoulders, raised her eyebrows, and opened up her palms for an explanation. She tried to keep the irritation from her face, knowing that if Nevin sensed it she would clam up tight, wailing something like, "I can never do anything right with you!" And so she refrained.

Nevin held up one finger. "Well, yes, I see, well I suppose it might take us a day or two to get things organized. But I don't see why not. I really don't. We'd be delighted in fact. So we'll be speaking in a day or two. Yes, give me your number, I'll write it down right here. We'll be in touch. Thank you so much." She carefully put down the phone with the dazed expression of a person who's just won the lottery. She clapped her hands. "Well, well, well, I just *knew* it. I knew if I just waited long enough the solution would roll right in through the front door. And here it is. Looks like that wonderful life we were just meant to have is going to happen after all."

"Mummy, for God's sake, what was that all about?"

You'll never guess!"

"*What?*" She popped her eyes. Her whole upper body shook with impatience.

Nevin chortled. "Well. *That* was Miss Geraldine Dodge herself!"

"Who the hell is that?" Cornelia hated that her use of profanity sounded more like Patsy than herself. Was she a chameleon, picking up mannerisms and phrases from people, trying them on to see if they suited? She yearned for the day when she would know who she was without having to copy anyone else. She hated that she had slunk into such lethargy around Nevin that even her inner voice was stilled. She felt lost without its guidance.

"Don't you know?" Nevin's expression was arch.

"Obviously no, I don't. Elucidate me!"

"Well, Miss Geraldine Dodge just happens to run the most preeminent modeling agency in all the world. Even I know that. She's been around forever. Even when I was a girl and not so bad myself, one of her people stopped me in an elevator and said I should come in for a test. But my father would have none of it. He said models were no better than hat check girls, and no girl of his was going to do anything like that."

"Mummy," Cornelia gritted her teeth. "Stop talking about yourself. What was the phone call about?"

Nevin flinched.

Cornelia felt a quick flash of guilt. "Sorry." She made her tone as sweet as she could. "*Please* tell me what the phone call was about."

"Okay then," Nevin giggled, "She *saw* your picture."

"What picture? What are you talking about?"

"Well now." Nevin grabbed at the back of Cornelia's rocker and gave it a push. "It *seems* there was a picture of you in the *New York Times* this Sunday past."

Cornelia waved her hand. "So? Mummy, stop rocking me. I'm not a baby you know."

Nevin withdrew her hands as if the rocker were on fire.

Cornelia snapped. "Oh for god's sake, stop it, will you *please* stop being so sensitive, it's driving me crazy. And *tell* me, I know you're dying to."

"Well, if you *must* know, there was a *picture* of you. In an article about Horace dying, don't you know? And *there* you were. And she saw the angle right away, being the Geraldine Dodge that she is."

"What angle? What does that mean?"

"Why you being a Woodstock of course."

"What are you talking about?" She dropped her head down into her hands. "This is so frustrating, just come to the point."

"Oh don't be such a ninny. They want us to come to New York. *Geraldine Dodge has asked us to come to New York*. What about that don't you understand? She's lined up a photographer and she's going to help launch you into the modeling world. And of course they want me too. That's important because you're underage, don't you know. So I will be your chaperone." She clapped her hands again and whirled herself around in a wild jitterbug. "Isn't it just *wonderful*?"

"But why? I don't understand."

"Well, *obviously* it's because you're being seen as a heiress, what else could it be? It's not your looks, anyone can see that."

Nevin's careless mention of her lack of looks had been so constant a theme of her early childhood that she had become, if not inured, then at least accustomed to it. But now as Nevin went on and on about how of course it had *nothing* do with her looks, Cornelia had a sudden insight that it had everything to do with her looks. For so many years, Nevin had been the sole inhabitant of the territory of beauty in their family. Now, perhaps, the only way she could still feel safe was to keep pushing Cornelia out of it. And yet, Cornelia thought with the first glimmer of hope she had felt in days, perhaps she would just fight, just a little bit, for her own space after all.

And with that she pushed herself up off the rocker, called the dogs to her with a snap of her fingers, charged out through the front yard, slammed the gate shut behind her and tossed her head at the catcalling man across the street.

For days now the deep sadness of her mother's betrayal had filled her with a metallic heaviness. It was clear that her mother did not love her absolutely. Nevin cared more about what other people thought than about whether her child had been hurt and needed protection. She thought back to the mother she had spied on in the jungle. Instinctively, she knew that mother would fight to the death for her babies.

Her own mother talked a good game. But there was something inside Nevin that kept her from putting her children's safety first. Her own emotional needs clouded her capacity to love.

As Cornelia walked now, new synapses sparked in her brain, forging connections that illuminated her own actions. This is why she had turned to the Moral Absolutes! She had been a child reaching out to a group with rules and parameters. And whatever she might think of where the group was now heading, they had kept her safe.

She continued walking until she found a grocery store and a pay phone. She called the DA's office in Michigan and found out, not a surprise, that because she was a minor, without her mother's support they would file the evidence but not follow through on charges against Hall Hamden.

At first, rage filled her. Then as she walked back toward the cottage, her quiet inner voice zinged in through a fog of emotion, as clear and bell-like as the call of a loon across chilly waters, "Trust in your self. Walk through the dark days. Follow your own light." The thoughts came in the same cadence as her stride and they comforted her.

Nevin spent the next few days in a tizzy of preparation. "I've got nothing to wear!" She would fool around with a pattern from Vogue, furiously pumping at her foot pedal sewing machine, then tear at her hair and say, "It'll never be ready," and then rush outside to the wringer machine to wash what few clothes she did have. Cornelia had her one black dress but little else.

"Didn't your father ever buy you anything? Oh why do I even ask? He might be a Woodstock, but he was always just so cheap. You'd think, given all the money there was, he could have bought his wife a new party gown every now and then, but oh no, I was expected to rework old ones. So I'd add feathers and some such frippery and hold my chin up and I was *still* the belle of the ball. Cornelia, you *must* have had something else besides this one black dress. Why *didn't* you bring anything else home?" She stamped her foot.

"I've told you, Mummy, I didn't have much of anything else anyway. Besides, you don't seem to want to understand that I was under the gun to leave the island as quickly as possible."

"Oh that's nonsense." Nevin twirled her hand. "I've had just about enough of that. Please don't ruin this opportunity that has presented itself with some ridiculous and unseemly need to flaunt to the world that *some* man, and I'm sure he *was* creepy, made a pass at you."

"I've *told* you, it was much worse than that. And I wanted to catch him. I wanted him to be punished."

Nevin held up her hand, "I just don't want to hear another word about it. We've *all* had men press unwanted attentions on us. You're not the first one this has happened to you know."

"Oh God, you'll never understand." Cornelia slumped, and her head fell into her hands. Anger, frustration and shame waged a war inside of her. Maybe her mother was right, maybe she had misinterpreted the whole thing. She suddenly had a vision of pointing fingers and jeering voices and the smugly triumphant smiles of Rudy and Patsy, and she sank once more back into that welcome lethargy.

"Whatever you want, Mummy, I don't care. Just do what you have to do."

Two days after the phone call, Ray dragged himself home. Nevin tucked him into bed, placed a gallon pitcher of water on the bedside table, pulled down the shades, closed the door, and then ignored him.

On the day of their flight to New York, Cornelia knocked on his door to say good-bye. "Just a minute," she heard him mutter. There was a clink of his dentures being removed from the glass by his bedside. "Come on in."

The light was dim, and he lay in bed, his face all droopy with apology. His unshaven face was grizzled with white hairs. "I must stink to high heaven."

"I've smelled better." Cornelia smiled.

He guffawed, "You always did have a sense of humor. Better than your mother."

"Well, *that's* not hard to do. Not that she's had much to laugh about."

"I guess not. I guess I've been something of a son of a bitch."

"You could say that."

His mouth tightened into a thin line. "What the hell do you think of this latest scheme of hers? Is there any truth to any of it?"

"Don't know," she shrugged her shoulders, "Guess we'll find out."

"Seems to me only fools think there's gold lying in the road just waiting to be picked up, but what the hell do I know."

She threw one right back at him, "On the other hand, you used to tell me, don't look a gift horse in the mouth."

"Tuhhunhhunh," he laughed. "You got me there. Guess you were listening to some of what I had to say after all." He struggled to a seated position, "Take care of the both of you, will you? Always thought you had more sense in your little finger than she does in her entire body."

"Do I have to?" She tried to laugh but it came out more like a wail.

"Guess we saddled you with more than you bargained for, didn't we now?"

She parroted back one of his other favorite sayings. "We don't always get to choose what life gives us, do we now?"

"Guess you were paying attention after all."

"Course I paid attention, sometimes you were the only grown up that made any sense to me at all."

"Despite the fact that, according to your mother, I'm a no good rotten bastard. Guess she told you I've got a two-bit whore."

"Something like that." She held up her hands, signaling she wanted no further information.

"Well, there's no excuse for it, I know. But the thing of it is, your mother has a way of taking me down a peg or two and goddammit, sometimes a man just likes to feel good about himself, know what I mean?"

"Yup."

He laughed, "Guess you do at that. I know your mother gives you a hard time, but she does love you, you know."

"Could have fooled me. She's got an odd way of showing it."

"Always thought you were the strongest of the three of you. Don't let her get to you. Don't forget that if you get knocked down into the middle of next week, you're way ahead of the game. You're stronger and smarter than you think you are."

She waggled her head and her mouth turned down into a bitter smile. "Well, smart anyway." Though the more she thought about what he said, she wondered whether he was right. Was she stronger than she felt? Maybe she was like a spindly long-legged mangrove tree. They might grow right next to open waters, but their roots sink far down beneath the sand to the cavernous limestone below. Even hurricanes don't kill them. They just bend with the wind.

And if they do break apart, their pieces drift for hundreds of miles, finally washing ashore on an incoming tide, up onto an alien beach, where up near the high-water mark, they sprout tiny appendages. Some go up to the sun; others root down into the earth. So perhaps for now, she told herself, she would drift along, watching the world, quietly observant, waiting to see where she might land up.

"Tuh hunh hunh," Ray chuckled, as if he somehow knew what she was thinking, "guess the old fellow hasn't been all bad, has he now?'

"Not at all," and then she couldn't look at him. Tears stung the corners of her eyes, "You take care of yourself too. Hear me now." And with that she stumbled around and left the room.

Their flight left at noon. Cornelia had on her black dress, somewhat faded and a bit shiny now from being pressed and washed. She carried her trench coat over her shoulder. Nevin's chin pointed high but she wobbled on her too high-heeled spectator pumps. With red lipstick lining her pursed mouth, and her tight travelling suit left over from the fifties, she was a brave relic of her younger years. She nodded pleasantly at the flight attendants, "We're going to New York, don't you know."

The snappy young woman responded. "That's a lucky thing then because that's where the plane is going, ma'am."

Nothing daunted Nevin's high spirits. She smiled and nodded at the seated passengers as she passed them. "Isn't this nice?" She spoke to no one in particular. She patted the seat cushion. "I think this occasion calls for champagne."

Nevin regaled the businessman across the way with tales of how wonderful their new life was to be. She told the flight attendant how very nice the amenities were and sent compliments to the pilot on the smooth plane ride. Cornelia slumped down, with her head turned to the window, pretending to be fascinated by the view. And indeed, soon, she was, as always, enchanted by the boiling landscape of clouds. And then she fell asleep.

By the time they landed in New York City, the champagne had made Nevin even wobblier on her feet. Her lipstick was in tatters and her jaunty little travelling hat had slipped down to a crazy angle. Cornelia grabbed her by the arm, hauled her off the plane, gathered up their luggage, and hailed a taxi to take them to the Barbizon Hotel for women, in the city.

The lobby was grand, and the famous clock looked just like she had imagined it from books. Their room was tiny, no bigger than a closet, with two twin beds jammed along each wall. A grated window looked out onto a narrow courtyard. Nevin passed out on the bed, fully dressed. Cornelia wiggled off her shoes, noting the red dents all along Nevin's swollen feet. She covered her with the extra blanket she found in the closet. She hung up her own black dress, shook out her trench coat, took a shower, brushed her teeth, put on a tee shirt and went to bed. Though it was only 6:00 PM, she wasn't sure what else to do in the unfamiliar city.

She lay down in bed and cleared her brain of all the muddy thoughts and impressions of the last few days. Whom could she trust now? Who would love her? Care for her? Protect her? She sent the questions out into that divine void and waited for guidance.

At first, floating in from the night, all she heard was distant sirens, the grinding of garbage trucks, and a steady roar of traffic and honking horns.

But then, finally, her divine connection plugged in. She was comforted, as always, by the return of her clear still inner voice. It seemed she was not alone after all. Though at times, she would be troubled and forget how to listen, she would always, at some point return to these words.

"Trust in your own self, child, that is absolute love. For if you don't cherish yourself, you will never be able to love another."

She snapped on the light and wrote down those words, then tore the sheet out and folded it up, putting in her wallet where it stayed for years until the folds darkened and cracked and became so much a part of herself that she no longer needed them.

She clicked off the light, sighed deeply, and fell asleep.

For better or for worse, she had floated ashore on a new island.

"Beyond Absolute Love" coming soon...

Those first weeks in New York were a blur of physical details, many of them painful. Cornelia was trotted about. People grabbed her chin, twisting her face from side to side. They ran their fingers over her body, pinching her stomach to see if there was any excess flesh. There was not.

Other people painted her face, then rubbed it off. They washed her hair, yanked it free of tangles, jerked it up into high, backcombed madness, then brushed it back out. People barked at her to take off her clothes, yelled at her when she squirmed, pushed her to stand taller, jump higher, project better. Lights flashed so bright they made her squint. Voices shouted to arch her back, open her eyes, angle her face, thrust out her pelvis. The only thing she would not do was smile. Whenever they asked, she scowled.

Geraldine Dodge, who, it turned out, was a bit of a comic nightmare, orchestrated everything. She was a parody of an aging fashion model, bony angles and paper-thin. Her lips had narrowed, but their ghost was still sharply outlined in crimson. She yelled at Cornelia to be grateful, poked at her posture, and kept track of every little penny she was spending on her, so that one day, when the "dollink gull" as she called her was earning her keep, she could pay her back in triple.

Nevin fluttered around, her face creased with worry. "Why *won't* you smile?" she begged Cornelia.

Cornelia had no answer. She hated the fittings and cuttings, the posing and reposing, and the endless rounds of makeup and hair pulls. She felt invaded, attacked, silenced, made fun of, and talked down to; anything but herself, whoever that was.

Acknowledgements

I would like to thank my parents for providing me with a bizarrely absolute upbringing. And to my beloved husband whose need to get up and go keeps life interesting. I would also like to thank David Smitherman for his help in editing *Absolute Cornelia.*

About the Author

Photo by Allegra Anderson

As a child, Lucretia loved books and making up stories. In their drama, they mirrored the misadventures thrust on her by her parents. Lucretia studied writing at Sarah Lawrence College in Bronxville, New York. Upon graduation, she went to Los Angeles, where she made a living as a free-lance travel writer and photographer. Her credits include publication in *Vanity Fair*, *Conde Nast Traveler*, *Travel and Leisure*, *Islands*, and *Saveur*. She was a frequent contributor, for many years, to both the *Los Angeles Times Magazine* and their travel section. She now lives with Jim Fitzpatrick, her husband, and writes novels in a grand shingle-style house on Long Island Sound.

CPSIA information can be obtained
at www.ICGtesting.com
Printed in the USA
BVHW031148181019
561496BV00001B/15/P

9 781950 544042